NATURAL LAW

Also by D. R. Schanker

A Criminal Appeal

For my father, Robert Frank Schanker

Acknowledgments

With profound gratitude, I acknowledge the extraordinary efforts of my editor, Reagan Arthur, and my agent, Laura Blake Peterson, and the kind assistance provided by Jennifer Lukemeyer, Barry Brumer, Jan Tarlin, Suzanne Buchko, Cheshire Schanker, the faculty and staff of the Indiana University School of Law at Bloomington, where I spent three years researching this novel, and James Wilson Jones, whose spirit and artistry influenced this work. I also wish to acknowledge my use as source material *The Taoist I Ching*, translated by Thomas Cleary, ©1986, used by arrangement with Shambhala Publications, Inc., Boston.

NATURAL
LAW

1

WEDNESDAY, DECEMBER 7

Hoyt Richey sat on the steps of his front porch and drowsily watched the sun rise in a smudge of color over his farm. It was 6:35 A.M., and during the night, a long-predicted cold front had moved down over central Indiana, dropping temperatures into the teens. Shivering, Richey took a sip of coffee from the tall porcelain mug he held between his stiff, chapped hands, then inhaled the crisp air with an eager anticipation of winter and its quiet joys. At long last, the harvest was done and the fields nearly cleared, and he would soon have time to hunt, to sleep, to breathe.

Richey took off his cap and smoothed back the few strands of gray hair remaining on top of his head, then replaced the cap and opened the sack lunch that his darling Melva had prepared for him to eat at midday as he sat beneath the ancient sycamore that stood at the intersection of his southern and eastern cornfields. The sack contained a chicken salad sandwich, three oatmeal cookies, and an apple, just as it had every day of his married life. For twenty-nine years, his Melva had awakened with him before dawn and made his lunch while he showered, and every day when he took his midday break, he savored that lunch and the tender devotion it represented.

Richey unfolded the paper napkin Melva had placed in the bag and read the message she had written there: I ♥ U.

Silly girl, he thought, smiling; it was a message that appeared in

1

his lunch sack whenever they had made love upon waking. Richey took one of the oatmeal cookies from the bag and chewed it absently as he replayed in his mind the sensations of Melva's warmth, her softness, the sweetness of her breath.

The sun was rising fast, and the temperature slowly with it. In the bright bolts of sunlight now streaming across his fields, Richey saw a circle of buzzards in the distance, swooping in and out of the stand of pine trees on the far side of his cornfield. He was pleased at the thought that he'd finally caught something in one of the traps he'd laid for the raccoons that had fed on his corn all summer. He downed the rest of his coffee, set the cup on the porch railing, then hurried over to his barn and mounted his tractor, carefully slipping his lunch into the saddlebag behind the seat.

Richey drove along the side of the field, which bore its prickly winter stubble of harvested corn, to where the buzzards were flocking. He dismounted and stepped into the grove of a dozen spindly pines. Before he got to the birds, he knew he'd never laid any trap in that corner of the field, and he wondered what creature might have crawled in there to die—maybe a hunter's wounded prey, maybe a sick dog or a skunk that had gotten bitten up in a fight. But he didn't smell any dead dog and certainly no skunk.

What Richey saw through the trees stopped his heart cold and made him cry out in a jolt of horror. It was a man's body, naked, bloodied at the groin and mouth and eyes; buzzards perched on his head and chest and legs, pecking at his flesh, leaving jagged pink tears in his skin. As he approached, the buzzards screeched, ripped last morsels from the corpse, and flapped noisily away.

Richey stood, transfixed, balanced between flight and a dreadful curiosity. The man's white hair was a tangled mess of dried blood and dirt. There was a pile of clothes nearby, neatly folded, and a pair of black shoes, a sock stuffed in each, side by side next to the clothes. The body was white like plaster, dead white, and nearly hairless. But between the legs was a dark mat of hair and clotted blood, and Richey's stomach constricted when he realized that the man's genitals had been slashed.

"Dear Lord," he whispered, "dear Lord."

As Richey turned his eyes away, he noticed something odd about the man's mouth, but he could not look again. The buzzards were still circling, screeching, and their number had doubled. He angrily tore a handful of sticks and pine needles from the icy ground and threw it up at them, then ran back through the trees to his tractor as the buzzards greedily descended.

2

"G emme the ffffuck out. Thass all I fuckin' want. Th' ffffuck out."
Kindness, Nora thought. Kindness first. Remember: She, too, is a creature of God.

The young woman sat before her, her hands clasped together between her knees as she rocked back and forth, babbling and cursing and spitting. A twenty-year-old white woman, she had a dull, wedge-shaped face, its triangularity accentuated by the blond hair that lay flat around her head, the too-short bangs, the small, narrow blue eyes. Her name was Stormi Skye, a name less playful than cruel, if names were destiny.

Stormi Skye did not look at Nora Lumsey, a woman some eight years older than she, a largish professional woman with a coil of brown hair on top of her head, who sat across from her in a folding chair; Stormi's eyes were focused on the square foot of linoleum floor between them, a pose that suggested remorse, but nothing more. The two women thus found themselves together for the second time in eight months, conferring in a stark meeting room in the women's lockup on the fifth floor of the City-County Building in downtown Indianapolis.

Hunched over, Stormi chewed her lower lip and picked at a scab on the back of her hand, a raw, bleeding scab at the end of a long trail of scabs scratched into her skin in lines across her wrist and disappearing into the cuff of her dirty suede jacket.

4

"Fffuck, fuck, fuck," she muttered, moving her head from side to side rhythmically, as though to ease the pain of keeping still. "I'm so fffucked."

Kindness first, Nora thought.

Nora Lumsey felt her stomach growl and closed her eyes. She had been awakened by a 5:45 A.M. phone call from an incoherent Stormi, who had been picked up for cocaine possession, and now, at 7:07, Nora's thoughts were drawn to the warm carrot muffin that sat on a corner of her desk nine floors above them, next to the mug of coffee she had hurriedly poured and sipped, in her cubicle in the office of the Marion County public defender.

Nora looked at Stormi's face and chased breakfast from her mind.

Her arms resting on the thin file folder on her lap, Nora leaned over in her chair and considered Stormi. Nora's heart, which was too compassionate, told her to reach out and put a hand on this woman's shoulder, arm, or knee to provide a measure of comfort, but Nora knew better. On the occasion of Stormi's last arrest, she had been in a similar state of drug withdrawal, and Nora had spoken soothingly to her, lovingly, and had attempted to put her hand on Stormi's hands, which had been clasped in a tight knot in her lap. Suddenly, Stormi had spat at her, a hot wad of saliva that landed on Nora's upper lip; Stormi did it quickly and then laughed, the flash of anger evaporating as quickly as it had come, and she then took hold of Nora's arm, at first affectionately, seeming to apologize, but her fingers continued to squeeze, digging into the flesh. It was a child's sadism, a sick joke. She had dared Nora to reject her.

Instinctively, Nora had slapped her hard, a solid slap that connected with the meat of Stormi's cheek, shoving the girl's head sideward. As Nora felt the sting of the slap on her hand, she experienced a sharp pang of guilt; it was a slap like the many she had received in adolescence from her father. And, as Nora had done, Stormi rubbed her cheek, eyes watering, and she did not give Nora the satisfaction of so much as a whimper.

Now, Nora sat silently, offering no compassion. She felt dizzy, not yet fully awake, reeling a bit, abruptly aware of being much bigger

5

than Stormi, a half-foot taller, weighing half again as much, and she felt as though she might topple over onto the girl and crush her.

Stormi was a prostitute. It is not a difficult concept to grasp, Nora thought, if one doesn't dwell on the physical realities of it. Sex for money. Not a way Nora could ever imagine using her body, but in the marathon year and a half she had served as a deputy public defender, the unimaginable had become routine. Murderers, child molesters, thieves, arsonists, pimps, drug lords, rapists, shoplifters, check-kiters, drunks, and dealers in coke, crack, heroin, marijuana, and sex; Nora had come to know perpetrators of these crimes and more, had shaken their hands, joked with them, embraced them. And she had, to her astonishment, found herself not just doing her dirty job of defending these criminals but also liking them—their nerve, their heat, their audacity. Their contempt for authority was so much like her own stubbornness, she could not help but empathize, horrified by her simultaneous attraction and repulsion to their criminality. But this was, others told her, precisely what made Nora good at her job; she truly believed in the humanity of these offenders, and thus it was no lie for her to humanize them for the jury.

Stormi slowed her rocking movement and stopped her mumbling and seemed to be falling asleep with her head in her hands. Nora watched and waited.

It is one of our neater legal distinctions, Nora thought, that rape is a sexual offense but prostitution is classified as a form of public indecency; prostitution seemed to Nora to be rather a kind of self-rape, an economic and sexual self-abnegation. In her short life, Stormi Skye had become a regular customer of the judicial systems in Indianapolis and its surrounding counties, and in the words of those who by virtue of their positions in the system had occasion to deal with her, Stormi was "a white-trash whore" and a "low-life junkie piece of ass."

To Nora, Stormi was a kindred spirit with a blasted brain and a warped heart, a reflection of Nora herself in a distorting mirror.

Nora reached out and touched Stormi's shoulder.

Stormi shook it off and raised her hand to strike Nora, then stopped herself. "Fuck you," she said, and she started to cry, angry sobs that were like explosive coughs.

A shiver of annoyance passed over Nora. The girl was amazingly selfish; even her tears were self-indulgently loud.

Nora opened the file folder and glanced at the affidavit of Cal Weeks, the police officer who had arrested Stormi while on routine patrol in the southwestern corner of the city, in the Campbellville section. It was time to drag Stormi back to reality.

"Stormi?"

"What?"

"I have to ask you some questions."

Stormi scratched an ear.

"It says here the police officer found you last night walking in circles around a car registered to your mother, which was parked by the side of Route Forty, and it was running, with the keys locked inside. Is that right?"

Stormi shrugged.

"It says you appeared to be drunk and under the influence of narcotics. Is that right?"

Stormi sat immobile.

"It says the police officer volunteered to open your car for you and you said okay, so he used a slim jim to get the door open, and that's when he saw the packet of white powder that appeared to be cocaine on the floor. Is that right?"

Stormi shook her head, though not in denial.

"It says here that when the police officer asked you about the packet, you denied knowing it was there."

Stormi shrugged again.

"It says here that you then offered to perform oral sex on the police officer if he would let you go. Is that right?"

Stormi tilted her head and smiled at Nora.

"Good move," Nora said.

The last time they met, Stormi had been arrested for prostitution, and the owner of the adult bookstore where Stormi worked, a businessman named Gene Lydon, had refused to provide Stormi with a lawyer to defend her, as he normally did. It seemed that Lydon was pissed off by Stormi's moonlighting at bachelor parties, where, for a small fortune, Stormi would provide oral sex to groups of as many as a dozen men. When she was arrested after one such event—following a tip from the father of the bride—Lydon had decided to let her hang out to dry. And so Stormi, who despite a sizable income had not a cent to her name, thanks to her drug habit, was forced to rely on a court-appointed public defender, a fall from grace that was, for her, a bitter humiliation.

Lydon's punishment lasted a week, during which time Nora represented Stormi in the initial hearing and had begun to interview the young men who had attended the bachelor party. Nora had been a deputy public defender for less than a year at that time, and she still labored under the delusion that every charge had a viable defense, or at least a mitigating factor that could serve to reduce the sentence or the degree of the crime. She had hoped that in the private nature of the bachelor party—it had taken place in an apartment occupied by one of the young men—there was a defense to the element of the prostitution offense that required proof of money or other property exchanged in payment for sexual services; it could at least be argued, she thought, that the money Stormi had received had been for her services as an exotic dancer. Not the kind of argument that easily passed the straight-face test, but keeping a straight face was a skill learned early by deputy public defenders who hoped to succeed at the job.

Stormi's case was yanked from Nora just as she had begun to research the issue. Lydon had relented, hiring James Barris, a law professor, to defend Stormi. Barris was an authority on law and personal liberty, particularly sexual liberty, and he had successfully defended Lydon when the city tried to shut down Lydon's adult bookstore on zoning grounds. Barris was somewhat less successful with Stormi. Lydon had hoped that Barris's mere presence would scare the prosecutor's office into dropping the charges—certainly, the city did not want an expensive, protracted, and high-profile trial over a bachelor party, particularly considering the damage to the reputations of the young men involved—but the city's new prosecutor, whose campaign for office the prior year had taken on the character of a moral crusade, was a hard sell. The best Barris could do was a plea bargain for a year's probation and a ten-thousand-dollar fine.

And then Stormi's call, these months later, awakening Nora, reminding her that she needed to get a new, unlisted number. Nora pushed from her mind her concern that she would begin to work on the case only to be replaced by Lydon's hired counsel. It didn't really matter to her; she liked Stormi, despite Stormi's utter disregard for her health, for morality, for the law. If Lydon came through again for Stormi, so be it. For now, Stormi was her client.

"They treating you all right?"

Nora spoke quietly as she examined Stormi's face, and there followed further expressions of concern. She gave Stormi a rundown of what would happen in the next few hours, days, and weeks, though she knew Stormi was familiar with the drill. Stormi would have an initial hearing at 9:30 that morning, at which time an automatic plea of not guilty would be entered. The court would then set an omnibus date, the date from which all other deadlines were derived—the deadline for the filing of an alibi defense, for evidentiary objections, and for other pretrial motions.

As she told Stormi these things, Nora watched Stormi's hands caress each other again and again, and the speckled skin of Stormi's hands came alive; there were white scars, like lice, black scabs, like bugs, brown irregular blotches, like spatters of stain. There were the bruised ridges of her veins, dark and mottled, and the many minute wrinkles and chafed and dry patches and bloody tabs of skin that had come loose around the nails, which were dirty and bitten down to the quick.

Nora shook Stormi's hand and took her leave, handing the girl over to LaTisha, the corrections officer who would escort Stormi back to her cell.

"I'll meet you in court in a couple of hours," Nora told Stormi. "Just stand with me and it'll be all right."

"All right? What the fuck is that?" Stormi said in a small, clear voice.

9

3

Luther Cox dreamed of fire and its terrible deafening roar. He dreamed of a house afire, his house, and of awakening to an orange light flickering beneath his closed bedroom door, of turning to his wife, next to him, and not finding her there. In the dream, Cox pulled open the door and nearly collapsed from the heat and smoke, covered his face with his hands, and dashed headlong through the flames to see his wife's body in the kitchen, a heap of fire on the bubbling linoleum, the charred gas can beside her. In the dream, he stumbled aflame through the kitchen door and out into the yard, crumpled onto the wet, cold grass, and fainted. In the dream, the noise was so loud, so continuous, like radio static, that he couldn't hear himself scream. Until it woke him up.

The sound rang against the walls of his cabin. He shivered, soaked to the skin, the mattress drenched with sweat. His mouth was sticky, his tongue swollen and dry. He reached for his pouch of tobacco, found a cigarette he'd rolled the night before, and lighted it.

"Sainted Christ, Spunk," he murmured through puffs of smoke, "another stinkin' day."

Spunk, always there on the corner of the mattress when Cox awoke, stretched his front paws in the tangle of bedsheets, then curled up again as Luther Cox smoked and stared into the near dark.

After a shave and the comfort of a hot shower, Cox stood at his easel in his red flannel nightshirt and prepared to sketch a self-portrait in charcoal. He began by studying the wreck of his features in a mirror taped to the easel, then quickly drew the landscape of arroyos, ruts, promontories, and craters that made up the jagged topography of his face. He knew he'd look a damn sight better if he could get a few solid hours of sleep. Not that there was much hope of that; the same dream had haunted his nights for nine years, leaving touches of gray in his drooping mustache and thick, close-cropped brown hair.

Spunk meowed and did a figure eight around Cox's legs. Cox bent down and scratched his brown-black-and-white piebald companion behind the ears, then took a sip of scalding coffee from the mug he used every morning, the one that said GOOD COP on one side and DON'T GIVE ME ANY SHIT, I'M HAVING MY COFFEE on the other.

Cox looked at the old grandfather clock in the corner—7:24— and was glad to have another half hour to draw before dressing and hustling off to work. He cherished this time, his hour or so devoted to art in the morning. It was an activity that centered him and provided perspective on the unsettling duality of a life lived half in seclusion, half in the turmoil and stress of his responsibilities as a cop.

Cox completed a rough sketch of his face, the expression guarded, weary, the eyes direct and probing, then outlined the background, a view of his one-room cabin that took in his stone fireplace, his old claw-foot bathtub, and his east window, an aperture onto a scene of late-fall desolation—leafless branches etched black against the pale sky. Cox had begun to put a bare network of lines on paper when the phone rang, always an unwelcome portent at that hour of the morning.

"Cox."

"Luther, sorry for the intrusion." It was Tina Farrell, Cox's assistant and the Harrison Police Department's evidence technician, calling from her cell phone with her standard apology.

"Uh-huh."

"Got a goodie for ya. Corpse in a cornfield. Up north side of town, off Regner Road. Got a positive ID. James Barris. Seems he's a law professor at BHU. Nasty job, too. Been slashed up."

"Any idea when it happened?"

"Wee hours. Maybe two or three. A farmer found the guy, nude, this morning. Been cut up, bad, at the mouth and privates."

"Who's with you?"

"Perry, Adams . . . and Quade."

"Quade?"

"Yeah, orders of the chief. And somehow, Quade managed to drag his ass out of bed."

Cox wrote down the location, hastily splashed a few drops of coffee into his cup, and picked up the medicine bottle that lay on its side on the kitchen window ledge. He spilled into his palm a small green-and-yellow capsule—a twenty-milligram dose of Prozac, his green-and-yellow savior—placed it on his tongue, downed it with the coffee, and stripped off his nightshirt. The cold air whistling through the cabin's barely insulated walls chilled his skin, raising gooseflesh, and Cox gritted his teeth as he contemplated the day that awaited him.

Cox drove north to the crime scene on Old State Road 60, a two-lane highway that cut through a landscape sanctified with fertility. From the thickly forested hills where he lived, the road wound past fields of turned-over earth, where, in the spring, a sea of deep green soybean would extend as far as the eye could see.

Cox slipped an old Grateful Dead tape into the cassette player; "Sugar Magnolia" sprang forth. The bright, ringing guitar cheered him slightly, but only slightly, as he pushed the gearshift into fifth and floored it, whooshing past wooden fences enclosing silos, barns, farmhouses, cows, goats, and horses. Above Cox, buzzards drifted in the chilly air. It was a season of famine for the black-shrouded scavengers, when the cold kept most creatures hidden and few animals meandered onto the blacktop to fall victim to the cars and pickups that rattled down those country roads.

Farther north, the farms gave way to the belt of stone quarries, deep gouges in the earth, piled with slabs of cut limestone. Beyond the quarries, the road cut through the industrial west side of Indianapolis and into neighboring Watkins County and the town of Harrison, which was heralded by a huge billboard reading BENJAMIN HARRISON UNIVERSITY SALUTES COACH DON HEDSTROM AND THE SAGAMORES! To the left of those words was a giant photograph of the grinning coach, bald pate gleaming, twirling a basketball on his index finger.

Cox raised his middle finger to the coach, a gesture that had become automatic, then sped across the north side of Harrison and into the country, where farms appeared again, nestled among dense groves of evergreen.

Hank Bieberschmidt stood with arms crossed, cradled atop his wide belly, and rocked from one foot to the other as he confronted the body of James Barris. The time was 7:55 A.M. and the temperature was well below freezing. Surrounded by a cloud of his own exhalation, Bieberschmidt silently gave thanks for the cold. If not for the damage done by the birds, the body would have been as well preserved as if it had spent the night in a drawer at the morgue.

The isolated patch of trees amid the fields of corn stubble was the scene of quiet, earnest activity as four of Harrison's finest processed the crime scene under Bieberschmidt's weary, watchful eyes. Few words were spoken among the officers, as if they were tiptoeing around a light sleeper. Murder was a rare occurrence in Harrison, and this morning was a nervous-making event for these cops, who had no regular experience with homicide. And so deference was paid, the dead man granted a certain respect as the business of preserving evidence was conducted.

Two rookies, Vaughn Adams and Doug Perry, laboriously paced a grid search of the area from the road through the pines and into the cornfield, while Tina Farrell, her muscular body compacted into a painful low crouch, moved cautiously around Barris and the unnervingly fastidious stack of clothes next to him as she examined the

13

ground surrounding the body, merrily attacking the pine needles and dirt with a tiny set of tweezers. "Beautiful, beautiful," she crooned. "A ton of fiber. Green acrylic, for sure."

Teddy Quade, the Harrison force's other detective, second in seniority to Cox, stood uncomfortably next to Hoyt Richey, who was seated on a crate he had brought over from the barn so he and Melva, who came out to join her husband once the police had arrived, could watch the proceedings. Hoyt and Melva huddled together for warmth as Quade nervously bit the nails on a pudgy hand.

Bieberschmidt glared at Quade with disgust. Hiring Quade had been his worst mistake in sixteen years as chief of police, and it was a mistake he had to look at every day on the job. Quade had been on the force in Chicago for ten years when he decided he didn't like being a cop, but thirty-eight was too early to retire, so he did the next best thing—he landed himself a job in Harrison, where the worst offenders he had to deal with were drunk drivers, rowdy frat boys, and a coke dealer once in a blue moon. Bieberschmidt considered Quade to be the laziest son-of-a-bitch he'd ever met, and he would have dismissed him long ago if Quade hadn't been the brother-in-law of Mark Andrews, city council president and boyfriend of Harrison's mayor, Faith Brodey. Bieberschmidt had hired Quade as a favor to Andrews, knowing it was wrong the moment he agreed to it. But doing favors for people was, as he had long ago discovered, a big part of his job.

Bieberschmidt glanced at his watch and wondered what the hell was taking Cox so long, then decided to look at the victim's car, a late-model blue Volvo that sat on the shoulder of Regner Road. Bieberschmidt didn't get the chance. Just as he reached the road, Cox's late 1970s–vintage Chevy came rumbling out of the morning sun, the peeling Deadhead sticker on Cox's rear window brightly backlit by slanting rays of sunlight.

"Luther." Bieberschmidt nodded, delivering his usual tight-lipped greeting as Cox approached.

"Somebody call Ivan?" Cox asked. Ivan Sarvetnikov, the county coroner.

14

"Yeah, he's on his way."

"Has the family been contacted?"

"We managed to get hold of his secretary, a girl named Connie, and the dean of the law school, Ernestine Hume. She says he's got no family in the area. There's a mother at a nursing home in Indy, a brother in Boston. That's it."

Cox nodded.

"I told the dean you'd be paying her a visit this morning."

"Right."

"That means a tie."

"Right." Cox glanced involuntarily down at his pants—black denim—and at his worn leather jacket. "I know I've got a tie . . . somewhere."

As the murder scene came into view, Cox stopped, took a cigarette, already rolled, from his shirt pocket, lighted it with his battered metal lighter, then proceeded. As the others noticed his approach, he took a few deep, lung-bruising drags and nodded to Farrell, Quade, and the rookies in turn. He glanced quickly at Richey, then strolled resolutely toward the body.

Cox stopped about a yard from the upturned feet and rubbed his cheeks as he inspected the corpse.

The upper torso was leaning against the base of a tree, the head tilted back and to the right. The lower portion of the body lay flat on a layer of pine needles, twigs, and dirt, the legs slightly apart. Slash marks, superficial sharp incisions crisscrossing like wide X's, had been cut into the abdomen, extending from just below the navel to the upper thighs. From Cox's vantage, it appeared that the penis was lacerated, although it had not been severed. The incisions looked as if the perpetrator had flailed in the dark with a knife or razor, cutting wildly back and forth.

Then there was the face. The eyes were half-open, staring sleepily or as if drugged. The mouth was a gaping bloody hole, slack-jawed, and the lips were oddly stretched at the corners, simulating an expression of surprised merriment. Blood had caught under the lower lip and clotted there, creating a swelled appearance, and some blood had spilled down the chin. The stump of tongue hung cartoonishly truncated in the middle of the mouth.

Cox stood stock-still and stared a moment, then crouched and began to examine the corpse closely. All activity among the other officers stopped as he inspected the wounds, the skin, the eyes, the hair. Cox worked rapidly but meticulously. The stink of the corpse, mild as it was, penetrated the cold air, and the very sight of the violence that had been done to it distressed him intensely. Yet he knew that physical evidence in and on the corpse would be the first to be lost if he did not preserve it now.

Death had occurred some six to nine hours earlier; Cox could tell by the general putrescence of the corpse, the mottled condition of the eyes, the degree to which the blood had congealed. The skin was pale—nearly white—exaggerating the varied ways in which the body had been damaged. Beside the abdominal slashes, there was the work the buzzards had done, bruises here and there, resembling sports injuries, scratches on the legs, and a long red horizontal indentation in the skin across the neck.

Cox motioned to Farrell. She scampered over to him.

"Have you got a good picture of that?"

"Yeah, it's a beaut. I did a whole roll on the neck. Looks like he was garroted with a bit of twine. Awful friction burns there."

"What about this?" Cox pointed to a smear of blood on the side of the chest near the right underarm. There, preserved in the dried blood, was a smudged fingerprint.

"Shit, got me there, babe," said Farrell. "It's not much, and there's no way to lift that; but we'll get in there and take some ultra-close-ups."

"Mmmm." Cox took a last drag on the cigarette, then pulled a thin metal can from his back pocket, unscrewed the top, stubbed the cigarette out in it, and closed it again. He stood and wiped his forehead on his sleeve, vaguely annoyed that his clinical detachment couldn't stop him from sweating.

Cox glanced over at Bieberschmidt and Quade, both of whom

had stepped out of the way as Perry and Adams ran bright yellow crime-scene tape around the tree trunks.

Cox turned and regarded Hoyt Richey, who sat bent over, his hands welded to the sides of a coffee mug, staring at the ground and looking for all the world like he was the repentant killer. Cox took the packet of tobacco out of his front shirt pocket, rolled another cigarette, then he and Farrell walked to where Quade and Bieberschmidt were waiting.

"Tina," he said.

"Yeah, sir," said Farrell.

"Talk to me."

"Looks to me like he was killed somewhere else and dragged here dead. The pine needles are pushed around like something was dragged through the trees. Looks like the strangulation killed him; there's petechial hemorrhaging in the eyes. The hackwork was done afterward, and probably here, because there's very little blood, and what's there is confined to the immediate area of the body. I've combed through the hair and the pubic hair and sealed samples, but it's such a mess, there'll be nothing to see until we can dry it all out."

Farrell flipped open her field notebook.

"I've got the tongue tip, which I found about three yards from the body. Also some fibers that might be from a blanket. We're still looking for a trace of whatever it was they used to strangle the victim. No footprints—the pine needles are too thick and the ground's too hard anyway. We do have some light tire prints on the shoulder of the road. We can deal with the car once it's been impounded. As for the body, I'll let Ivan have first crack at it."

Cox nodded and looked around. The sun, streaming unfiltered out of the cloudless sky, made vision painful. He watched Farrell as she examined the victim's clothing.

"The wallet was emptied of cash but otherwise undisturbed." Bieberschmidt handed Cox a thick trifold leather wallet. Cox surveyed its contents, pausing to look at Barris's driver's license photograph.

17

"Anything else in the pockets?"

"Change, Life Savers. Car looks relatively clean. Keys are still in the ignition."

Cox said, "Before I go to the law school, Tina and I will pay a visit to Barris's residence."

Bieberschmidt took a breath. "I want the three of you working together on this."

Cox shifted his gaze from Bieberschmidt to Quade.

"There's a first time for everything, kids."

Bieberschmidt smiled wanly at Cox, who did not return the smile, and then at Quade, who shrugged.

"I'm going to have to release the news within the hour. We're not going to mention anything about the condition of the body. The victim was asphyxiated. Period. I think Mr. Richey will cooperate."

Cox glanced at the farmer, who looked shell-shocked, and at Melva, who stared lovingly at her husband, patting his hand.

Bieberschmidt went on: "The dean at the law school says Barris has been teaching there for years. No doubt he's got a lot of friends in town. They're going to want answers."

Cox listened impatiently, hating the implication that he'd do anything differently because this particular corpse happened to have had friends.

Bieberschmidt went off to tell the rookies that it would be their job to guard the crime scene until relief came. Gritting his teeth, Cox asked Quade to wait for Ivan, then told Farrell to meet him at Barris's residence, where he hoped to learn something about Barris's personal world—his habits, his interests, his appetites, his circle. A little knowledge would give him the confidence to offer comfort to Barris's grieving colleagues, to ask indelicate questions delicately, and to distinguish those upon whom suspicion rightly fell.

4

It was a metal-framed cubicle with walls of baby blue fabric; at times, it felt to her like a prison, but for Nora it was her home by day, her refuge, the place where she toiled for justice. She had long since given up pining for a window or a real office; such perks were exclusively for supervisory attorneys and for the public defender himself, so Nora contented herself with a calendar photograph of a sunrise over the Alaskan tundra, a far better view, at any rate, she told herself, than the one available from the fourteenth floor of the City-County Building. Nora stared at the calendar too long, having glanced at it to note the date and gotten lost, wandering the tundra. Reluctantly, she turned her attention to Stormi Skye's file.

There was little there—the charges, the affidavit of the arresting officer, the police report, Polaroid photographs of the drugs, a state police record search showing Stormi's lengthy list of prior arrests and convictions, and the presentence report from Stormi's last conviction. Nora sighed heavily. As in so many cases, there was nothing for her to do but negotiate for a plea bargain with the deputy prosecutor assigned to the case. It was a little dope, that's all. Just possession, not even dealing. Certainly nothing to waste the county's taxes prosecuting.

Of course, the taxes paid Nora's salary, too, a not-quite-living wage for her services as champion of the likes of Stormi Skye. A nasty

19

job, but somebody's got to do it—her mantra, though there were times when she wished it wasn't her job to do.

In the commission of her duties as defender of the indigent accused, there was a layer cake of rationales to be swallowed, and lately Nora had found herself choking on it. There was the "keeping the cops honest" rationale—that it was her job to make sure the police obeyed their constitutional responsibilities in the manner in which they investigated the crime and made the arrest. There was the "one in a hundred is innocent" rationale—that all her effort and heartache were worthwhile if she uncovered that one poor bastard unjustly caught up in the system. There was the "every person deserves a vigorous defense" rationale—that her clients, the lowest of the low, the poorest of the poor, the dregs of society, the habitual offenders and miscreants, living lives of drug- and booze-addled confusion, of permanent unemployment, of political and cultural paranoia, existing beyond the fringe, perpetually in trouble, victims of their own ignorance and stupidity, without hope of change, should receive the same level of legal advocacy as those middle-class criminals who had the good fortune to be able to afford their own attorneys.

And the icing on the cake was the "all God's children" rationale—that there is an essence of goodness and love in everyone.

And this last was the foulest, the hardest to swallow, the rationale that was closest to her beliefs and the least susceptible of proof.

There was a point in each case when it was possible for Nora to believe in a client's innocence; usually that point, which began when she was assigned the case, ended during the initial meeting with the client, when she saw for herself the whipped-dog look on the faces of the habitual criminals—that they'd been caught again and knew it, and all they wanted from her was the best-possible deal.

And that's what she got them.

But if Nora came to care too much about her clients, her defendants, it was because somewhere not too far beneath her skin she felt herself as much a social outcast as they were. Her antisocial bent was directed inward, however, a cruelty toward herself that told her she was too big, not lovely enough to be loved, too book-smart and lacking even a farmer's common sense, too brash, too needy, too awkward.

In Nora's view, this sense of being *too much* sprang from an early immersion in the sensations of life at their most elemental; her world growing up was wild with the stink of the farm and all the varieties of shit to be handled each day—cow manure and chicken shit and hog excrement, the shit of her dog Jack and her cat Scratch and the shit of her baby brothers and sister, even the shit of her grandmother. All these shits had their own stink and texture, and, as Nora was the one to clean up the shit wherever it came from, she came to regard herself as a kind of connoisseur of shit, inured to manure. And then there was blood, the blood of the slaughterhouse, the blood of a severed finger, coughed-up blood, menstrual blood, blood in shit, bloody scalps, broken arms. The burden of raising all three of her siblings, after her mother left, and of working the farm hardened Nora to messes, to stress, to reality, and it made her feel that it was her place to serve, to clean, to make things right, and that when she wanted something for herself, it was because she was greedy, selfish, wanting too much.

Too much. It was not making friends easily; it was living a perpetually lonely existence and alienating the few friends she had with her pushiness, her meddlesomeness. Yet all she disliked about herself, she regarded as inseparable from her, part and parcel of her bigbonedness, her rural upbringing. She could not help taking care of people, mothering, sometimes suffocating.

And that made Stormi Skye *her* prostitute, just as the others were *her* crack dealers, *her* rapists and burglars and thieves, *her* multitudes of poor bastards who just need, need, need that TV, that necklace, that cocaine, those running shoes, need these things enough to steal them, or who hate enough to beat, rape, murder. Ninety-nine percent of them committed the crimes of which they were accused—that was a given—and the charade of rationales was wearing on Nora, burning her out to the point where she just didn't have the strength to create in herself the illusion of belief in the humanity of her clients.

When she won a case, it didn't make Nora's day to think that another piece of shit parasite was back on the street; when she lost, she hurt with the tragedy of another wrecked life spent behind bars.

On the wall of her cubicle, held in place by two pushpins, Nora kept a photograph of a black teenager named Dexter Hinton, the photo cut out of the *Indianapolis Standard* on the day following Dexter's death. Dexter had been convicted of murder, wrongly, and Nora, who was working for the judge who was to decide Dexter's appeal, had investigated the crime, in violation of her duty to refrain from contact with parties to cases before the court, an ethical violation that earned Nora a six-month suspension from the practice of law and a certain status among members of the bar as a socially conscious rebel and a bighearted fool.

For Nora, Dexter was her first client and her first success: Her meddling got Dexter out of prison. And then he became her first tragedy: Dexter was shot to death within weeks of his release.

There were times when Nora needed to remind herself that it was Dexter's death that got her here, to this job, and she would look into Dexter's face, into the eyes she had once found fearsome, and think about him, how his innocence had inspired her to fight for his freedom, despite the danger to her career and to her life.

But Dexter Hinton had been innocent. He was a *cause*, a reason to fight the system, to fight for justice.

Stormi Skye was guilty as sin.

Nora pulled from the file the presentence report from Stormi's conviction for prostitution and skimmed it absently, turning the mundane, obscene facts of the case over in her mind. What was the case about? A twenty-year-old girl giving blow jobs to men for money.

Why is sex the road to ruin? Nora thought. It invariably was so for girls like Stormi, girls who had lost their virginity at fourteen to an uncle, a stepfather, a father, an older boy at school. From there, somehow, it was straight to the streets and straight to hell—homeless, turning tricks to survive, and then the girl, if she was particularly unlucky, attracted the attention of a pimp, who'd use her like a cash cow in exchange for a modicum of safety and ready access to drugs, drugs paid for with sex, sex, and more sex, sex with the pimp, sex

22

with the pimp's friends, sex with johns, sex with other whores, sex for the camera, sex for the Web site.

The presentence report on Stormi Skye included the following under the section titled "Evaluation":

> Stormi Skye is a twenty-year-old white female who is presently before the Court for sentencing on a charge of prostitution. She pleaded guilty after an initial plea of not guilty. She was born the fourth child of Louise "Weesie" (Spencer) Skye and has an identical twin sister, Sunni Skye, who also has been convicted of criminal offenses, including prostitution and possession of a controlled substance with intent to distribute. Her father is Levon Skye (deceased), who was, prior to his death, convicted of child molesting and was serving a sentence at the Pendleton Correctional Facility.

A twin sister. Nora had never met Stormi's sister, Sunni, but she remembered hearing from Mark Gautier, the deputy prosecutor who had prosecuted the last case against Stormi Skye, that Sunni made Stormi look like an angel.

Nora read on:

> The defendant attended school in Indianapolis until the second semester of the tenth grade, when she was expelled for selling cocaine to classmates. She has earned seventeen high school credits. Ms. Skye is single and has no children. She states that she would like to be a mother someday.
>
> Her employment record consists of several jobs held for short periods of time, including a job as a waitress at a Bob Evans restaurant and at the counter at a McDonald's. She has worked at an adult bookstore, Pleazures. Her income has come primarily from illegal activities such as prostitution and drug dealing. She was unemployed at the time of her arrest.
>
> Ms. Skye has a charge of cocaine possession on her juvenile record, for which she spent two months at the Indiana

23

Girls' School. In addition to traffic charges on the defendant's adult record, she has a conviction for second-degree burglary, for which she received a six-month probationary period, with a satisfactory discharge. She also has one prior conviction as an adult for cocaine possession, for which she received a six-month probationary period and drug counseling. She has two prior convictions for prostitution, for which she received probation and a six-month term of incarceration, respectively. The defendant's term of incarceration was discharged after ninety days of good time.

Regarding the instant offense, the defendant is in desperate need of psychological counseling, drug-rehabilitation treatment, and removal from the environment that has resulted in her repeated convictions for prostitution. It is apparent by Ms. Skye's past behavior that imposition of the maximum sentence of incarceration will benefit society the most and is consistent with the goal of rehabilitation.

She did not serve a day for that offense; Barris's intervention—and skill—saw to that.

And Stormi Skye would like to be a mother someday.

Cox pulled up in front of Barris's Art Deco limestone cottage to find Farrell already seated behind the wheel of Barris's black Jaguar, which was parked decoratively in the driveway.

"Get a load of this damn car," Farrell yelled as Cox moved up the flagstone walk. Farrell, who raced peewee cars on the stock-car circuit on weekends, had a love for vehicles of all kinds, which Cox, who was reluctantly coming around to the idea that he'd have to replace his twenty-some-year-old Chevy, found irrational. "Whoo-wee! Now here's a guy who was *real* secure about his manhood."

"So what does my car say about me?" Cox asked cautiously.

Farrell grinned. "You don't wanna know."

The house was small but elegant, a one-of-a-kind architectural gem situated on the prettiest block of Harrison Park, a neighborhood of expensive homes populated almost exclusively by long-established professors and university administrators. To Cox, Barris's place epitomized a brand of midwestern upper-class pretension—a European aspiration, typified by the red tile roof, the beveled glass in the ornate iron-framed windows, the slate-floored patio in front with its low stone parapet. Cox squinted as he regarded the picture-perfect scene—a magnificent home, complete with black Jag in the driveway. The only thing missing was an ascot-wearing playboy, circa 1927, bounding out the front door, waving a tennis racket.

Cox and Farrell approached the glass front door and peeked through the slats of the miniature blinds on the other side as Cox gave the doorbell a perfunctory ring. Without waiting for a response, he pushed in the likeliest of Barris's keys and swiftly opened the door.

The interior of Barris's home was plush and immaculate, and both cops stopped short just inside the doorway, as if hesitant to disturb the fastidiousness of the furnishings.

"The ultimate bachelor place, eh?" Farrell said, smirking. "Pillows on the couch arranged just right, fireplace, *Architectural Digest* on the coffee table, CD player in the wall. It's too perfect, man, too perfect."

Cox went over to a long, low glass table in front of the living room window; it held a few small Mexican pottery figurines and a huge Nigerian ebony bust. Pleasant stuff, ersatz folk art, he thought. The walls had the usual Gorman print, an anonymous oil, no doubt bought on a street corner in Montmartre, and some innocuous watercolors.

But in the dining room, across from the gleaming mahogany table, was a portion of wall dedicated, like a shrine, to the career of one instantly identifiable individual. Cox shook his head in amazement as he approached the multiple images of Don Hedstrom, here exhorting his team from the sidelines, fist extended, there receiving an award, and elsewhere posing with his arms around a couple of sweaty seven-footers in basketball shorts. In the center of the wall was a framed eight-by-ten photograph of Hedstrom and Barris shaking hands and grinning.

At the left side of the shrine, a high shelf held a trophy—it read

"MVP, 1988 Faculty-Student All-Star Game"—and a basketball on a tiny wooden stand. Cox picked up the ball. The autograph scrawled across its nubby surface read "To Jim Barris, keeper of the faith. Don Hedstrom."

Cox replaced the ball and joined Farrell, who had ventured into Barris's bedroom, where she was exploring the cubbyholes in the headboard of a king-size platform bed.

"Anything?"

"Condoms, pornography, a vibrator, a small Baggie of pot, novels, nail clipper. Nothing you wouldn't expect."

"Uh-huh."

"Well, I take that back." Reaching into a cubby, Farrell pulled out a tiny Ziploc bag containing a fine white powder.

"Hmm."

Farrell opened the bag, examined the powder closely, then sniffed lightly at the bag.

"Cocaine."

Cox nodded, then poked his head into the bathroom, which was smallish and functional and tiled in white and gray. In an adjoining room, he found Barris's at-home office.

Cox went first to the file cabinet, which stood behind a long, narrow, cluttered antique desk, and flipped through the files. He found the usual mortgage, receipts, and correspondence files, and other files labeled with the titles of law journal articles and several chapters of a book Barris had apparently been writing—*In the Beginning: Law Before God*. He found no will, no safety-deposit box key.

Cox glanced through the contents of Barris's desk drawers and through the papers on top of his desk. There was no Rolodex, and nothing of immediate interest. The bookshelves were crammed with legal texts and journals, and the floor was piled high with stacks of magazines, books, and file folders overflowing with photocopied pages.

Cox sighed. The room contained a veritable mountain of paper, and all of it, relevant or not, would need to be sifted through.

But then he spotted a briefcase crammed between a floor lamp and the wall.

It was a boxy Coach briefcase in burgundy leather. Cox opened it with two quick snaps. Inside, a small gold mine of information was laid out before him, the three keys to the life of any well-organized individual: checkbook, address book, and appointment calendar. He took a moment to thumb through each, feeling the pressure of time passing and knowing he'd better get home, get changed, and hurry over to the law school.

But first a cigarette. He sat at Barris's desk, took out his pouch of tobacco, deftly rolled a cigarette, and lighted it. He pulled the can out of his back pocket to use as an ashtray, then surveyed the pages of names in Barris's address book. A few were familiar to Cox: Hedstrom, of course, then Al Hickey, the county prosecutor, and Faith Brodey. A few women's names, names unconnected to spouses or places.

Cox decided to take the appointment calendar with him. He told Farrell, who was admiring the Lladro golfer in Barris's breakfront, to get a thorough ID and alibi on everyone in the address book.

As Cox stepped outside into the cool morning air, his thoughts were momentarily distracted by the quiet beauty of the sun glinting off the leaded glass in Barris's windows and burnishing the limestone to a golden glow.

It was ten minutes after nine when Cox arrived at the law school, an imposing Gothic-styled structure at the edge of the BHU campus. He was now wearing his dark blue wool suit and his fake Burberry raincoat, too neatly pressed and smelling like dry-cleaning fluid. Searching for the building directory, he pushed through a bustle of students crowding into the law library, which had just opened its doors. Did they know about Barris? Somehow, he didn't think so.

He spotted an elevator and took it to the second-floor administrative offices. When the elevator doors slid open, he found himself looking down a long corridor in which clusters of men and women stood chattering excitedly outside a series of office doors. As Cox stepped out of the elevator, the heads turned toward him slowly, a ripple of attention passing through the crowd.

He approached the pleasant-looking rotund man nearest him.

"I'm looking for Dean Hume," Cox said evenly.

A short bookish woman wearing green tortoiseshell glasses stepped toward him out of the group. "I'm Dean Hume," she said in a tremulous voice.

"Detective Luther Cox of the HPD. May we speak privately?"

"Of course."

Cox followed the dean as she moved swiftly past the others and down a narrow hallway, through a waiting area with couches and magazines, and into her office. She motioned to a studded leather chair, murmured, "Please," then walked to the window behind her desk. Folding her arms, she stood motionless, with her back to Cox. He waited, scanning the bookshelves, surveying the purposeful disorder of the room.

"I've just told the faculty, those who are here," she said finally. "I haven't made any other calls yet. There's an enormous number of things to do."

"My condolences to you," Cox said softly. "And allow me to apologize in advance for the intrusion I'm going to be during the investigation."

"No need," she said flatly, turning to him. The skin around her eyes and nose was raw, her eyes tinged with red. "What can I tell you?"

"Talk to me about Professor Barris."

"What do you want to know?"

"What kind of person was he? Was he liked? Disliked? By whom? And why?"

She smiled weakly. "He was a good friend of mine and a genius. He could also be difficult. He graduated from Harvard Law School at the top of his class, clerked for Justice White, and could have taught anywhere in the country. He came back out here, where he grew up, because he loved Indiana, and loved basketball. He was

28

married when he started teaching, ended up divorced three years later. His ex-wife lives in Austin, Texas, if that's any help."

"Do you have any idea who might have murdered Professor Barris?"

She shook her head. "No, not really. . . . I mean, you could imagine people who might want to do such a thing. Like students he gave bad grades to, like girlfriends or ex-girlfriends he mistreated. Like husbands of wives he'd slept with. I honestly don't know. . . . I know he pissed off a lot of people. . . . But that's not so unusual, is it?"

She sat down distractedly and made a bridge with her fingers. "I think he had a real problem, sexually, psychologically, however you want to view it. I mean, other than that, he was . . . sweet, really. A nice guy. Helpful to students. A brilliant scholar in the area of criminal procedure and constitutional law. He deplored the judicial activism of the Warren era, a constant bugaboo of his, yet he applauded the same sort of activism when it came to Rehnquist. He's Scalia's biggest fan. Truly passionately conservative."

Cox smiled blandly and nodded.

"Jim was a social Darwinist," she went on. "Natural law . . . survival of the fittest. He believed society had no responsibility to help the underclass, just to create a world free of impediments to economic success. Of course, Jim was born to a quite wealthy family in Indy. But we all have our blind spots."

"You mentioned a sexual problem a moment ago."

"Yes, I quite forgot what I was saying." She put her hand to her forehead and closed her eyes. "Umm. How shall I put this? He came on to students. Subtly, most of the time. I mean, I think he had a certain knack for picking out the ones who might be interested and who wouldn't make a fuss, you see. And he could make his own interest apparent in such a way that if it wasn't reciprocated, the approach would pass off harmlessly. But not always. Over the years, a number of secretaries complained of being hit upon by Jim, a couple of the research and writing instructors, and several students. The word *harassment* was used in three cases, but he was too careful, really, maybe too clever. The ones he slept with didn't seem to have

29

any complaints, and the ones he didn't sleep with were generally content to let it go." She paused, then added, "Of course the law school would have taken action had a particular instance merited it, but that simply hasn't happened."

"Of course."

"But to get back to my main point—Jim had a problem with women. . . . He just couldn't keep his hands off. Maybe it gave him self-esteem to win at seduction. Maybe he was just a selfish prick. I think he saw himself as living under a kind of natural law of sex— that whatever woman he could win was his, by rights, that under the law of nature we are as free to copulate with one another as any creatures of the forest." She smiled, seemingly at the notion, then, as if remembering the gravity of the circumstance, looked down at her hands, which had again begun to tremble.

"You'll want to speak with his secretary, of course. Her name's Connie Slaybaugh; she's out in the secretarial pool on this floor. Harvey Blau, an old friend of Jim's, is also on this floor. Louis Robertson, the dean of students, might be able to tell you something of the sexual harassment complaints. Other professors—you might try Judy Rosen, a friend and ideological opponent, and Monty Mtoyo, another crim law professor, who would occasionally have a beer with Jim over at Rick's."

"Do you know anything about his relationship with Don Hedstrom?"

The dean raised her eyebrows and frowned. "Oh, Jim was a buddy of Hedstrom's. I don't know the man myself, but Jim was very proud of that friendship. Went to all the games, even on the road, when he could."

"What about girlfriends? Did you know any of his girlfriends?"

"Oh, I'd see him around campus with this one or that one. He never introduced them to me."

Cox stood. "I'm going to need the freedom of the building for today and probably days to come. I hope you don't mind."

"It's a public place, Mr. Cox." The dean walked to her door and paused before opening it. "I forgot to ask you, Mr. Cox. Do you have any idea who murdered Jim?"

"Not at the moment." Cox faced the dean. "I'll need to speak with some of the staff, and with some of his students."

"Certainly. You can use one of our interview rooms on the first floor. In fact, there's going to be a meeting today at one in the Moot Court Room—an impromptu memorial, of sorts—for students and faculty who want to express their feelings about Jim's death. Dean Robertson will be conducting it. We might arrange with him to set up a room for you and then announce at the meeting that you would like to speak with past and present students of Jim's."

"That would be a start."

"Yes. Of course we can also provide you with lists of names."

"Let's see how it goes," Cox said mildly as the dean pulled the door open and stepped aside.

At 9:30 A.M., Nora sat alone at the defense table in an empty courtroom. She always tried to arrive there first, to have a moment alone to center herself in the stillness of the place where her clients—the accused—came face-to-face with their accusers and judge and jury. The courtrooms in the City-County Building had furniture of a peculiarly utilitarian kind—circa the mid-1960s—which made this ritual of Nora's particularly important to her, as though in possessing the room alone, she dissipated its coldness, took control of it, and gave herself a measure of confidence. The judge's bench was of plain blond wood, and behind it there was a plain wood-paneled wall with a bronze-colored state seal of Indiana centered above the judge's throne. On one side of the judge's bench was a desk for the court reporter; on the other, a witness stand. To one side of the room was the jury box—thirteen leather swivel chairs, and in the center of the room were the tables for the attorneys—one table for each opposing side. Behind the attorneys' tables were the rows of seats for the sixty or so spectators the room was designed to hold.

There were no spectators in court that morning, no one to watch

Stormi Skye be brought into the courtroom by LaTisha and her cohort Greg, a black man of sixty who had worked for the court for nearly forty years. When he saw Nora, Greg winked at her, as he always did, and in return, she met his eyes and smiled tightly.

"Hey, Greg."

"How are you, counselor?" he asked jovially, and he pumped her hand once, a comic routine intended to put the defendant at ease.

Stormi Skye was not at ease. She stared at Nora, her face a sallow shade of pink, blotched, as if she'd been crying. At Greg's direction, Stormi took a seat next to Nora at the defense table, and then she put her hands in her lap and stared at them.

Nora saw that Stormi was biting the inside of her cheek, and she began to put her hand on Stormi's shoulder, but then stopped herself and said, "It's all right, Stormi. You don't have to say or do anything today. Just sit here quietly."

Stormi nodded, bit down harder, and wondered if the woman from whom she had bought a fix on her last stay in the lockup was still around.

The deputy prosecutor, Mark Gautier, entered from the back of the courtroom.

Nora followed him with her eyes, knowing that Gautier's eyes would not meet hers until he was close enough to look down at her. Gautier was thirtyish and conservative, a dark-haired, heavy-bearded man whose cheeks were always red from shaving too strenuously.

Smiling his politician's smile, Gautier caught Nora's eyes as he held out his hand to her. She shook his hand like a good fighter and introduced him to Stormi, who did not avert her gaze from her hands in her lap.

"Nice to work with you again, Nora."

"You, too, Mark," Nora lied.

At 9:45, the judge and court reporter entered the courtroom through a door behind the bench. Judge Stonebreaker, a heavy, ungainly man with large plastic glasses and a slick of greasy hair falling into one eye, cleared his throat loudly as Mark and Nora rose.

"Forgive me," he intoned, "but I'm ill. It's some damn flu bug, and I'm feeling a bit flushed. So don't get too close."

Nora said warmly, "I hope you're feeling better soon, Judge."

"Same here, Your Honor," Gautier said quickly.

"Thank you, so do I." Judge Stonebreaker, who looked about to die—his breathing was labored, and sweat shone on his face and forehead and forearms—opened a thin file folder on the bench in front of him.

"We are here this morning for the initial hearing on the case of the *State of Indiana versus Stormi Skye,* cause number four-nine-D-oh-eight-one-oh-oh-three-CR-oh-eight-five-two. Stormi Skye has been charged with the felony possession of a controlled substance, cocaine, and with public intoxication. An automatic plea of not guilty is hereby entered." He coughed loudly and glanced at Nora over his glasses. "Let's talk about dates."

"The prosecutor's office will be ready for trial in three months, Your Honor," Gautier said.

"And the defense?"

"We would prefer a six-month calendar, Your Honor. There is investigation that needs to be done." Which was code, they all knew, for "I'm not going to roll over on this one; we'll plea, but the sentence had better be light."

"Any objection from the prosecutor?"

"None, Your Honor, except that it must be understood that the defendant waives her right to a speedy trial by setting a six-month calendar."

"Understood, Your Honor."

Judge Stonebreaker glanced at Nora impatiently, then pronounced the omnibus date—thirty days from that date—and dates for pretrial motions.

"Bail will be set at fifty thousand dollars, considering the defendant's record. Anything further?"

Judge Stonebreaker cast his eyes for the first time at Stormi, who lifted her gaze to meet his.

"Nothing further here," Nora said.

"Nothing further, Your Honor," Gautier responded.

The judge banged his gavel once and rose swiftly. "So entered," he said. "See you in a month. If I'm still among the living."

5

After handing Stormi over to LaTisha, Nora returned wearily to her desk, wishing she had a door to close so that she might lean back in her chair and rest her eyes.

As she entered her cubicle, Nora saw that the message light on her telephone was blinking.

She dialed her voice mail and took a sip of stale coffee as she waited for the message to play. "Nora, this is Marjorie. I've just had some awful news. It's about Jim Barris. Please call me."

The voice belonged to Marjorie Paugh, a law school classmate of Nora's who now taught legal research at BHU. Nora frowned. She had no wish to speak with Marjorie, who had never been a close friend, not even a friend at all, really, until Nora had begun a relationship with Jim Barris seven months before. It was then, on jaunts to Harrison and stops at the law school, that she had found herself bumping into Marjorie, and their awkward hellos and polite suggestions that they lunch together had gracelessly evolved into actual lunches.

Marjorie knew something was going on between Nora and Jim Barris, despite Nora's white lie that she was there to do research in the law library, and before long, Marjorie took it upon herself to "be there" for Nora, wanted or not, a wary, watchful eye, a vaguely mocking voice of reason.

Nora was well aware of how ridiculous it was to be sleeping with a man nearly twice her age, and a law professor to boot. Though she had not been his student—Nora had gone to Indiana's other state law school, in Bloomington—the fact that he was a law professor somehow made the relationship an even greater sin, and thus all the more desirable. Nora was just a couple of years out of law school herself and still under the peculiar spell of the tantalizingly quasi-parental taboo on sex between student and professor. So what if he was fifty-two and she twenty-eight? She wasn't thinking about marriage, she told herself, and even if she had been, she knew that she would not, could not, be his wife. He was too selfish, too mean, and if he ever chose to get married, it would be to some pretty little girl, a trophy wife, not to someone like her. She was not pretty enough to be a trophy of any kind, and even if she had been, she was too loud and abrasive and unruly to be anyone's possession. She would be more like an albatross, something stuck to one's shoe, a clinging embarrassment.

No, they would be lovers for as long as it suited them, which, as it turned out, wasn't long.

They had met when he took over Stormi's defense. Was that what Marjorie's call was about? Had Jim again been hired by Lydon? But how would Marjorie know?

And then Nora telephoned Marjorie, who told her through sobs that Jim Barris had been found dead in a cornfield on the outskirts of Harrison.

After a brief, unproductive interlude with Barris's secretary, Connie—a tearful young woman almost beside herself with fright—Cox was escorted down to Dean Robertson's office by Dean Hume.

"I don't envy you your job," she said. "You have to pry into such painful events when the wounds are at their freshest. At least we lawyers have the distance of time when we do our prying."

"Yes," said Cox. "And people are less likely to tell us the truth."

Dean Robertson, a muscular former wrestler with a pencil-thin mustache, greeted Cox at his office door with a closed-lip smile and a handshake that felt oddly soft to Cox's touch.

"Thank you for being here," Dean Robertson intoned as Dean Hume motioned that she was going back upstairs. Cox nodded to her quickly, then faced Robertson, whose strangely robotic expression suggested a studied presentation of sincere but not overwhelming grief.

"May we speak privately?"

"Certainly." Robertson nodded to his secretary and led Cox into an area of his office assembled like a living room, with a couch, two plush chairs, and a coffee table with a large metal ashtray containing two cigarette butts.

"May I smoke?" Cox asked quickly.

"Certainly."

"Thank you." Cox took out his tobacco and rolled a cigarette as he spoke. "We estimate that Professor Barris was murdered by asphyxiation at one or two A.M. last night. As you may have heard, the body was found among some trees near a cornfield north of town. Do you know who might have murdered Professor Barris?"

"No, not at all," Robertson said in a voice so carefully modulated that Cox felt his bullshit antennae instantly move into position. "Or let me put it another way." He licked his lips. "Jim Barris had people who did not care for him, as we all do. People who were insulted by him or were hurt by him. But we never imagine that these people are capable of killing us. Do we? No. If you asked me to name people who disliked Barris, I would begin with about seventy percent of the faculty, including myself. He had only a couple of solid friendships here. And then, of course, there's Don Hedstrom."

"Why didn't you like him?"

"Because he was . . . arrogant, unpleasant to deal with. God's gift to the law, or so he thought."

"Who were his solid friends?"

"Harvey Blau. Monty Mtoyo, perhaps. And he had a solid professional relationship with Dean Hume."

Cox was distracted by a large portrait photograph of Robertson with a pretty wife and three blond children. Robertson turned, noticed what had drawn Cox's attention, smiled broadly, and was about to speak when his telephone rang, a sharp electronic siren.

"Yes. . . . Uh-huh. . . . Put it through." He handed the receiver to Cox. "For you."

"Cox."

"Luther, sorry to trouble you." At the sound of the distinctive voice coming across the wire, Cox couldn't help but lean back in his chair; there was an ineffable relaxing quality to Ivan Sarvetnikov's loping, slightly syncopated Russian-inflected speech. In the seventies, Sarvetnikov had emigrated from Russia, where he had been an eminent surgeon, to teach an international relations course at BHU under a federal grant. By the time the grant ran out, Sarvetnikov had fallen in love with the verdant Hoosier heartland, which reminded him of the countryside around his native Kursk. So the university president pulled some strings and got Sarvetnikov the coroner's job, a position for which he was well suited by morbid temperament. Sarvetnikov could deliver the most gruesome information in a fashion that was easy on the ears, deceiving the mind into a calm acceptance.

"Talk to me, Ivan."

"The man died of a heart attack, probably while being asphyxiated. Blood tests positive for cocaine, which is perhaps a contributing factor."

"Uh-huh."

"As for the . . . ah . . . condition of the body, those touches were merely for amusement. Clean and superficial. Likely done with razor or very sharp knife, hunting knife perhaps. From the angle of the cuts, look for a right-handed butcher."

Cox held the phone for a moment in silence. "Nice work, Ivan," he muttered finally. "Anything on time?"

"Judging the condition of the body and the weather, between twelve and two A.M."

"Fluids?" Cox looked at Robertson, who regarded him with unabashed curiosity.

"An ejaculation took place not long before death. Can't say when yet. Within an hour, most likely."

"Thanks, Ivan. Keep this down, okay?"

"Will do."

Robertson took the receiver anxiously from Cox. "What is it?"

"Coroner's findings." Cox crushed out his cigarette. "We're going to need someone to come down to the morgue to identify the body, just for the record. Would you?"

"Yes, I'd be happy to do that," said Robertson, seeming heartened by this official role.

"I've been expecting you. Please, sit down."

Harvey Blau rose slightly from his chair and gestured from an awkward stooped position toward the red swivel chair on the other side of his desk.

"Thank you." Cox turned the chair toward himself.

"I mean," Blau continued, "it's so incredible! So terrible! Lord! I must tell you, I am deeply wounded. I have lost a man who was at times my dearest friend in the world! But—Jesus! This is so *shocking!* How did it happen?"

"He was strangled to death at an unknown location; then the body was dropped out in the country," Cox said. "Near a cornfield."

Blau stared a moment, then shook his head. "That's all you know?"

"Essentially." Cox took a breath. "Professor Blau, tell me who you think might have killed James Barris."

Blau looked down at his hands, which were resting in his lap, then out over Cox's shoulder, as if engaged in mental calculations too complex for speech.

"No one," he said finally. "In fact, I don't think he was killed. I think he's playing some sort of shitty practical joke on us all."

Cox looked point-blank into Blau's face to see if there was any hint of macabre humor. There was none. Blau stared back in peremptory silence.

"No, Professor Blau, there's no doubt."

"Of course." Blau's eyes watered. He picked up a pencil and rolled it between his fingers. "He arrived here the year after I did. We played a lot of racquetball in those days. Not so much lately." He slapped his wide belly and grunted a laugh. "We drank a lot of beer, too. Saw a lot of basketball. Used to go to Amsterdam each year for the Law and Society Conference." He tapped the pencil on the desk. "What else can I tell you?"

"Women in his life?"

"Ah, now there's a subject. Of course there's his wife, Jane, a marvelous woman. She's a political science professor in Austin now." He paused. "Somebody ought to call her, I suppose."

"Recent girlfriends?"

"I don't know. We never talked much about women. Just the usual succession of pretty girls. He'd introduce one to me now and then, but I didn't remember their names for an instant. Why bother? There'd be a new one the next day." He paused. "We really didn't talk much at all. Really. Hadn't for years. Life's too busy. No time for friendships."

Cox rose and searched his pockets for a business card. "Call me if something comes to mind, would you?"

"Sit down another moment, please." Blau looked pleadingly at Cox as he motioned him down. "I ought to tell you before Jane does that Jim had an affair with my wife some years ago. That was shortly after he and Jane first moved here. I don't think it's significant, and I wouldn't mention it except in the interest of full disclosure . . . but this was back in the mid-seventies, and I was fooling around some myself in those days—it was the times, you know." He smiled. "You might just be old enough to remember those days. . . ."

Cox nodded. "I am."

"It wasn't a long affair. Three months, I believe. You might question my wife about it if you like, though it's one of those dead and buried things we prefer to keep that way. I can tell you that I think it contributed to the Barrises' breakup. Of course, Jim didn't have a faithful bone in his body."

"I appreciate your honesty, Professor Blau." Cox rose again.

"You're much too polite to ask me for an alibi, Detective," Blau went on. "But I'll give you one anyway. I was at the University Opera last night with my wife. *Rigoletto*. It ended at eleven-fifteen; then we went home and went to bed." He smiled. "And stayed there till morning."

6

<hr/>

Their relationship had been a kind of offense against reason.

He had invited her to dinner during an afternoon spent loitering in the hallway outside criminal court; it had been the afternoon of Stormi's sentencing hearing, when Nora happened to be there on another case that was stacked up behind Stormi's case on that day's long docket. Nora and Barris had been waiting among the dozen or so other attorneys crowding the hallway, and they had found themselves sitting together on a bench otherwise occupied by men in handcuffs. They sat there and talked for three hours.

Barris was handsome. He was lean, muscular, and graceful, his figure crowned by a mane of prematurely white hair that billowed back from his high forehead. Nora thought him to represent, almost comically, an idealized image of the legal professional: dynamic, brilliant, and pugnacious. As he spoke, he smoothed back his hair for emphasis, gazed at the ceiling with theatrical impatience, and stroked his short white beard like an aged preening lion. Nora thought he was very pretty.

Over dinner, he continued to charm her, smiling a lot, showing off his perfectly shiny white teeth, until, gazing gently into her eyes, he said, first, "You are very beautiful," and then, taking her hand, "I would love to spend the night with you."

She replied, "I would like it if you would," keeping the tone serious but light, in the spirit of the thing, their casual sophistication.

So she drove to his house, followed his black Jaguar in her car, rejecting the opportunity to change her mind, looking forward to the night with cool excitement.

He had drinks poured when she entered his house—Jack Daniel's, which by then he knew was her preference—and she noticed in the crystal ashtray on his coffee table a joint rolled and waiting.

When he took her coat, he kissed the back of her neck, and the sensation of his lips on her skin went straight to her knees and she knew she would have him, regardless of the reservations she was now constructing in her mind.

The joint was the first thing. He said, "Would you like some?," lighting it, not waiting for an answer, which was no—first because she had no interest in marijuana, but no less because she was subject to random drug testing and would not be so foolish as to jeopardize her career for a puff of pot. She declined, grateful to have a reasonable excuse, and he took a few hits on the joint, medicinally, it seemed, just enough to relax him, while he undid his collar button and reached over and undid her collar button and smokily kissed her neck.

She sipped the Jack Daniel's, a bit dizzy from the smell of the pot, enjoying the attention, yet feeling somewhat like she felt at the beauty salon when she was being worked on by a particularly solicitous hairdresser. She closed her eyes, catlike, and let him work on her. He lifted a breast out of her bra, wetting the nipple with his tongue and blowing on it softly, then kissing it warm again, taking it into his mouth, hot with smoke. And then he said, "Let's go to bed."

He stood on one side of the bed and undressed completely. Nora stood on the other side, undressing to her panties, and then he sat cross-legged on top of his forest green down comforter and reached back into a compartment in the headboard of his bed and removed a tiny Ziploc bag of white powder and a mirror about four inches square. Nora's heart sank when she saw it, appalled at the stupidity, the indulgence, and she was relieved to have already provided an excuse for not partaking. It seemed such a passé thing to do, so at odds with his intelligence, but she merely watched him with a mild dismayed curiosity.

"I'm worried about kissing you now," she said. "I don't want to get any of that stuff in my blood."

"I'm sorry," he said, and he leaned over and kissed her stomach. "I want so much to kiss you."

He snorted one short line into each nostril, then leaned back on the bed and took his penis, which was semierect, in one hand while he swept up the remaining specks of cocaine with the fingers of his other hand. He rubbed the cocaine into the head of his penis, then gazed heavy-lidded at Nora.

"Do you need to do that?" Nora asked gently.

"No," he murmured.

"Then why do you?"

"Waste not, want not."

"Do you want for anything?" She smiled as he kissed a nipple.

"No," he said.

He was an odd sort of lover, she thought later. When he had entered her, he raised himself up on his arms, stretched full length, and flexed his whole body as if to make all of him hard, his legs and buttocks and abdomen and chest and shoulders and arms—all of him was tensed and hard and his penis was just the leading part of him, as if all of him were fucking her, as if all of him would go inside if only he could fit.

It was not wonderful. She did not enjoy his determined style of lovemaking, his insistent effort to wring an orgasm out of her. It was like torture, like tyranny, like an ultimate possession. He would not be done, would not be satisfied, would not come or let her rest until she came.

And so she faked it for him, annoyed with herself for doing so, but by the time he was done, she was sore and she'd had enough.

44

She stayed with him that night, sleeping fitfully on her back as he curled against her in what she would have considered the female position—his head on her shoulder, her arm around his back, his arm draped across her chest, her other arm lightly holding him. She breathed the scent of his shampoo, or perhaps it was something he used to keep his hair in place, but it was strangely floral, like dried, scented flowers, potpourri.

Sometime in the middle of the night, they found themselves simultaneously with eyes open, the kind of moment when with some other man she would have pulled him to her and made love again, but Jim looked up at her once, softly kissed the side of her breast, and began to talk.

"You are marvelous," he said.

"Thank you," she replied. "You, too."

He raised himself up on an elbow. "Tell me about your first love," he said, grinning.

"Why? Are you taking a poll?" she asked, taken aback, cautious.

"No. I want to know. Research of a kind. It interests me to know women's lives."

Deciding to play, Nora said, "First love or first lover?"

"Not the same?"

"Of course not."

"First love."

"A boy in preschool. Ben was his name. I used to bite him, make him cry."

"First lover."

"Does the boy I jerked off in back of the high school football stadium count?"

"Sure."

"You like to talk about sex, don't you?"

"Yes, I do."

"That would be Martin. A tall boy everyone thought was gay because he was so unconventional. He was a musician, an oboist. Quite serious about it. I played the piano then."

45

"You made beautiful music together."

"Indeed we did. I've told; now you tell me."

"Love or lover?"

"You decide."

"I was a senior in high school and she was an exchange student from Italy. She was small and voluptuous. She had a pretty face and huge hair, so curly, it was kinky, hair you could grab on to." He closed his eyes. "And she had beautiful breasts, like yours."

Nora gazed at him, feeling strangely invisible. "Her name?"

"Francesca."

"And she went back to Italy?"

"Of course." Opening his eyes, he touched Nora's navel. "We wrote back and forth for a time, then I flew over to see her the following summer, the summer before I started Harvard. She hadn't the slightest interest in seeing me, but I convinced her to go camping with me, a bicycle trip into the Castelli Romani, the hills south of Rome. We slept together, in a single sleeping bag, but she wouldn't make love with me. She was done. Done. And it was as though she could barely tolerate being near me. Sort of like the female spider who bites off the head of her mate once he's performed for her."

He smiled sadly at Nora, seemingly in an afterglow of nostalgia.

"I'm not going to bite off your head," she said.

They met again, at her place, a couple of weeks later; Nora thought she'd give him another chance because she was fair, and alone, and because she was at the point in her life when the first answer to any proposal was not Why? but Why not?

There were no drugs, just the two of them and a bit of wine, and so she told him exactly what she would like him to do. He was more than pleased to do anything she desired, because although she was not conventionally pretty—she had a wide, doughy, country-girl face and a fleshy, big-boned body—she gave off a sexual heat that made him absolutely crazy with need; he had to fuck her (as he told her while fucking her), *had to,* and just the thought of her made him hard (he said), practically coming in his pants.

The sex was good for a while, so long as they were not at his house. So long as there were no drugs. But as per the pattern Nora knew well, after a couple of months, it was maintenance sex, and then they did not see each other for weeks at a time.

By the time of Barris's death, they had not seen each other for more than two months.

She had never been in love with him. She had been lonely and horny and not particularly high on herself, disgusted by the things with which nature had blessed her—her face, her hair, her body. He was refreshingly honest about desire, and his lust for her was a pleasant antidote to her negativity.

There were times when she thought she hated him—his arrogance, his conceit, his claim to existing above morals, manners, the law. Most of the time, though, she found him amusing—sexually too much the *Playboy* sophisticate manqué, but intellectually, conversationally, a challenge, something too few men offered her.

Nora's reverie was interrupted by a phone call from the court clerk, who informed her that Gene Lydon had posted bail for Stormi and that Stormi had been released.

"Did someone come for Stormi?"

"Her mother."

Nora put the phone down slowly, still lost in thoughts of Barris, when it occurred to her that Barris had been found dead west of Indianapolis, in Harrison, where Stormi lived, and not far from where Stormi had been picked up. Nora wondered if Barris had ever slept with Stormi Skye. It certainly would not be beyond him to violate the rules of professional conduct by sleeping with a client or to break the law by hiring a prostitute; Barris's legal representation of Gene Lydon's prostitutes and porno store had seemed to Nora to be a dangerous game, of which Barris was entirely too fond.

What is it about men? she puzzled. Why this attraction to pornography, to dirty games, to ugliness—the way little boys play with insects, crush worms in their fingers, set fires? As men, they played these games hidden from women, as though fearful of their mothers. For one another, however, men displayed the pride of who's nastiest, who's grossest, who's screwed the most women, who's behaved the worst toward them.

She wondered how much she did not know about Barris. At first blush, she figured it was the cocaine that had done him in—that he'd been killed in a deal gone awry. But why naked? Why the mutilation? Why in a cornfield?

She picked up Stormi's file and found an address for Louise Skye. Nora felt a strong intuition that she needed to see Stormi now, to tell her what had happened, and to find out if she had had more than an attorney-client relationship with Barris.

Nora telephoned Marjorie Paugh and told her brusquely that she was driving out to Harrison to speak with a client and wanted to meet her for a drink afterward.

"Yes, of course," Marjorie said, sounding hurt. "I'm sorry I didn't say something earlier. . . . I thought perhaps you preferred to be alone."

She thinks I'm upset about Barris, or she thinks I should be, Nora thought, offended by the idea.

"I'm fine," Nora said. "More than fine."

Cox met Farrell for a quick bite to eat in the tiny law school canteen a few minutes before the memorial service was to begin. Farrell had nothing of substance to report, only the results of what had become, for her, a study in the delivery of bad news: "About two-thirds of the people I reached said nothing when I told them. Silence. Then it was always something like 'How'd it happen?' The other third can't shut up. They say, 'Ohmigod, he's dead. I can't believe it. I just saw him three days ago at the mall; he looked so healthy. . . .' "

Cox nodded sympathetically as he bit into a soggy tuna on white.

"And then, after an hour of trying to get through to Don Hedstrom, his secretary puts me on hold for twenty minutes. He comes on the phone. Knows who I am—his secretary had to have told him—and says, 'Whaddaya want?' I tell him the news. He's quiet for a minute and then says, 'What're ya callin' me for?' I ask him where he was last night. He told me he hung around Aberdeen Hall for a couple of hours after last night's game, then went home and didn't go out."

"That's the trouble with your two A.M. murders," Cox said, stifling a burp. "Everybody's fast asleep when it happens."

Farrell frowned. "There's somethin' really weird about this one. There's too much evidence at the scene. The corpse right out in the open. It looks too easy."

Cox watched her face move as she spoke, listening, but at the same time admiring her sharp, dark, vaguely Appalachian features. He would enjoy painting that face, he realized.

"How's your pa?" Cox asked softly. Farrell's father, a retired factory worker with whom she lived, was in the hospital with emphysema.

"He's not so good," she said soberly. "He's fuckin' dying, as a matter of fact."

"Your ma coming in?"

"Yeah, she'll drive down from Lansing this weekend."

Cox nodded sympathetically. "Let's hope we can wrap this sucker up by Friday."

Farrell rolled her eyes. "Dream on."

In the Moot Court Room—a wide lecture hall encircling a high judge's bench, flanked by the Indiana and United States flags—about fifty students, a couple of secretaries, and a handful of faculty and administrators gathered at one o'clock. Cox and Farrell stood at the rear of the room, surveying the somberly murmuring crowd as Dean Robertson prepared to speak. Near him, milling about at the front of the room, were Hume, Blau, and four other dark-suited men and one attractive silver-blond-haired woman. Judy Rosen, Cox thought, recognizing her from the faculty photographs in the law school lobby.

Robertson tapped the microphone, cleared his throat, and began, "As you have all heard by now, early this morning Professor James Barris . . ."

Cox whispered to Farrell, "Have a seat and stick around." Farrell grimaced and nodded, and Cox slipped out. He walked through the hallways, quiet now, and took the elevator to the second floor.

An hour of rooting around in the maelstrom of papers in Barris's office yielded nothing, as did a check of the contents of the directories on the hard drive of Barris's computer. Cox pocketed a couple of diskettes found in the top drawer of Barris's desk. He sighed. So far, nothing anomalous, nothing pointing anywhere.

On a corner of the desk was a pile of reprints, neatly bound, of an article Barris had apparently just published in the *Hastings Journal on Law and Society*. Cox picked up a copy of the slim paperback and opened it gingerly.

ON SEX AND JURISPRUDENCE:
A PROLEGOMENON FOR A CONSERVATIVE RESPONSE
TO THE POSTFEMINIST TURF WARS

JAMES BARRIS

It's ugly out there. The sexual marketplace, like the marketplace of ideas, has become a hazardous place to shop. AIDS and sexual violence are the evils society seeks desperately to control, and innovative legal tools have been proposed and, in some places, implemented to achieve that end. At Antioch College, a code of sexual conduct prescribes specific language to be employed in the dating rituals students use to bed one another down. From the halls of legal academia, we have proposals for an end to pornography by making sexually explicit material actionable as a civil rights violation. In courtrooms across the country, in the chambers of Congress, and in the never-ending press conferences of alleged victims, we witness tales of sexual mutilation, sexual molestation, sexual harassment, seduction, rape, and revenge. It is a world of sexual predators, where words are indistinguishable from deeds, where all men are rapists, and where one's eyes are simply not to be trusted.

Welcome to the new millennium.

In this era, we are confused about sex, and there's no dearth of theories to go around, particularly among the heirs to Millett, Greer, Friedan, et al. In today's postfeminist turf wars, Camille Paglia and Kate Roiphe defend assertively the robustness of female sexuality against the neopuritanism of Catharine MacKinnon and Andrea Dworkin. The men have weighed in, too, of course; Richard Posner's *Sex and Reason* is the most prominent example, but there have been notable murmurs from Ronald Dworkin and Larry Tribe.

Nonetheless, there has been no unified conservative response to the disparate voices emerging from both sexes, and the time seems right for this writer to enter the breach. The sexual-intellectual climate has not been so overheated since 1971, when, in the midst of similar geologic stresses, Norman Mailer published *The Prisoner of Sex*. In this article, I hope to synthesize the strands of my own theories on sex and the law, along with the disparate rumblings in the souls of my colleagues, into a preliminary critique of contemporary sexual jurisprudence. The work of the individuals noted above will provide a battering ram for breaking through the doors of the feminist fortress. On the way, I take a brief side trip through Foucault World, the postmodern amusement park, where our hosts, Derrida and Lacan, take us on a fragmented, digitized ride into the future of sex and the law, in all its virtual reality.

Cox grinned as he read, enjoying the language and Barris's comic belligerence, despite the academic name-dropping. He was unfamiliar with the legal references, but he understood the cultural ones, and he sympathized with Barris's wry view of the state of sexual relations.

He had long ago ceased doing business in the sexual marketplace, but he could see in the lives of those around him how antagonistic and downright perilous the act of mating had become.

Cox pocketed the reprint, thinking he had learned more about Barris from four paragraphs than from anything Barris's colleagues had told him.

He sighed and tried to shake off the tingling sense of annoyance he felt creeping over his skin, a physical manifestation of the frustration gnawing inside him. He never doubted for a moment that the killer would be found, or that a logical explanation would be deduced. In every one of the twenty-three murders he had investigated for the HPD, the identity of the killer was apparent within hours. Most often it was immediately apparent—the boyfriend, the ex-husband, the guy in the bar whom the victim had been getting drunk with and fighting with for years. But this case was different; so far, nothing was apparent.

One nasty chore remained to be done. Cox took the scrap of paper with the phone number of Barris's ex-wife out of his wallet. He hesitated, rehearsing the words, and dialed.

"Hello." The voice was pleasant, unaffected, and even. Cox would have guessed from the greeting that she hadn't yet heard about Barris's murder, but when he identified himself, she interrupted to say, "Oh, yes. Harvey Blau said you'd be calling."

"Yes," said Cox, caught off balance.

"I'm not sure I can be much help. It's been years since I spoke with Jim."

"Well, what would be helpful would be to know from your perspective about old grudges or patterns of behavior that might have developed into something dangerous. I mean drug use, alcoholism, gambling, involvement in a crime of some sort, like securities fraud or extortion."

"Oh, God no." She laughed. "I mean, aside from the numerous affairs he had before and during our marriage, there was just the usual pot smoking when we were younger and drinking lots of white wine. We were . . . gentle people. You know, working in academia is like being a hippie with a steady job. For a while there we were full of ourselves, not caring much for convention. Except that I wasn't really the sexually adventurous type. I wanted a real marriage and children and a real life. Which I have, by the way—two kids, a terrific husband, and a great job. James Barris was in my life for about six years from start to finish. And that six years was over thirteen years ago."

"Thank you. I appreciate your—"

"I mean, I'm sorry he's dead. And maybe tomorrow it will hit me that he meant a lot to me and I'll be able to cry about it. But maybe not. I really hated him for cheating on me. Especially with Blau's wife. Harvey told me he told you. If you want to know something that might get him into trouble, there's a good one for you— the way he treats his friends. Or, that is, treats himself to their wives. He was an amazingly selfish person who didn't care very much about the way his behavior affected others. At least he was that way when I knew him. I don't imagine he was capable of changing."

"Whose wife besides Blau's did he have an affair with?"

"Two I know of. . . . There was a Professor Jack Hinkle, who has long since moved on, and Leo Rothstein, who left his wife when he found out about it. Poor guy was devastated. But that was—what, fourteen years ago? A long time to hold a grudge. Harvey Blau's the only one who's still around, and though I'm sure he was hurt by it, Harvey's a very forgiving kind of guy." Her breath came heavy over the phone, an impatient sigh. "I don't know, honestly. It's a long time ago."

The interview room provided by Dean Robertson was tiny and windowless, with off-white walls, an efficiency desk, and a pair of swivel chairs. Cox sat behind the desk and waited as Dean Robertson funneled students who showed up at the memorial service into a neat line extending up the hall.

Cox played with a rubber band and a paper clip, the only two items in the desk, as he waited for the first of Barris's present and former pupils to knock. The day had hardly begun and he already felt worn-out, indecisive, apprehensive. Speaking with the students was a long shot, he knew, but it was something that could be accomplished now. Later, he'd go through the painstaking business of reconstructing Barris's movements during the previous evening.

The parade of fresh faces began, and one after the other, the bright, intense young men and women answered his questions with earnest seriousness. At first, it stunned and delighted Cox to see how much they cared about providing the complete information on their whereabouts, their feelings about Barris, their guesses as to the reasons behind his murder and the identity of his killer. Then it began to disgust him as he realized that not one of them gave a shit about Barris or about catching a murderer; they viewed the entire event as a learning experience, staged, just possibly, for their benefit—what a marvelous way to view the whole range of criminal law, from the murder through the investigation and then the trial. Barris couldn't have taught them more if he were alive.

Ultimately, the students' responses to Cox's questions were little more than gossip and the venting of complaints about Barris's classroom personality, as Cox expected. The first-year students were in awe and scared half to death of the man; the second-year students were sarcastic and bitter, the angriest of the lot, feeling the fresh bruises of the beating they'd taken as first-years; the third-year students were the most charitable, a few even expressing sincere sorrow for the loss of a life-shaping mentor, an influential teacher and friend—the Kingsfield of Benjamin Harrison. After a time, Cox gave up looking for clues and listened as sympathetically as he was able, though he was bored silly with the sameness of their stories, the banality of their feelings. Toward the end, he used the Zen trick of allowing the boredom to form a kind of white noise in his mind, so that he needn't listen any longer and his mind could be off doing other chores. When something unusual reached his ears, it would rise above the static like a piccolo trumpet in an orchestra and he would tune in again.

But then an attractive young woman walked in, a tall, well-built brunette, oddly nervous; she identified herself as Margaret Sanderson, and it was like a fanfare, played fortissimo, snapping him to attention.

Cox knew immediately that the face was familiar, and importantly so, and his heart pounded as he struggled to remember why. It wasn't until he stood up and shook her hand and she began to say her name that the switch got thrown in his brain and he knew it all in a rush of mortification.

"Sit down, please," he mumbled.

She sat, obediently, and looked blankly at him. Cox looked back at her with what he knew was a ridiculous mixture of confusion and pain. He wanted desperately to mention it, to apologize somehow, even to explain it all, to tell her the whole filthy truth.

"We're speaking with students today to find out if anyone has any information. . . ."

He said the words mechanically, and Margaret responded evenly, with a restraint that was obvious to Cox. She hated him. He saw it in the set of her jaw, the directness of her gaze.

"And there's little I can tell you," she said forthrightly, the words seeming rehearsed, "except that Professor Barris's abilities as a professor were overshadowed by his personality, which was . . . abrasive, to say the least. . . ."

He heard her words without listening, just as she seemed to be speaking without consciousness of meaning; all of their energy was engaged in a separate, unspoken conversation of blame and regret.

Then suddenly she was quiet, her words having ceased, and he said, softly, "I will always be sorry about everything that took place at your trial."

If Cox had hoped his show of contrition would have a healing effect, he was far wrong, and he watched, horrified, as her face instantly flushed bright red and she began to cough and gasp for breath. He stepped around the desk to help her, but she thrust out her arm, shook her head violently, and fled.

Cox dropped back into his chair, cursed, and punched the desk with his fist. In a stroke, he'd managed to reopen the wound, deep and bloody as it ever was. What had he been thinking? He punched the desk again, then rubbed his throbbing knuckles.

7

She won't be there, Nora thought, not at home, not after being bailed out by Lydon and having to endure a long car ride home with her mother. She'll be out—at Lydon's store, or at a bar, or on the street. She will be out where twenty-year-old prostitutes go on their off hours.

Nora hadn't the faintest idea where that might be, but she was determined to find out.

She knew from Stormi's file that she was available to customers through an escort service that was run out of the back room of Pleazures; the adult bookstore was conveniently adjacent to a seedy flophouse. Customers would call ahead or simply ask in the bookstore if Stormi or one of the other girls was available. The whole operation was laughably obvious, a tribute to the ineptitude and corruption in the Harrison Police Department, reputedly the worst police force in central Indiana.

Driving amid the rush-hour traffic around downtown Harrison, Nora felt suddenly exhausted and depressed. It was nearly 5:00 P.M. A Steve Earle tape played softly on the stereo in the cab of her pickup, and as she drifted past the storefronts and the corner bars, she followed the rise and fall of Earle's gritty voice and picked at the worries crowding for space in her heart.

She had to see Stormi now, had to talk, finally, about Barris, to find out everything she knew, everything that had gone on between them. Nora drove across the grid of Harrison's streets to a place where the traffic thinned to a trickle, and she found herself on the back streets behind the business center, where the factories and auto-body shops were set among lots crowded with tractor-trailers. The streets were rutted and full of chuckholes, and Nora was about to turn back toward town when she saw a brightly painted cinder-block building a few streets ahead. She drove slowly toward it, carefully avoiding the chuckholes, until she saw the neon sign—Pleazures—and the big frosted panes of glass and the notice on the door, which read ADULTS ONLY. Next door was another building with a neon sign; this one said SLEEP TITE MOTEL.

Oh, Lord, Nora thought. What else would it look like?

She pulled up in front of the building and parked among the five or six cars in its tiny parking lot. Trembling in the cold air, she turned off the ignition and waited for the courage to go inside.

Five minutes later, Nora entered the building. Two sets of doors at the entrance led to a short flight of steps down to a high-ceilinged room about the size of a triple garage, containing six or seven rows of racks filled with magazines and paperback books. The walls were old and cracked and painted light blue, the floor was spotted gray linoleum, and next to the entrance was a high counter with a cash register, behind which a man with a ponytail and mirrored sunglasses sat on a tall stool. He looked up from the book he was reading and nodded down at Nora; if he was shocked to see a woman in this place, he didn't show it. She nodded back to him and entered the center aisle.

There were three college-age guys laughing around a circular rack of magazines. An older man was staring into the pages of a paperback book.

Nora looked around and noticed an unfinished wooden door at the back of the room. The door had a small square window in it, illuminated from behind.

She had seen pornography, but she'd never been in a porno store. She glanced at the magazines, embarrassed, her eyes roving the myriad images of sex on the covers. Most of the magazines were sealed in plastic. Nora picked up an unsealed magazine titled *All-American Girls,* the cover featuring one of the blond, blue-eyed type she had always envied; in the photograph, the young woman lay on a locker-room floor, cheerleader regalia arranged around her nude body, the blond pubic hair exposing genitalia displayed as if she were modeling for an anatomy class.

Nora looked at the pictures in the magazine for a few moments, then put the magazine back and drifted around the aisles, hoping Stormi would materialize.

She did not.

Nora approached the counter. The young man looked down at her expectantly. She asked, "Where can I find Stormi Skye?" and the man's eyes widened.

"She'll be around later," he said.

"Can you give her a message?"

"Maybe."

"Tell her her lawyer needs to speak with her." Nora handed him a business card. "Have her call me."

The man shrugged and put the card in his shirt pocket.

At a quarter after six, Cox strode wearily into the station carrying a pair of white take-out containers from the Shanghai Garden: lo mein and fried dumplings. It was comfort food, and he was contentedly anticipating the animal pleasure of wolfing the greasy stuff down with a hot cup of coffee when he noticed a light on in Bieberschmidt's office. Bieberschmidt was never in his office past five if he could help it, and Cox knew Bieberschmidt was waiting for him.

As he approached Bieberschmidt's door, Cox saw Mark Andrews sitting across from Bieberschmidt, reading the newspaper while Bieberschmidt shuffled papers.

Cox tapped on the office window and pushed the door open.

"Hank . . . Mark."

Andrews glanced at Cox and nodded. Bieberschmidt exploded with impatience.

"Shit, Cox, you could call me now and then with a progress report!"

"There's no progress," Cox said dryly. "Where's Tina?"

"Damned if I know. Nobody tells me anything."

"Fine." Cox turned to go.

"Detective Cox." Andrews regarded him with an odd serenity. "Is there anything I can tell the mayor?"

Cox shrugged. "Tell the mayor it's not going to be over soon." He glanced at Andrews, whose face remained impassive, then left the office, Bieberschmidt trailing behind.

"That son of a bitch has been camped out in my office all day," Bieberschmidt whispered. "It's like a damn wake."

"Throw him out."

"I can't do that."

Cox shrugged. "Sure you can."

Bieberschmidt shook his head. "You never understood politics in this town, Luther."

"Damn right. I do my best to stay clear of politicians."

"Yeah, but even you can't always have your way."

Cox shot him a hurt glance.

Bieberschmidt gestured pleadingly. "I'm not asking much, Luther. Just be polite to these people."

Cox did not reply. He pushed open the door to his office and let it swing shut behind him.

Cox made himself his much-desired cup of coffee with the office microwave and a heaping teaspoonful of instant Maxwell House, then returned to his office and shut the door. The station was blessedly quiet in the evenings, and his office was far enough in the back, near the interrogation rooms and the evidence lockup, that he almost never heard the commotion at the front desk.

He rolled a cigarette—a little thicker than usual—then lighted it and exhaled smoke slowly as he flipped open the carton lids and split the disposable chopsticks. He deposited the cigarette on the edge of a seashell ashtray, careful not to get any grease on the cigarette paper, and hoisted a dumpling with the chopsticks, dipped it in the savory sauce the restaurant had provided, then bit deeply into it. The taste flooded his consciousness, making him feel instantly happier.

Cox alternated bites of dumpling, sips of coffee, slurps of the lo mein noodles, and drags on his cigarette, aware that he was engaged in a process of filling himself up, of closing a gap, of creating a buffer between his mind and a sorely empty spot inside him. He felt the food slowing his body down and the cigarette and coffee simultaneously sparking his brain, replacing anxiety with a calm contentedness. It was the kind of feeling he'd once had with Julia—whatever they'd done, they'd done it with a sense of quiet pleasure, a calm joy in living. At least it had been that way in the beginning, before he became a cop, before things fell apart, before their marriage changed in ways that reflected the growing distance between them and the coming of age of the demons that destroyed her.

They had met as art students in Chicago when he was an undergraduate, but they didn't connect romantically until two years later; by that time, she was working intensely toward a doctorate in art history and he was supporting his painting by scrounging from one odd job to the next. Their salad days lasted seven years, until Julia got her Ph.D. By then, their long struggle had soured them on urban life, so when Julia was offered a faculty position at Benjamin Harrison University, they jumped at it. For Cox, it meant coming home to Indiana, where he'd grown up in the little town of Milford, just north of Evansville. It was then that he decided to become a cop; it would be, he thought, a decent way to support his art habit while putting his sixties-holdover idealism to a practical application— that is, taking some responsibility for making the world a better place.

The first year was heaven. They found their forty acres, built their cabin, and lived among nature in verdant Morgan County, south of Indianapolis. Cox put in his weeks at the police academy in Terre Haute and joined the Harrison force.

The discovery of his passion for police work was a revelation to Cox. He loved the interaction with the other cops and the sense of his place in the community, but most of all, he loved the confrontation, the turmoil, the speed, and the power to give effect to his sense of justice. It was far more satisfying than the Sisyphean task of trying to achieve perfection on canvas, and soon his brushes went dry from disuse.

But a year later, Julia began to spend nights in the studio she rented off campus, a loft over an antique store on the west side of town, toiling prodigiously on the mural that was to be her final work. It was a political piece, like most of her paintings, exploring the dynamic of male and female creative forces through the lives and work of Diego Rivera and Frida Kahlo, melding their styles into a collage of indigenous, colonial, and immigrant peoples and of their labor and the cycle of their lives. The painting obsessed Julia; it had importance for her not only because of the level of difficulty of executing her ideas but also because she saw in it an opportunity for wider exposure, for fame. She stopped sleeping, fretted over it, fought with Cox over the time she devoted to it, fought with the other faculty members of the Fine Arts Department over the resources she devoted to it, and tried not to hate the work for causing so much pain in her life. She drank while she worked, taking hits of mescal from a bottle she kept among her paints; she missed classes, went for days without eating. It was then that she began to disappear, first for a night or two, then, once, for twelve days. It turned out she'd gone to Mexico City to the national museum. She had told no one. Cox had put out a national search for her; television stations from Chicago to Nashville appealed to viewers for help in finding her. When Julia returned, it was to her studio, not to Cox, and then began the terrible months of psychiatric examinations, of lithium therapy, of a separation that made real what had already occurred, of a suicide attempt, of Julia institutionalized, and then of reconciliation.

Through it all, Cox had drifted like an actor forced to play out a drama in which he had no real part. His life was a reaction to Julia's life and the roller coaster of tension and release that propelled her. But he loved the woman, her genius, and he respected the violent, volcanic nature of creativity. When she was released from the hospital, she came back to live with him, and he took care of her, treating her like a traditional wife for the first time in their marriage. She accepted it at first with some humor, but then as she began to ponder her future and the thought of returning to her painting, she was beset with depression. He talked to her about children, about her joining the life he'd found for himself by abandoning his struggle to live as an artist. But she couldn't do that, wouldn't do that. The shakily constructed facade of domesticity collapsed. Cox watched her fall apart, and he held himself responsible. He knew he was pushing too hard to keep them together. Then one night, she awoke at 3:30 in the morning, went out to the garage, got the gas can Cox used to fill the lawn mower, doused herself, and lighted a match. Cox found out later that she'd been three months' pregnant.

Cox stopped eating when the food was gone, and he knew he'd eaten too much. He rolled and lighted another cigarette and stared at the burning tip of it, then reached into his pocket and took out Barris's law journal article—forty pages of tiny print, 287 footnotes in tinier print. Impatient for distraction, he skimmed the article, waiting for something to catch his eye. After two minutes of furrowing his brow at the opacity of the jargon, something did.

> Suicide is arguably the ultimate act of self-determination, belonging strictly to the sphere of individual concern. Yet suicide may have a substantial effect on loved ones and society, which can be said to be diminished by the loss of the individual. As John Stuart Mill put it: "No person is an entirely isolated being; it is impossible for a person to do anything seriously or permanently hurtful to himself without mischief reaching at least to his near connections, and often far beyond them." In a similar vein, Aristotle and Saint Thomas Aquinas weighed in against suicide; David Hume, foreshadowing Kevorkian and Humphrey, felt otherwise: "Should I prolong a miserable existence because of some frivolous advantage which the public may perhaps receive from me?"
>
> The societal benefit/harm calculus pertinent to suicide has

analogues in pornography, prostitution, and what I call the "free market in sex"—the unregulated, fend-for-yourself dating game.

We are all free agents at the start of the game, regardless of whether we were born with a silver or a plastic spoon in our mouths. When we reach the age of sexual maturity, somewhere hopefully in our late teens, we begin to interact sexually with others. We pursue the objects of our prurient interests, obeying, like a junkie obeys his particular "jones," the chemical commands of our biology.

In the unreal world, we all find love and lifelong mates by this process. In the real world, by dint of unattractiveness, disability, age, or other defect, many are forced to shop the sexual marketplace with empty pockets. For these poor souls, despite sharing the urges of the sexually well-heeled, there is no release. Thus, a demand exists for sexual services that can be acquired with money rather than with sexual attractiveness. Hence, pornography and prostitution.

Contrary to the assertions of some, not all women who participate in the production of pornographic films are raped in the process. Aside from economic duress, which also forces some of us to work as law professors, by and large the men and women who participate in the production of pornographic films do so as a matter of free will. Likewise, the men and women who work as prostitutes have chosen to do so out of the range of available employment options. Thus, it may be said that participation in pornography or prostitution is within the sphere of individual action, and the state should not be involved in the individual's choice to work in these fields.

At the same time, the societal mischief generated by pornography and prostitution places these activities within the societal sphere. I would agree with the antipornography feminist on this point only to the extent that drugs, organized crime, child molestation and exploitation, and sexual vio-

63

lence—all of which are already crimes—and disease attend pornography and prostitution. As Mill wrote, "Fornication, for example, must be tolerated . . . but should a person be free to be a pimp?" Of course, a person *should* be free to be a pimp, just as we are free to be employers in other fields of endeavor. Mill felt, however, that if the protection of society requires maintaining the prohibition on prostitution, then the restriction on liberty is justified, so long as brothels "are available for those who seek them." In other words, society saves face by making laws against prostitution, but acknowledges its necessity by winking at its existence.

Suicide, pornography, prostitution. Society's winking eye. For Cox, understanding the law meant confronting questions of when the line between legality and illegality was crossed. It was sometimes difficult to find the line, but the basic assumption was rock-solid: The law was there to be obeyed. He found it astonishing and somewhat liberating to witness Barris's playfulness with the law, his fascination and high regard for the abstractions underlying the law, and his clear contempt for the law itself.

Cox wondered if Barris had taken Mill's belief in individual autonomy too far. Had Barris disregarded the consequences of his actions? And harmed someone or so angered someone that murder was the result?

Barris's philosophy now seemed coldly ironic; if there was ever a restriction on sexual liberty, on individual autonomy, it was surely murder.

8

Marjorie Paugh sat staring tearfully into her Bloody Mary as Nora covered Marjorie's hands, which were clasped together on the tabletop.

"Strange . . . I was so envious of you," Marjorie murmured, her lips quivering.

Nora gazed at her friend, amazed and disgusted, desperate to summon even a speck of sympathy when she couldn't help thinking, You fool, you idiot, you stupid, childish thing.

It was Marjorie who had needed comforting but had been ashamed to ask, Marjorie, who was married—happily, everyone supposed—to a classics professor but who'd been pining away for Barris, bitterly envying Nora's freedom.

"I had to have been the only woman at the law school he didn't proposition," Marjorie lamented. "I don't know what I would have done. But I thought about it. Often. Much too often."

"Oh, you wouldn't be unfaithful to Frank," Nora said. "That's just not you."

"I don't know about that," Marjorie sniffled.

She was a reasonably attractive woman, Nora realized, searching Marjorie's face, her pert, pointy nose, her sweetheart lips, her big brown eyes under long brown bangs. But she was not Barris's type; she had the imagination of a stone, and she exuded domesticity. Nora thought that the romantic fantasy Marjorie had constructed around Barris was the most interesting thing she'd ever done.

Nora asked softly, "Do you have any idea who might have killed Jim?"

Marjorie shook her head. "I have no idea. Except . . . that he was so alive, so . . . out there, you know? You always knew where he stood, and when you have strong opinions and you express them, you're bound to make enemies."

The girl's got it bad, Nora thought, suddenly weary.

"There was a detective here today asking questions," Marjorie went on. "Of course I didn't say anything . . . about how I felt. Maybe I should have." At this, she started to break down again. "But I couldn't."

It occurred then to Nora that she would need to contact the Harrison police. She'd have to tell them about her relationship with Barris, unpleasant as that might be. "Did you tell them about me?"

"No. I should have, I know. I lied." She stared at Nora, terrified, as though suddenly aware that she had done something horrible. "I lied! I did! They asked me if I knew anything about his personal life, and I said no! Why did I do that?"

"You were upset. Don't worry about it." Nora smiled comfortingly at Marjorie. "I'll call them tomorrow. Do you remember the name of the detective who spoke with you?"

"He gave me his card," she said. "It was Luther something . . . Luther Cox."

Stormi turned the card over in her hand, noticed a hangnail, and bit at it. The man at the counter, whose name was Larry Crowder, watched her, amused. "Got yerself a lawyer. Good deal." He smiled. Stormi shrugged and stuffed the card into the back pocket of her shorts.

There was a boy watching and waiting, a college boy, red-cheeked, bushy-eyebrowed, nervously fingering a magazine as he clutched the wire frame of the magazine rack, looking furtively through it at Stormi.

Catching his gaze, Stormi moved toward the boy as he replaced the book on the rack and turned as if to leave. She approached the magazine rack and stood a few feet from the boy, inviting him to look her over. And as his eyes met hers, she smiled and said softly, "Hi."

"Hi," he responded, and turned away, his head swimming.

"Ya look lonely," Stormi said, and she leaned against the magazine rack and looked up at him.

The price was forty-five dollars for a half hour of her company, and by the time it came to terms, he would have agreed to anything.

Stormi led him out the back door, nodding to Crowder as they left. The boy followed her down a cold passageway and through a set of doors to the motel next door. She stopped at a room on the ground floor, opened it with her key, and pulled him inside.

It was a small room with a single double bed, a TV bracketed to the wall, and a couple of small end tables. One of the bedside lamps was on, throwing a dim yellow illumination over the dirty turquoise wallpaper and matching bedcover and carpet. She sat on the end of the bed and patted a spot beside her.

"C'mere, darlin'," Stormi said. "Take your shoes off."

The boy did as he was told, and he sank into the creaking old mattress, his mind reeling with the utter craziness of what he was doing. A prostitute! Good God! Yet he slipped off his loafers, pushed himself up on the bed, and lay back, resting his head on a soggy, foul-smelling pillow.

Stormi pulled off her tank top and shook her hair wildly—it was part of the show—then took down her shorts, leaving on the grayish threadbare panties, and turned to him, her small breasts with their pallid nipples suspended over the pronounced ridges of her rib cage, made emphatic by the shadows cast by the single lamp.

"Ya want me to do the undressin'?" she asked.

He was looking at her skin with an expression of dismay on his face, and he reached out to touch a cluster of small round scabs on her left side, about twelve inches below her armpit.

"What's that?" he asked.

"I got hurt," she said.

"By who?"

"None of your damn business."

He looked closely then at the rest of her torso, at her arms and sides and ribs and breasts, and he saw that there were scars and scabs and wounds all over her, in different stages of healing.

"Ya want me to do the undressin'?" she repeated.

He nodded. He watched her as she undid his belt buckle and unzipped him. She pulled his pants down a short way, played briefly, perfunctorily, with his penis and balls, then took his pants all the way off and started to unbutton his shirt.

He liked her and pitied her, and seeing the violence that had been done to her did nothing to dissuade him from having her. He liked the quiet, matter-of-fact way about her. He would have preferred her to be fuller, not so skinny, and to have a prettier, fresher, more girlish face. Her face looked old to him, like a grandmother's face, stern and unyielding.

"Ya put awn a rubber, okay?" she said, and glanced up at him, vaguely apologetic.

"Okay."

Stormi opened the nightstand drawer and took out a condom.

"What's your name?" he asked.

"Stormi," she said.

He entered her and kissed the side of her face as he moved, and she kissed him back, strangely like a real lover, and held his ass tightly, moving forcefully against him. He soon felt the orgasm coming, but he didn't want to come, not yet, and so he stopped moving, and then she stopped moving, and he pushed himself up on his hands and gazed at her.

Stormi smiled at him and pushed away the hair that was matted to her sweaty forehead. She wanted to say something like "Ya want t'get yer money's worth, hmm?" but she wouldn't. Repeat business was essential in a town like Harrison, and this one had a decent body and was clean and didn't want anything perverted, which was rare

68

enough and always a great relief. Besides, he was a bit pathetic; she could tell he was the kind who bruised easily, the kind who wanted something resembling love. She saw the illusions in his eyes and knew how important it was that she say the right words to make him feel that she wasn't in a hurry, that she was enjoying this, that she was his girl, if only for a half hour.

The boy looked down at her and wished he hadn't stopped. He withdrew from her and lay back on the bed, chilled by his sweat and the awful turquoise glimmer of the room.

Stormi leaned over and touched his cheek. "What's wrong?"

"Who did those things to you?"

"It's none of yer business, cowboy. Maybe I did it to myself."

"Bullshit."

"Come on and finish up, honey."

"It's okay. Don't worry about it." He rubbed his forehead and sighed.

"What's your name?"

"Joe Tyler."

She laughed. "Well, ya didn't have to tell me yer last name."

"Oh, yeah." He smiled.

"You a student?"

"Yeah, I'm a grad student. In business school."

"Ya gonna be a businessman?"

"That's what most people go to business school for."

She touched his chest and snuggled against him. "You like me?"

"Yeah, I like you."

"I like you."

She kissed his stomach and belly, her breasts grazing his skin, and his penis grew hard as she stroked it through the condom. He pushed her down on the bed and entered her again, but this time with a lust that sought its resolution in her body.

All in a night's work.

Poor Marjorie, Nora thought over and over as she traveled from Harrison to her old jewel box of a home in the heart of Indianapolis.

Somehow, she could not now spare a thought for Barris; it was Marjorie and her broken heart that occupied Nora's mind, Marjorie, who despite her husband and two children had lusted for a slick piece of work like Barris and now grieved for him.

Nora did not feel grief, a fact that upset her only when she contemplated her inevitable interview with Detective Luther Cox of the Harrison police. She would be too cool, she feared, not to be suspected of involvement in his death. At the very least, she would be thought a slut for carrying on with a man she cared nothing about.

By the time Nora reached her house, it was nearly ten o'clock. She lived alone now, after having shared her home for more than a year with a roommate, a teacher of the deaf named Owedia Braxton, and though Owedia had been gone six months, Nora still felt a small hurt, a moment of disappointment, when she pulled into her driveway and the house was dark.

Nora had befriended Owedia in the course of investigating Dexter Hinton's murder conviction, and after a time, the differences the two women had submerged in their struggle to free Dexter rose to the surface, impossible to ignore. Owedia was black, Nora white—that was the main thing. Owedia knew that Nora was a racist—a recovering racist, Nora insisted, a racist fully and agonizingly attuned to the hatred hard-wired in her heart and brain, struggling one day at a time to overcome that heritage—and Owedia forgave her for it, but it was an irritation that accentuated their differences. Owedia was pretty and slender, Nora tall and big-boned and plain as a dirt road. Owedia was urban, Nora country. Owedia was a devout and practicing Christian, Nora a heathen and a practicing hedonist. Owedia didn't drink; Nora drank too much. Owedia had a boyfriend in Atlanta around whom she orchestrated a perfectly paced romance; Nora fell into bed with the wrong men too soon.

Around the time Nora began to date Jim Barris, Owedia received a hoped-for job offer from a deaf school in Atlanta. The two women said good-bye to each other with many regrets for the way their relationship had gone sour, and Owedia moved to Atlanta—though not into her boyfriend's apartment.

Owedia did not call, as promised, with her Atlanta telephone number, a fact that Nora was reminded of as she arrived home each evening.

Once inside, Nora threw off her coat and poured herself a Jack Daniel's, neat, medicine for her perpetually aching heart, then sat in her living room in her oversized rocking chair, sipping it slowly.

I'm going to have to tell the police everything, she thought miserably—the marijuana, the cocaine, the sex. Then the thought occurred to her briefly that perhaps she could postpone going to the police; after all, they didn't know she existed.

But no.

Big-boned women don't hide, she told herself. We can't hide; we're too fucking obvious. She resolved to tell Luther Cox everything.

9

THURSDAY, DECEMBER 8

Cox awoke to darkness at 5:59 A.M., enveloped by a soul-churning dissonance, an indefinable anxiety. He flipped on his bedside light just as the clock clicked to 6:00 A.M. and the radio alarm began to blare the hour's news. Out of the corner of his eye, Cox saw something move quickly at his window. In an instant he grabbed his revolver from under his bed, rolled into a crouch, and approached the window cautiously.

He relaxed when he realized the culprit was a banana spider, a female, huge and dramatically marked with streaks of brilliant yellow on her black body. The spider had skittered to the corner of the intricate web she'd spun across Cox's window frame, and there she hung, startled by the sudden light. Cox examined the web and wondered at the spider's tenaciousness, her quest for prey so late in the year.

He rubbed his arms, took his tobacco pouch into bed with him, rolled a cigarette, lighted it, and turned off the lamp.

"Sainted Christ, Spunk, another stinkin' day."

Cox scratched his cat companion under the chin, then scratched his own itching neck. Spunk yawned and batted Cox on the forearm, annoyed at the pause in attentiveness. Cox took a deep drag on the cigarette, watched a long ash fall into Spunk's fur, then frantically tried to brush it out. The cat sprang away, furious.

"Sorry," he mumbled.

Cox sat on the edge of the mattress, sighed smoke, and rubbed his leathery face. The morning was coming on like a dull headache; the sky outside his window throbbed dark gray and darker gray, looking like one of those days when rain was impending, impending, impending, but never came, and the air, heavy with moisture, added to the weight of everything else his body and mind would carry through the long day.

Spunk sat on the windowsill, sniffed at the spider on the other side of the windowpane, then followed a sparrow with swift jerks of his head. He looked at Cox.

"Good morning," Cox said. Spunk turned away.

An hour earlier, Cox had awakened shivering, sweat-covered, having dreamed the nightmare that was his nocturnal companion, the terror of which was undiminished by time. He had gone to the refrigerator, taken a drink of bottled water, and returned to bed for the forty-five minutes remaining before the alarm went off.

In that time, he drifted in and out of a light sleep, his mind embroidering thoughts around two faces that kept surfacing in his consciousness, two names he had hoped not to hear for a while, and certainly not linked in a homicide investigation.

Don Hedstrom. Margaret Sanderson.

The connection between Barris and the two of them was coincidental, even arbitrary. But there it was. Sanderson just happened to be in the part of the alphabet assigned to Barris's class; Hedstrom was Barris's friend. But by virtue of that slim connection, the sad history of Cox's own near disgrace, his dishonor and self-betrayal, came surging back into his consciousness with a sting as painful as a year before, when the stains on his reputation were fresh.

Donald Gunnar Hedstrom had been a college all-star who in the sixties had led North Carolina to an NCAA championship his senior year. It was at North Carolina that he got the nickname that stayed with him throughout his career—"the Skater"—a reference to his

73

Scandinavian ancestry and his unique style of play. He was, for those years, impossibly tall at six-eleven, and all of him was leg. As if on stilts, he moved across the court with giant strides, and he hardly needed to pick up his feet. He just slid, glided—skated—from one basket to the next, and the ball seemed to flow between his palm and the floor as if caught in a magnetic field. He was slick, an effortless scorer, and the crowds loved his gangly movement, his country-boy smile, his "Aw shucks" manner.

During his brief career in the NBA, the Skater showed promise as a guard for the Celtics, but a back injury in his second year put an end to his playing career. After a five-year stint as assistant coach at Florida State, Hedstrom was handed the head coaching job at BHU. The gangly kid had long since disappeared by then, along with most of the hair on his head.

What remained of the hair was cut short, military-style, a look that fit Hedstrom's uncompromising, win-at-all-costs attitude and his imposing, imperious, indomitable ego. He became known for the rigorous training he imposed on his players, with a schedule of work-outs that bent every NCAA rule just short of the breaking point. "Hedstrom's Heroes," as they were later known through succeeding generations, endured a Spartan regimen of five-mile runs at dawn, ice baths, three-day fasts, and, of course, Hedstrom's patented "drill till you drop" marathon sessions of ball passing, free throws, and rehearsing the meticulously structured zone defense that was Hedstrom's trademark. Hedstrom's Heroes were expected to become inured to verbal abuse that would straighten dreadlocks and to psychological abuse comparable to POW survival training. A player guilty of a fumbled play, a missed shot, a mental lapse, or a tactical error would merit humiliation before the assembled team, and if the mistake were sufficiently egregious, he'd be given a sticker, a six-inch letter *F*—which stood for "Fuckup" or "Fuck me," depending on Hedstrom's mood—to be worn on the backside of his uniform during practice. The players were kept in a continual state of attention, expectation, and fear.

His first five seasons were dismal: His teams lost twice as many games as they won, and each year campaigns were mounted among the alumni to get rid of him. But Hedstrom was tenacious, and his teams improved to the point where he began to receive invitations to the NCAA tournament. Then, in his eighth year of coaching, by a series of quirky wins, the BHU Sagamores made it to the Final Four.

Harrison was delirious with pride and b-ball fever as the Sagamores upset one team after another on their way to that coveted moment in the national spotlight, and Hedstrom was instantly canonized, all sins forgiven. It hardly mattered that the Sagamores' drive for the NCAA title ended with a creaming by Arkansas. From then on, Hedstrom could do no wrong. Almost.

Two incidents marred the gleam of Hedstrom's career, and one of them almost cost him his job.

The first had been the suicide of a player, Van Walters, in 1989. The team had played a brilliant preconference season, perfect but for one irksome loss to Kansas, and they were undefeated in their first five games of conference play. Then, suddenly, the team's fortunes plummeted, and BHU endured four straight losses. In those days, hopes for Hedstrom were in their post–Final Four inflation, and he rode the team hard, employing drill-sergeant tactics that he said would either "make my boys champions or kill them."

Nobody saw it coming. Van Walters was, like the rest of Hedstrom's Heroes, a stoic kid with brains and talent, but he was quieter than most and a loner, though nobody knew why until the end. He was found dead, his neck slung forward in a makeshift noose that he had attached to a wall fixture in his dorm room. A note pinned to his shorts contained a rambling monologue of adoration and hatred of Hedstrom and of his abject sorrow at having failed his teammates. The note also revealed Walters's homosexuality and his love for a certain religious studies professor. But what hurt Hedstrom's public image was the revelation that he knew about Walters's sexuality and had used it against him:

Dear Coach—*faggot* and *cocksucker* are words you used to wound me and motivate me, I know. But those words are not all I am, as you know.

Half of Harrison was outraged that Hedstrom would knowingly allow a homosexual to play on the team; the other half found it appalling that Hedstrom was capable of such cruelty. Everyone agreed that his treatment of his players was too harsh, though no NCAA rules had been broken. The incident succeeded, nonetheless, in making Hedstrom a nationally recognized figure and one of the most feared and hated men in college basketball.

But the second incident, the Margaret Sanderson rape, left deep scars.

It took place nearly a decade after Van Walters's suicide, and long after the Hedstrom legend had taken shape. By then, Hedstrom's face had become ubiquitous in Harrison—on calendars, posters, oil paintings, and autographed eight-by-ten photos displayed in stores, in the mall, in restaurants, bars, and barbershops, and in many of the offices of city hall, including the mayor's.

After the furor, a few of those portraits were removed. But only a few.

Hedstrom's handling of the incident, his public comments in defense of the rapist and denouncing the victim, and his win-at-all-costs defense of Chappelle during the trial created the public perception that Hedstrom's grasp of reality was shaky, at best, and that the level of competitive spirit he fostered had psychological roots that were not entirely healthy. Here was a man who took partisanship to the point where he would not consider that a player of his could do something so heinous as to rape a girl, where he would defend that player passionately, no matter what the evidence, where he would publicly denounce the girl as a publicity-seeking whore. Harrison, a town with relatively liberal leanings amid conservative Indiana, was outraged. Campus feminist and antirape organizations picketed the university president's office and home, demanding that Hedstrom be fired. President Abbott, who had come to the position from Colgate

University only the year before, was caught between those most vocal opponents of Hedstrom and the vast majority of Hoosiers, who were shocked but preferred that Hedstrom get his wrist slapped and be sent back to the gym. Despite his lack of tenure as a Hoosier, Abbott knew that there was no choice to make—BHU's basketball program was far too important for fund-raising and alumni relations.

And basketball, he knew, was the heart and soul of every true Hoosier.

The nightmare for Hedstrom had begun with a 911 call from a frantic young woman. It was the eighteenth of December, early in the season, after a winning game against Penn State. Against Hedstrom's wishes, Chappelle and a group of friends had gone out to Hoops, the Harrison sports bar that had become an unofficial team hangout. There Chappelle struck up a conversation with Sanderson, who had been at the game with a couple of girlfriends. It was 2:00 A.M. by the time the party broke up; they were all drunk by then, and Sanderson, who was in no condition to drive, accepted a ride from Chappelle, who was equally drunk but managed to get her home. He walked her to her door; took over when she fumbled so badly with her keys that she couldn't get her door open; supported her as she moved unsteadily toward her bed; then took off her clothes as she lay there, head spinning, murmuring, "That's enough, okay thank you, good night, stop, please, don't, please, no . . ." And she began to fight, consciousness emerging out of the sickening swirl, punching him, trying to move her knees up to kick him. But his body was so huge, so heavy, his thrusts so hard and painful. She bucked at him, tried to turn over, crawl away, but mostly she just wanted it to be over.

Afterward, she threw up, got back into bed, locked the door, which he'd left wide open, then lay there blaming herself for getting too damn drunk, and wondering what to do. Just let it go, she told herself. Save yourself the pain. Don't make a fuss; just let it go. But then she got angry. She was angry to think that he thought he could just fuck her without even asking, without caring what she thought about it. It occurred to her that he thought he could do that because

77

of who he was. It dawned on her slowly, the reality of it: He took me by force. He raped me. He raped me. Understanding seeped through, her mind clearing. Then she dialed 911.

It didn't matter that she'd been so drunk that she needed to be carried home and put into bed; it didn't matter that her body was sexually alluring and that she dressed to show it off; it didn't matter that she liked to get drunk; it didn't matter that she had been in relationships with other athletes at BHU. None of that mattered a damn to the law, and that just about killed Don Hedstrom. As he watched the judicial process eat up and swallow his star player, he fumed with frustration. Chappelle was arrested and charged within hours of the rape; Hedstrom got him Harrison's best criminal attorney, Chad Turner, and paid his bail.

Chappelle was a brilliant basketball player, but he was no rocket scientist. When he was awakened by police several hours after the rape, he denied ever touching Margaret, said he'd taken her home, walked her to the door, and that was it. It was an absolutely transparent story; it hadn't occurred to Chappelle that he could be identified by his semen. But with an idiot's persistence, he stuck by his story through hours of questioning, even against the advice of his lawyer. It turned out to be a brilliant strategy. Had Chappelle admitted having sexual intercourse with Margaret that night, the prosecution would only have had to prove the element of force, which was a matter of Margaret's word against his. But now the prosecution had to prove that sexual intercourse had taken place between Chappelle and Margaret in the first place. The semen sample, obtained from Margaret at Harrison Hospital within ninety minutes of the rape, was taken by the Harrison police and placed in the freezer in the evidence room. There it would remain until sent, if necessary, for DNA testing to determine if a certain number of chemical markers could be found to match those of a suspect. It was an expensive process, one the HPD sought to avoid if possible, so samples were never immediately sent for testing.

Hedstrom, frantic over his team's chances without Chappelle, knew that his best hopes lay in pulling a few important strings. Unaware of the HPD's evidence-handling techniques, he didn't know precisely what could be done on his behalf by Harrison's powers that be, but he knew something would be done if he screamed loudly enough at the right people. First on the list was Mayor Brodey, then President Abbott, then Mark Andrews. That's all it took. Bieberschmidt got a call precisely seventeen hours after the rape. "Do something," the voice said. "Just do something."

Bieberschmidt knew exactly what to do. He found another semen sample of recent vintage in the freezer, one from a case disposed of with a plea bargain. He repacked it in a fresh evidence bag and marked it carefully to match the Sanderson sample, forging Cox's initials across the seal. He placed the Sanderson sample in the incinerator.

Simple, perfect, and utterly undetectable; now, when a blood sample from Chappelle and the semen sample were sent to the lab, no match could possibly be found.

Except that two days later, Cox noticed the change while preparing to send the samples to the lab. He went straight to Bieberschmidt's office.

"Somebody's been screwing around with this Sanderson sample," he said, knowing intuitively that Bieberschmidt had had something to do with it.

"What makes you think so?"

"Don't fuck with me, Hank. You may have your reasons for doing what you do, but it's my ass out there on the line, too."

Bieberschmidt was silent for a moment. "You amaze the hell out of me."

"You don't have steady hands, Hank. And you're impatient. The blue tape on the bag was crooked. The handwriting was shaky, like an old man's. You'd make a lousy forger."

"And I always wanted to be a forger." Bieberschmidt ran his tongue along an abscess in his left cheek. "Close the door," he said.

"For Christ's sake, Hank," Cox mumbled, closing the door.

"We're letting the boy off the hook," Bieberschmidt said softly. "A favor's been called in. . . . That's all there is to it."

"He's no boy."

79

"I beg you, Luther, don't make this hard on me. It's got nothing to do with you, and I didn't want anyone else to be involved. Understand? Please. Forget it ever happened. Just forget about it."

"But I'm the son of a bitch who's going to have to get up there on the stand and swear to the chain of custody on this piece of evidence! You're asking me to perjure myself, Hank. Do you realize that?"

"That wouldn't be the case if this conversation never happened."

"It's too late for that." Cox turned, disgusted, and started for the door.

"Wait a minute."

Cox stopped, but he could not turn to face Bieberschmidt.

"I gotta know. Are you gonna do me this favor?"

Cox muttered, "Yeah, sure," and left the room.

It was the kind of thing he thought he'd never do, not in a million years. To perjure himself? To lose evidence as a favor to somebody? To free a rapist as a favor? And he wondered if it was the guilt, the corrosive guilt with which Julia's suicide had scarred him, that had collapsed a moral barrier inside him. He had failed Julia, he knew, failed to love her enough to save her, had not been kind enough, not willing enough to bend.

Now he would bend. He would do what he was asked, whatever it was, to smooth everything over, make it all right.

But it wasn't long before the shit hit the fan, and Bieberschmidt caught it. As expected, when the DNA test results came back from the lab, the sample was shown not to be Chappelle's. But skin cells and tissue shreds in the sample showed that the person the sample had been taken from could not have been Margaret Sanderson—it was an African-American woman.

The *Harrison Herald* and the Indianapolis papers and TV news crews were all over Bieberschmidt, as were the mayor and the city council president, who looked outraged for the cameras and demanded an explanation. Bieberschmidt chewed a lot of Rolaids and fretted about his future employment, but he knew there were only two things to do: apologize and explain. Look stupid, look bumbling—but look sincere. One thing Bieberschmidt wouldn't do was to hang Cox and Farrell out to dry. So he held a news conference, at which he presented a cockamamie story about having taken charge of the evidence himself because it was such an important case, how he'd put the sample into the freezer without doing the usual paperwork because he wanted to be sure it wouldn't break down before freezing, how he'd put Cox's initials on it because it was Cox's case, how he'd put a temporary label on it that hadn't stuck properly, how he'd taken the wrong bag from the freezer, how only he and Cox and Farrell had keys to the evidence locker, how the freezer was cleaned out while the other sample was at the lab, how the true sample must have been destroyed, and on and on. By the time he finished, he looked like a complete ass, but the reporters were glassy-eyed with confusion. And Bieberschmidt was reasonably sure, by virtue of the mayor's involvement in the cover-up, that he would keep his job.

The prosecutor, Al Hickey, went forward with the case. The farce over the evidence made his job easier—how to lose the case while appearing to do everything in his power to win it. While the loss of the semen sample eliminated indisputable evidence of the element of sexual intercourse, it wasn't the only evidence. The time of the 911 call, a tape of which the prosecution would introduce in court, was only a few minutes after Chappelle took Margaret home, and hospital personnel would provide evidence that sexual intercourse had taken place shortly before Margaret arrived at the hospital, that genital bruises, as well as bruises on her forearms and wrists, indicated the use of force, and that Margaret's behavior was consistent with that of a rape victim.

The trial was, by Harrison standards, a media event matched only by the round-the-clock coverage accorded its championship sporting events. Chappelle, who as a junior had already become a nationally recognized player, was supported by the testimony of character witnesses from among his classmates and teammates. More impressive to the jury was testimony from Jared Mateo, the NBA superstar and

Hoosier hero. Chappelle had met Mateo while the star was doing color commentary during the NCAA championship the year before. Their conversation—entirely before the cameras—had lasted about eight minutes, but it was enough, evidently, for Mateo to testify to Chappelle's honesty and integrity.

Don Hedstrom testified as to what a model kid Chappelle was, and he insisted that he'd worked Chappelle so hard during the game that night and the practice that afternoon that he didn't believe that Chappelle would be clinically capable of sex at the time of the alleged rape, stressing the word *clinically* as if his opinion were scientific. And, as if to refute that testimony, Chappelle's girlfriend testified that they'd had sex at her apartment at 5:30 P.M. that day, just before Chappelle joined the team for the ritual pregame dinner.

There was character testimony on Margaret's behalf, as well. Her political science professor, who was also her career adviser, testified, as did a pair of her sorority sisters, and her parents. Their testimony could do little in the face of the Chappelle onslaught. Hedstrom and his lawyers had orchestrated a lavish and aggressive defense. Most damaging to Margaret were leading questions asked of her on cross-examination regarding other sexual relationships she'd had, particularly with student athletes. Objections were raised immediately each time, and the questions were stricken from the record under Indiana's rape-shield law, but the jury heard it all. The questions only confirmed allegations made in the media. One wag suggested that Margaret had been paid by the Purdue team to accuse Chappelle. A particularly vicious rumor had it that she had had sex with nine members of a fraternity in one night during her sophomore year. The portrait painted of Margaret was that of a sex-crazed brat, a sorority slut whose wild ways had finally caught up with her.

Testimony was also heard concerning the botched evidence. Bieberschmidt testified, as did Luther Cox, who for the first time in his career perjured himself in trying to make his story consistent with Bieberschmidt's. Fortunately, the evidentiary details were by then an incomprehensible sideshow to the circus of personalities, but something happened in the retelling of Bieberschmidt's lies that made it appear that Bieberschmidt wasn't really responsible for what had happened—that he was, in fact, covering up for Cox.

It took only a few seconds for that impression to be created, but once it was done, the onus for the prosecution's failure to convict Chappelle fell squarely on Cox. It started when Bieberschmidt admitted that it was usually the responsibility of Cox and Farrell to maintain the integrity of the chain of custody of evidence.

Defense counsel Turner picked up on this and asked, "When was the last time you took responsibility for a piece of evidence?"

"Ah . . . it's been some years, sir," said Bieberschmidt.

"Who is primarily responsible for the investigation in this case?"

"Detective Cox is, though it's not entirely his case."

"But you, rather than Cox or Farrell, were responsible for the chain of custody of this particular piece of evidence."

"That's correct."

On the stand, Cox repeated Bieberschmidt's story, but the taint of incompetence had shifted perceptibly, enough for the *Harrison Herald* to hint that Cox had purposely destroyed the true semen sample.

Chappelle was acquitted. The team would not be torn apart after all. Margaret Sanderson retreated, with great bitterness and anger, into her studies, and started the process of applying to law school.

But something had happened to Don Hedstrom in the course of the rape's aftermath, and, as Hedstrom changed, so did his relationship with Chappelle. Chappelle had failed him—first by doing something so stupid as to take advantage of a drunk girl, and then by blowing game after game once he rejoined the team. Something had entered Chappelle's performance that hadn't been there before—self-consciousness. He had become aware of the eyes of the crowd and of the TV cameras upon him, and he knew that with every shot, he was asked not simply to succeed as a basketball player but to succeed so well that it didn't matter what he'd cost the town in self-respect. As for Hedstrom, he came to hate Chappelle for what he had been forced to do to save Chappelle's ass and save the season. Hedstrom loathed asking anybody for anything, and Chappelle had made him humiliate himself before the mayor, expending valuable political capital and, worst of all, creating the potential for future disaster should the cover-up ever be discovered. It was no secret that Don Hedstrom had political ambitions; rumors had circulated for years that he would make a run for governor, and it was assumed that the Republican nomination would be his for the asking. Now all that was in doubt. It could take a good many winning seasons to rebuild the public's faith and adoration.

Cox stood shakily, his brain still congealed with sleep and confusion; the nicotine was producing its usual relied-upon effect of smoothing the morning's rough edges, but he craved caffeine and a hot shower. He started the coffeemaker and took three steps toward the bathroom, when the phone rang.

"Yeah," Cox murmured.

"Good morning, sir!" Farrell's voice, chipper as ever, tore into Cox's ear like a chain saw. "Sorry about the hour, but I wanted to catch you before you left."

"Yeah, wake me up anytime. What is it?"

"First, the bad news—the bar search turned up nothing. Barris is known in three places—Rick's, Hoops, and Niedermeyer's—but he wasn't in any of them Tuesday night. Nothing on gas stations or convenience stores, either."

"Okay."

"Second . . . I hear you'll be dropping in on Don Hedstrom today."

"Yes."

"Mind if I tag along?"

"No, provided you don't bring a basketball to be autographed."

"Aw shucks, sir."

"I'm not scheduled to see Hedstrom until ten. Look for me in my office at about nine-thirty. I've got a shitload of paperwork to do until then."

Cox hung up the phone and reached for the Prozac.

Nora awakened facedown, sprawled, inhaling the fragrance of her pillow, and she saw in her mind, as if lingering from a dream, for the first time since his death, his face. His face. His handsome face, his white mane, his muzzle of white beard. His smile—toothy, the teeth small, too perfect, the grin infectious. He had been a devilish sprite, a satyr, a naughty man.

Nora conjured his face, held it before her, tried to look into the eyes, thought of his penetrating stare, his seductive smile. And she felt for the first time a responsibility toward him, an odd, begrudging obligation to the truth, despite him.

First love, first lover. By virtue of that bedroom conversation, James Barris had become connected in her mind with that first boy, and she could not think of Barris without the shadow of Martin playing in her mind, a peculiar scent of joy among the complex flavors of her relationship with Barris. Martin. He was a red-haired boy, a burly boy from the other side of the Unity Consolidated School District, a farm child, as Nora had been, and he was, like Nora, big-boned, a bull to her cow, thick everywhere, his body hairless but for a patch of pale orange corn silk around his penis and the flames in his armpits. Dull of mind, inarticulate with hormones, a mumbling fool who used the wrong words for things, spoke in clumps of words, not sentences, standing there blinking his eyebrowless eyes, his lashes transparent, and he'd try to talk while Nora waited as long as it took, admiring his effort, his beauty.

It had been a natural courtship, he and Nora waiting after school at the bus stop, going in absolutely opposite directions; sometimes they would meet at the school door and walk the distance from the school out past the football field to the edge of the school grounds, where the buses stood by waiting. And there were times when they walked too slowly, talked too intently on that road past the football field, and they missed the bus, and in the hour before the next bus, they'd walk to the football field to a place behind the cinder-block concession stand and they'd get on the ground and kiss and stick their hands in each other's pants and play and play until they came in hot messes.

Blushing virgin that she was.

He had seemed dangerous to her; that was the funny part now. He had seemed dangerous because he was so unlike her father and brothers, big but gentle, an artist of focused passions, putting all his big soul through the tiny reeds of his oboe and out into that thin snake-charmer sound.

Martin. Barris. Odd how one's notions of danger evolve.

Barris must have gotten himself into some deep shit.

Nora thought then of Stormi, whose image in Nora's mind elicited an entirely different sort of visceral reaction—sympathy and sorrow. It came to Nora as a revelation that she liked Stormi, cared for her unexpectedly much, wanted her not only to survive her troubles with the law but to prevail over her addictions, her upbringing, the men who manipulated her.

I care too fucking much, she thought. As always.

She pushed herself out of bed, put her feet on the cold hardwood floor, and, half-asleep, made her way to the bathroom, where, as she was peeing, she cataloged the work to be done that day. Waiting on her desk was a stack of files to be closed and another stack to be opened, but she had no court appearances scheduled for that day or the next, Friday, so she decided that she would go straight to Harrison without stopping at her office. If she got to Harrison early enough, she reasoned, she would catch Stormi at her mother's address. And while she was in Harrison, she would submit herself to Luther Cox for questioning, a matter of killing two birds with one stone.

She decided to try Cox before showering, so she went back to her bed and sat crosslegged in her T-shirt and nothing else and looked up the number for the Harrison police. She took the phone from her night table, punched in the number, and when she asked for Detective Luther Cox, she was put through, without comment, to his voice mail. Cox's greeting was mumbled below the range of human audibility, and his voice struck Nora as so strange and unsettling that by the time the beep sounded, she could not think of a thing to say.

How does one confess to an electronic device that one was the recent lover of a recently murdered man?

So she repeated the process, this time listening with mild pleasure to Cox's gravelly yet warm southern Indiana–accented voice. When the beep sounded, she simply left her name, phone number at work, and the message that she had been a friend of James Barris.

Nora took the interstate southwest from her home in downtown Indianapolis and exited twenty minutes later into the immaculate residential neighborhoods surrounding the BHU campus. From there, she drove west past the industrial zone toward Stormi's address—2317 Vermillia Road.

The sun was rising behind her when Nora saw the sign for Vermillia Gardens, a huge trailer park. She turned and drove past a succession of short alleyways, each of which formed the site for four trailers. Most of the trailers appeared to be permanently fixed to the ground, others were on cinder blocks, but all were in varying states of dilapidation. Nora was unnerved and appalled by the poverty, the shabbiness of everything. Aluminum panels flapped forlornly in the wind and plastic flowers twirled ridiculously on sticks in the ground as dogs rooted among the trash cans. Christmas lights blinked on the trailer frames, and from the roof of one trailer, a Rudolph with a broken tail broadcast an eerie cheer.

Stormi's trailer was near the end of Vermillia Road, which deadended into a wide ditch that separated the trailer park from the back of a plastics factory. The trailer was about twenty-five feet long, permanently affixed to the ground, and in better shape than most. An American flag hung over one end, and near the metal steps that led to the front door, a boy of about four was playing in a plastic swimming pool filled with sand. Nora pulled her pickup in behind an old Impala and parked.

The boy, who was blond and very pale, stopped his playing and looked up at Nora as she strode toward the trailer.

"Howdy," Nora said. "Your momma home?"

The boy stared at her silently.

As Nora ascended the steps, the door behind the screen door opened wide, but not wide enough to reveal the whole of an obese middle-aged white woman in a flowered housedress.

"Whut kin ah do fer ya?" the woman asked, more pleasantly than Nora expected.

"Good morning. My name is Nora Lumsey. I'm the lawyer who's been representing Stormi."

"Oh Lordy, is she in trouble agin?" The woman wiped her hands on her housedress, smiling and shaking her head as if she had made a joke, then pushed the screen door open. "I'm Weesie Phipps." She grinned, revealing a jagged line of broken bottom teeth, and held out her hand to Nora. "Nice ta meet ya."

Nora shook her hand. Weesie had a mop of frizzy blond hair, slightly balding in front, surrounding a wide, pleasant face, cherubic and weathered. A long scar ran from above her left eyebrow down nearly to her ear.

Nora held the screen door open but did not attempt to enter the trailer.

"Is Stormi here?"

"No, ma'am, she's not."

Everything changed with the use of the word *ma'am*; now they were adversaries, the class gulf opening abruptly between them.

"She does live here, doesn't she?"

"Now and agin."

"What about now?"

"Yeah, but she didn't make it home last night."

"Where is she?"

"Couldn't say."

"You came and got her at the lockup yesterday, didn't you?"

"Uh-huh."

"Did you bring Stormi back here?"

"Yes, ma'am."

"And where did Stormi go after you brought her here?"

"Out. Ya know how it is." Weesie rocked back and forth on her heels.

"Do you expect her back anytime?"

"I 'spect she'll be here ta eat."

"When will that be?"

"Five or six."

"Would you mind if I came back around that time?"

"Suit yerse'f."

Nora dug in her purse, found a business card, and handed it to the woman. "Have Stormi call me immediately if she gets in before then. And if she's not going to be here for dinner, have her leave a message where I can reach her."

"Yes, ma'am."

Nora descended the trailer's metal steps and smiled at the boy in the sandbox, who had watched Nora's conversation with Weesie attentively.

"You have a nice day, now," Nora said.

The boy did not respond other than to follow her solemnly with his eyes. When she got to her truck, Nora turned around and looked again at him, the beauty of his young face in these piteous surroundings, and she knew suddenly that he must be Stormi's son.

Stormi awoke at 11:30 A.M., alone in Joe Tyler's big warm bed, the morning having slipped by her. After their initial encounter, Joe had decided to purchase Stormi's company for the entire night, and so he took her home to the shiny new house where his father, an Indianapolis cardiologist, had set him up in a development off campus. Joe's father had also provided a lavish bankroll with which Joe could entertain himself.

In the morning, Joe was gone, somewhere—Stormi didn't know or care—and she liked it that he was gone and she had the run of the place.

She sat up in bed, lighted a cigarette, and looked around the big empty beige-carpeted bedroom, sun pouring in through gauzy curtains.

The room was absolutely quiet. Stormi breathed slowly. She smoked. She picked a shred of something from the corner of her mouth.

The notion came flickering into her mind that she might live in a place like this someday, a clean, bright place, and she would have a big bed and children to play with, children who would jump up on the bed and snuggle softly with her. She would have a husband like Joe, a good-looking, irresponsible man, and she'd be the responsible one.

She'd always been responsible. She'd been good with money since she was a child. She never saved it, but she knew how to get it—how to steal it, how to beg for it, how to sell herself. She spent too much to get high, she knew, but it was her pleasure, the thing she did for herself and nobody else, and her proudest accomplishment was that she always managed to get a fix when she needed one. That was because she knew people, and people liked her, and people did favors for her because she did favors for them.

That was the way the world worked.

She thought of her sister, who'd never learned, Sunni, who expected too much and lived in angry disappointment.

They had been separated as four-year-olds after the trauma of having both been taken from their mother's home when their father, Levon Skye, was arrested for having molested them. They were shipped off to live with cousins, the Gribs, in Danville, a few miles to the west, until Levon Skye was permanently out of the home and the county social workers had determined that Weesie was fit to raise them. By that time, Weesie was pregnant again by Levon, and being that the Gribs had only two children of their own and Weesie had four, with one more on the way, she let Sunni stay with the Gribs while she raised Stormi.

She had seen a TV program about how twins who had been separated ended up growing up just the same anyhow, and so she figured it wouldn't make too much difference if she didn't raise Sunni. It would even be good for them, she thought, to be given the chance to develop as individuals, even though each could see the other twin anytime they wanted to.

But things weren't so good at the Gribs'. John Grib was a subsistence farmer and tax protester, whose refusal to recognize the sovereignty of the federal government did not prevent him from spending his family's welfare check on whiskey and cigarettes. He and his wife Georgia, Weesie's sister, worked their twenty acres, selling vegetables out by the road in the summer, and the rest of the time, John diddled one of their old trucks and Georgia puttered around the house and yelled at the kids, who were home-schooled, or so she would tell people. When Georgia was young, she had imagined a life like *Little House on the Prairie* or *The Waltons,* but it didn't turn out that way, just dirty and cold and poor, and as years went on, there was less and less time when they weren't sitting drunk in front of the TV.

The kids grew untended, filthy, and stupid; the Gribs' older son, Mark, four years older than Sunni, caught and tortured small animals and the pets of their neighbors, a hobby that got him a juvenile conviction for animal cruelty. The younger son, Tom, Sunni's age, was withdrawn and neurotic, bullied by his brother, and he would spend his days sucking his thumb and playing with himself in front of the TV.

Sunni was raped by Mark when she was eleven. It happened twice more, and when Sunni was thirteen, she ran away.

Indianapolis was only thirty-five minutes by car from Danville, but it seemed to Sunni, who had never been outside the orbit of her parents' home and that of the Gribs, like the Emerald City. She hitchhiked there one July afternoon and was neither seen nor heard from by her parents or the Gribs for three years.

Where did she sleep? Alleys, park benches, doorways, heating grates, and shelters, when she was desperate.

How did she eat? She foraged in downtown Dumpsters and trash cans and begged for money for food.

What did she do? For a while, she hung out around the bars and restaurants in the neighborhood known as Speedway in the vicinity of the Indianapolis Motor Speedway. When she tired of that scene, she migrated to Broadripple, a district of rock clubs and coffee bars and stores that sold crystals and hemp products. She made her way among the teenagers who hung there, congregating on the old bridge that spanned the narrow canal that ran northwest to southeast across the city. She became one of them, one of the "bridge kids," as they were called, and she hooked up with a boy named Lonnie.

Lonnie was a middle-class fifteen-year-old who lived with his parents in Carmel and dreamed of being in a band like his heroes Phish. He had white-boy dreadlocks and a scruffy beard, a ring in his nose and a stud through a pierced eyebrow, and tattoos of snakes on his arms.

And he introduced Sunni to heroin.

She had done everything else, and so she would do it because it was there, because Lonnie seemed so mellow and happy when he did it, and because there was something so wonderfully cool about the *works*—the needle and spoon and strap and candle and cotton—this little kit that Lonnie carried around to get him high. It was so *professional,* like a draftsman's pens, a cop's utility belt, a barber's scissors.

Have works will travel.

She did it and loved everything about it, but most of all she loved the needle, filling it and tapping it and pressing it through her skin. The pain of the needle breaking her skin felt to her as good as the pleasure that followed.

Sunni lived like this for a long time, seeing Lonnie every day when he got out of school, hanging with the bridge kids the rest of the time, scoring heroin with money Lonnie would give her. The two of them spent their evenings searching for places to get high, to fuck, to sleep, until Lonnie would head back home to see his parents and Sunni would crash somewhere, sometimes with other boys she picked up in Broadripple bars.

Later, Sunni would think of this time as the happiest of her life. It ended when Lonnie got busted and was sent to the Indiana Boys' School for a year under the county's zero-tolerance-for-drugs program, which did not allow plea bargains for hard-drug offenses.

Sunni kicked around Broadripple for a couple of months, until she discovered she was pregnant, and then she decided to go home. She was sixteen.

The reunion was bittersweet. Weesie was already raising a houseful of felons, and Stormi, who was spending more time away from home than in it, was managing only by the grace of a lax attendance policy and the lowest grading curve in the nation to stay in high school. A pregnant Sunni was the last thing Weesie wanted joining her brood.

But Sunni moved in and found herself again sharing a room with Stormi, just as they had more than a decade before. On her first day there, she introduced Stormi to heroin, and Stormi took to the habit just as readily as had her sister.

Stormi's addiction had the unexpected salutary effect of freeing Sunni from her addiction, fortunately for Sunni's child. It was as if Stormi served as caretaker for Sunni's addiction while Sunni was busy being pregnant.

Garth Brooks Phipps was born on a Sunday night. By Tuesday, Sunni and Stormi were shooting heroin together.

Stormi wandered naked into Joe's kitchen and examined the contents of his immaculate refrigerator—milk, beer, Coke, containers of Chinese takeout. She scooped up some cold fried rice with her fingers and nibbled at it, licking her fingers, then washed it down with milk and wiped her fingers on her hips.

In the bedroom, she picked up her pants, discarded next to the bed, and felt in the front pocket to make sure that the wad of twenties—six of them—Joe had given her was still there.

It was. Stormi skipped happily to the bathroom, where she would have just enough time for a shower before she was to meet her sister for lunch and a fix.

10

Cox and Farrell took a squad car out to Hedstrom's ranch, if only to provide a semblance of authority. Product endorsements, a salary in the hundreds of thousands, and sizable bonuses had given Hedstrom an incentive to stay at BHU and had long ago made him a wealthy man. Hedstrom owned two hundred acres to the west of town, a setting of rolling woods and meadows, with a twenty-seven-acre pond, tennis courts, and nine holes of golf.

Hedstrom's compound was surrounded by a high stone wall with glass shards set into the top surface. Farrell drove up to the iron gate, hopped out, pressed a button on the intercom, identified herself to an anonymous "Who is it?" and then jumped back into the driver's seat as the heavy doors swung open. The two cops drove about three hundred yards through a wooded processional, and as they approached the clearing ahead, the house came into view—a white three-story antebellum-style home fronted by four tall, square columns.

"Holy shit, it's Tara," said Farrell.

A curving driveway brought them to the front door, where they stopped and got out of the car, half-expecting liveried servants to greet them. The front door slowly creaked open as they approached, and a tall young woman stepped out and stood in front of the door.

Cox had seen her before, sitting next to Hedstrom in the courtroom during the whole Chappelle mess. She was an extraordinarily beautiful woman in the Hoosier mold—blond, blue-eyed, with a perfect porcelain complexion.

"I'm sorry," she said curtly, "Don isn't here. He had to go down to the gym."

"We had an appointment to speak with him here."

"I'm sorry."

"He should have called the station to let us know," Farrell complained. "Or you should have."

"Coach Hedstrom makes his own appointments. If you have a problem, please take it up with him." She stepped back into the house and began to shut the door.

Cox stepped forward and put his hand on the door handle. "Call Hedstrom at the gym. Tell him we're on our way. And that we expect to speak with him."

"I'll try to reach him," she promised, and she pushed the door firmly shut.

Twenty-five minutes later, Cox and Farrell arrived at the university's health and physical education complex, a sprawling assemblage of gymnasiums, tennis courts, racquetball courts, swimming pools, mat rooms, locker rooms, weight rooms, and more—a $200 million testament to the exalted position occupied by athletics at Benjamin Harrison University. Cox let Farrell, who'd gotten her bachelor's degree at BHU and had run track for the school, lead him through the building—down corridors gleaming with green-laminated cinder block, around corners, through tunnels, up and down twisting stairways.

With every step, Cox felt his jaw getting tighter, his teeth grinding with fury and frustration. He knew that Hedstrom was pulling his chain, deliberately wasting his time. He wanted to scream. More than that, he wanted a cigarette, and he was now deep in the center of Harrison's largest no-smoking zone.

Finally, at the end of a long corridor in the building's subbasement, they saw a green metal door, windowless, on which was spray-painted, graffiti-like, THE HOLE. A single basketball court with six rows of bleachers along each side of its length, the Hole was Don Hedstrom's lair, the private gym where the worst of the tantrums were thrown. It was a place to work out the boys before the team took over Aberdeen Hall on October 15, the first official day of practice under NCAA rules. It was to Aberdeen Hall, the team's showcase, what a chapel is to a cathedral—the real thing, but in miniature, pristine, stark, unadorned, a place where the essence of the game could be evoked without distractions. It was, most of all, a place where NCAA eyes could not penetrate.

Cox threw the door open and strode angrily onto the court. Hedstrom was standing at midcourt with two giants, holding the ball and getting ready to toss it for a tip-off. He glanced at Cox as he entered, but continued to talk to the players. He held a riding crop in one hand—it was one of his more exotic motivating devices—and he thwacked it against his thigh for emphasis.

"All right! Heads up!" Hedstrom balanced the ball on his palm for a second, then heaved it upward and stepped back to watch.

The players sprang up, competing for height, and the better jumper snatched the ball out of the air and was moving toward the basket before his feet touched the ground. Six quick strides, a slam dunk, and the player hung from the basket, the ball bouncing noisily away. The player swayed for an instant, then dropped, the other player left gaping at midcourt.

Hedstrom taunted the losing player: "Reed, you jump like you got a sore asshole from being fucked all night! Go soak your butt, pussy!"

Hedstrom nodded to the one who had sunk the bucket, then walked off toward Cox, chuckling to himself. "Take five," he yelled behind him.

"You got two kids there going in opposite directions," Hedstrom mused as he approached the cops. "Breaks my heart." He shook his head. "That Harris is a fuckin' genius, could be better than Shaquille. Or Chappelle, eh?" he grunted, looking at Cox, smiling slightly. He held out his hand. "Detective Cox"—he grinned—"strange that we've never been officially introduced. Of course, I know *of* you."

Cox shook the man's hand and tried to ignore the bait. "Officer Farrell and I are investigating the murder of James Barris. Any information you can give us regarding your relationship with Barris would be appreciated."

"I'm happy to help in any way I can, sir," Hedstrom said unctuously. "Let's have a seat, shall we?"

Hedstrom led the two cops to the bleachers, where he sat, put his hands together as if praying, and touched his fingertips to his nose.

"Jim Barris was a damned good guy. He was a fan, a real fan, the best kind. He cared about the team, loved the game. He was a winner. Came to road games, supported the team. And more than that, he did the charity things, too, the Rotary Club dinner, the Boys Club, Big Brothers. Put his money where his mouth is. A terrific guy, what can I tell you."

"What about women in Barris's life? Know any of them?"

Hedstrom shook his head and shrugged. "Nah. Never talked about women. You know, I think that's a misconception about men—that we brag to one another about our conquests. It's not that way, in my experience. I couldn't have cared less who he was with."

"Who do you think murdered him?"

"I think it was some kind of botched kidnapping or robbery, frankly. Or extortion of some kind. I think somebody wanted something from Jim or had something on him, and Jim wouldn't give in. Maybe Jim had a skeleton in his closet. You know, did something wrong and let the wrong person find out about it. Know what I mean?"

Cox looked Hedstrom squarely in the eyes. "Are you aware of anything like that?"

"No."

"How close were you to Barris?"

"Friends. Not close, really. Like I said, he was a fan. We'd have an occasional drink after a game. Dinner together once a year. He'd occasionally give me a little friendly legal advice."

"What sort of legal advice?"

"Personal matters."

"What sort of personal matters?"

Hedstrom looked at him with annoyance. "I believe that information is confidential."

"Was he your attorney?"

"No."

"Then no privilege exists, and you can be called upon to testify under oath as to the content of your conversations with Barris."

"I see. Well, I don't think that will be necessary, Cox. We didn't really talk about anything of importance. I happen to have three ex-wives, sir. Do you have any idea how difficult it is to live with three divorce settlements? He helped with that, and a question or two about my will and some investments of mine. Of course, we had a couple of fascinating conversations about the law of evidence—this was during the Chappelle trial. Do you remember that one, Cox?"

Hedstrom stood and stepped out onto the court, where his players had begun shooting foul shots. "Amazing what a difference a piece of evidence can make in a case. Like how a single missed shot can destroy a perfectly played game. Or one foul too many."

Outside the Hole, Cox rolled a cigarette, fingers moving swiftly, as he stared ahead and tried to cool off, wondering why Hedstrom would bother to taunt him.

Cox lighted the cigarette and inhaled deeply. Farrell watched him, then tapped his arm and pointed to the NO SMOKING sign on the wall a few feet away.

Cox exhaled, and they started their journey back to the surface. "I need a cigarette. There's nobody around. And frankly, Tina, I don't give a shit what the rules of this place are."

Farrell nodded. "So that's the great Don Hedstrom. A bit of a disappointment. He seemed so . . . small."

"He's a bitter man. I wonder what he has to be bitter about."

"But he's a great coach. How can he be such an asshole?"

Cox stopped walking and glared at Farrell. "Grow up," he said.

At 11:10 A.M., Cox ascended the law school steps, having arranged with Dean Robertson to speak with two professors who had been unavailable the day before, Monty Mtoyo and Judy Rosen.

Inside, the building was quiet. The eleven o'clock classes were in session, and the lobby was deserted except for a couple of women who were setting up a card table outside the library. One of the women began to pull bundles of white cloth from a large cardboard box and spread them out on the table. When Cox glimpsed the name Barris stenciled on the cloth, he blinked, then walked over to take a look.

The students were selling T-shirts. Cox nodded to them and picked one up. On the front, it said in large black letters I KILLED JAMES BARRIS; on the back, it said TOP 10 REASONS I KILLED JAMES BARRIS, and listed them:

    10. He gave me a D in Crim Law
    9. He didn't give me a D in Crim Law
    8. It was Dr. Kevorkian's golf day
    7. Only the good die young
    6. Penis envy
    5. If I hadn't killed him, he'd still be here
    4. Harvey Blau was on sabbatical
    3. A 2.20 curve is a capital offense
    2. This world was not meant for one as beautiful as he
    1. He was a mean sexist asshole and deserved to die

Cox put the T-shirt back on the pile. "You didn't waste any time, did you?"

One woman, in a tie-dyed T-shirt, smiled and said, "Why should we? It's for a good cause—the Women's Law Caucus. And I've got a feeling these are going to sell really well."

"Was Barris hated all this much?"

"Sure he was. I mean . . . are you saying, Is this in questionable taste? Well of course. But does that matter? I don't think so." She looked away suddenly, eyes flashing angrily. "I had Barris two years ago, okay? And you see this reason number one down here? That's the truth."

11

Cox took the elevator up to the faculty offices. As the elevator doors slid open, he found Dean Hume waiting. She looked up quickly and stepped back when the opening doors revealed Cox.

"Oh! Hello," she said breathlessly. "Forgive me, I didn't expect to see you there."

"People rarely do." Cox stepped out of the elevator and held the doors open for her.

"So . . . is there any news?"

Cox shook his head as the elevator doors began to close, banging against his arm. "No, nothing concrete—yet. I'm looking for Professors Mtoyo and Rosen."

"Down the hall," the dean said, stepping onto the elevator. "They've been expecting you."

The nameplate at the side of the door read MONTY MTOYO; inside, a rotund, bald African-American man of about fifty was thumbing through a thick volume. Cox tapped on the door frame.

Mtoyo raised his chin and eyebrows. "Yes—may I help you?"

"Sorry to disturb you. I'm Detective Luther Cox of the Harrison Police Department. I have some questions, if you have a few moments."

"Yes, of course. Please, sit down."

Cox sat on the edge of a straight-backed leather chair and explained his purpose. As Mtoyo listened, he matched the fingers of one hand against the fingers of the other and tapped them silently.

"James Barris. There was your beautiful scoundrel," he began. "He was an extremely charismatic and charming man. I enjoyed his company very much, though I was constantly aware that he was a virulent racist. You know, you can send an Indiana boy to Harvard, but you can't take the Klan out of the boy. Or let me put that another way. You can send an Indiana boy to Harvard and hope that he'll pick up a wider worldview—that is, an attitude of toleration—but chances are if he comes back to Indiana, it's because he prefers a segregated society to the more pluralistic, integrated society you find in eastern cities. Hell, he told me himself that as a child he'd watch his father and uncles putting on Klan uniforms. Now, I think Barris liked me, despite himself, because we found ourselves in the same camp, politically speaking, on occasion. I'm a conservative, what I call a 'bootstrapper,' because I share the view that the welfare system is inherently bad for black people—that this intravenous money supply just keeps blacks comatose and unable to wield economic power. And I happen to be the only faculty member at this school who thinks Clarence Thomas was a terrific choice for the Supreme Court."

Cox smiled and was about to open his mouth to ask a question, when Mtoyo rolled on.

"But I'm way off the track. Forgive me," he said amiably. "I don't know if you've already gotten this impression, but there aren't two people who actually like each other on this faculty, and few who can even agree on the weather, never mind what the law is or should be. You have your critical legal studies bunch, who say that law is built on shifting sand, and then your common law liberals, who say it's built on solid rock. You have your communitarians, who say the law has got to make us all responsible for one another, and your libertarians, who say we're only responsible for ourselves. You have your law and economics crowd versus your multicultural liberals versus your federalists versus your feminists. Of course, then you get Jews versus Gentiles and men versus women and straights ganging

102

up on gays and blacks versus whites and liberal blacks versus conservative blacks. But of course, on law faculties, blacks are still one-at-a-time performers, and everybody here is too cool to do anything but patronize me. Do I seem unhappy to you?"

Cox grinned, and again tried to speak.

"Of course," Mtoyo went on, "I am thought less of. Particularly by people like Barris, who just burned with the thought that I'd received this position, and eventually received tenure, because it is necessary in this political climate for law schools to hire black faculty to remedy inequities of the past. Do I seem angry to you? Of course, Barris is dead, and here you are, come to question the nigger on the block, the most probable suspect."

"I've spoken with quite a few faculty members."

"Of course . . . forgive me. I suppose the bottom line is that I was pretty damn sad to hear of Jim's death. I'm going to miss our arguments; he was a great adversary."

As he approached the door to Judy Rosen's office, Cox's nostrils caught the sweet aroma of cigarette smoke, and he sensed his body prepare ecstatically for a nicotine onslaught. He knocked, and a voice rasped, "Come in."

Cox pushed the door open into a fog of blue smoke, brightly illuminated by the tall windows at the opposite end of the small office. Silhouetted in her chair, knees pulled up to her chest, was the attractive woman with long silvery blond hair he'd seen at the memorial service. It took his eyes a moment to adjust to the blinding optical effect of the smoke and the window light, but he managed to reach out his hand to meet hers coming across the desk.

"Detective Luther Cox—"

"Yes, I'd heard you would be coming by. What can I do for you?"

"I need to ask you some questions about James Barris."

"Yes, of course. I—"

"Would you mind if I smoked?"

The woman smiled, then barked a phlegmy laugh. "Sorry, there's

103

no smoking here." She took a long drag on the cigarette she was holding, then reached into a drawer and passed Cox an ashtray.

"Thanks," he said softly, and quickly rolled a smoke.

"A hand-rolled man," she commented. "Either you're a vestige of the Wild West or a radical bomber in cop's shoes."

"Neither, I'm afraid."

She put one hand to her forehead, seemingly caught up in emotion. "Right. Okay. Jim. Do you have any idea who might have done this to him?"

Cox shook his head.

"Can you tell me more about what happened?"

"His body was found in a cornfield north of town. He'd been strangled with a piece of plastic twine, something like a cheap dog leash."

"God, how awful." She looked away, then asked, "What was he doing in a cornfield? Is that where he was killed?"

"We think not."

"I miss the bastard." She fought back tears. "Shit." She fished another cigarette out of the pack on her desk, lighted it, and inhaled deeply. "He tried to get me to go home with him a couple of times. Not that that was anything to brag about."

Cox watched her closely. She was, he thought, a melancholy soul, like he was; like him, she felt too much, regretted too much. The cigarettes were the self-medication for their common disease.

"I don't know how familiar you are with the academic culture," she went on, "but it isn't surprising that violence does occur. You know, like the stressed-out assistant professor who brings an Uzi into the department office and mows down the faculty, all for the sake of not having received the grant he'd counted on. In some ways, faculty life is better in law schools. There's far less pressure to publish, and once you're in, it's nearly impossible to get you out. But the competition for recognition, for status among the faculty, is tremendous. There is a definite pecking order, a hierarchy of respect, that forms the basis of relationships. Accomplishments—like important publications, appearances before the Supreme Court, citations of your work in the books or articles of important people—those accomplishments determine who your friends and enemies are. Your friends, of course, are those people who might benefit from your success; your enemies are the ones who fall a notch because of it. They resent you; they disparage your work behind your back; they sabotage your future when they can."

She paused. "For example, imagine that you're in the last stages of writing a book about rape, a book called *Rape as Metaphor*, a kind of intellectual meditation on rape in society, in literature, and in the law, with the concept borrowed from Susan Sontag's *Illness as Metaphor*."

Cox listened intently, sensing the pain of revelation in her voice.

"And this book is, say, given a more personal dimension by your having revealed and described in it your own rape, which had taken place a decade before, but which you'd only begun to deal with, emotionally and in your work."

"Yes."

She took a deep breath. "And that you had shared this manuscript—that is, large chunks of it—with one of your colleagues, a man known to be on the opposite end of the political spectrum from you, but whose views and intellect you greatly respect."

"Yes."

"And that this man, before discussing the book with you, criticized it harshly to other faculty members here and professors at other schools whom he happened to run into at a conference in Washington, in the process exposing and distorting the facts of your rape, and that some of these other professors, as he knew, had connections with your publisher, and they jeopardized the publication by raising doubts about the book's integrity and scholarly depth."

"When did this happen?"

"Last summer."

"Will your book be published?"

"The decision has been postponed. I won't know until January."

"I'm sorry."

"But I didn't kill Jim, in case you're wondering. I just stopped talking to him for a while."

"I see."

"And everything I said to you before is true. I liked Jim . . . most of the time. And I was attracted to him, despite myself. That's the awful burden of being a heterosexual woman—you love men, and want them, desire them, despite the fact that most of them are jerks or immature, selfish assholes. Need I go on?"

"No," Cox replied.

On his way out of the law school, Cox passed the T-shirt concession, which appeared to be doing a brisk business. A few of the students chatting in the lobby were already wearing them.

I KILLED JAMES BARRIS.

Cox smiled at the utter bleakness of the humor in those words, then was momentarily irked by the thought that the words mocked his failure to find Barris's killer. There they were, dozens of walking confessions.

He bought a T-shirt.

On his way back to the station, Cox breathed deeply and thought about the stone wall they were hitting and why they couldn't get past it, see through it, or climb over it. The crime-scene evidence—and there was a ton of it, from fibers to tire prints, to fingerprints, to hairs—was useless until a real suspect emerged. Then a warrant for probable cause could be issued to search the suspect's home and property to find evidence connecting the suspect to the crime scene. Briefly, Cox had hoped that the answer lay with the law school faculty, but his sixth sense told him no. He felt that he needed to strike out in an entirely different direction, but he hadn't the slightest idea what it might be.

Then Cox walked into the Harrison Police Department headquarters and found Nora Lumsey sitting on the bench outside his office.

Nora had spent the morning doing legal research at the law school library. She had called the Harrison police several times and checked her own voice mail repeatedly, hoping to connect with Cox before the end of the day. Finally, at 2:00 P.M., she decided to leave the law school, intending to sit outside Cox's office until he showed up.

As it turned out, he was only moments behind her.

Nora stood, unnerved to find the man approaching the door to Detective Cox's office to be a tall gray-haired man, his mustache badly in need of trimming, wearing a battered leather jacket and black denims. Yet she knew before he opened his mouth that he was Cox, knew by the way he looked at her inquiringly, sensing that she had a purpose in seeking him out.

For his part, Cox found it perfectly unsurprising that this young-ish woman—looking older perhaps than her years, tall and ample, too ample to be called statuesque—should be there for him, as if materialized out of his need for an answer.

"Detective Cox?"

"Yes."

They shook hands.

"Nora Lumsey. I was a friend of Jim Barris."

Cox opened the door to his office and threw his notepad on his desk.

"Would you like to have a coffee?" he offered. "Not here, I mean. Next door, at the café."

"Yes," Nora said, relieved at not having to sit in the stuffy, mal-odorous confines of Cox's office. "I'd like that very much."

12

The Mad Hatter was one of the few restaurants in Harrison to preserve a smoking section; here, it was a cluster of three tables set in an alcove near the kitchen. Cox knew the restaurant well; he had been displaying his artwork on its walls for years and had been smoking there since the days when the *non*smoking section was a knot of out-of-the-way tables.

At Cox's sheepish insistence, he and Nora took a table in the smoking section. Once seated, he immediately rolled a cigarette, lighted it, and watched Nora grimace as he exhaled the smoke up and away, as gracefully as he knew how. Then he tapped the ash from his cigarette into a tiny glass ashtray and smiled the smoker's apologetic smile.

Nora watched him perform these rituals, vaguely disgusted, yet feeling sorry for him, as though he were an elderly incontinent who had just shit his pants.

Nora ordered cappuccino, Cox an espresso.

"I should start by telling you that I'm an attorney," Nora said abruptly. "I'm a deputy public defender for Marion County."

"I see," Cox said. "The enemy." He smiled.

"Yes," Nora replied. "Some cops see us that way. But not most."

"No. The way I see it, each of us has a job to do."

"Right. And I thought I'd make your job a little easier by coming to you instead of waiting for you to find me."

"Much appreciated. Tell me about it."

Nora took a deep breath and looked down at her hands on the table; she was about to speak when she was jolted by a mental image of Stormi doing the same thing. She straightened her back and confronted Cox's gaze. "I met Jim about eight months ago. I was representing a prostitute named Stormi Skye when her pimp hired Jim to take over the case."

"I see."

"I got to know Jim after I transferred the case to him. I gave him the girl's files, and then I would run into him in the City-County Building. Occasionally, we'd chat about the case."

"Uh-huh." Cox watched Nora's face expectantly, wondering what the woman had waited all day to tell him.

"We started dating," Nora said, and then, after a pause, added, "though it never got serious."

"What do you mean?"

The waitress brought their drinks. Nora stirred the froth on her cappuccino.

"We . . . spent time together. There wasn't any particular . . . emotional connection. I didn't love him and he wasn't in love with me."

"You slept together."

"Yes."

"But you didn't care much for him."

"I didn't say that. I said I didn't love him. I liked him. I enjoyed going out with him. But no, I didn't care *much* for him."

"Is there anything else?" Cox sipped the espresso, feeling vaguely irritable. "You didn't come all the way out here to tell me you slept with the man."

"No," Nora said, relaxing now, feeling somehow that the worst of it—admitting to the affair—was behind her. "There are a few things you ought to know. First, he was a user of cocaine and marijuana. I know this because I saw these things in his house and I saw him use them. I don't know where he got them, however."

"Okay."

"Second, I know he had some involvement with Gene Lydon. Jim defended Lydon in an obscenity case a few years ago, and Lydon was the pimp who hired Jim to defend Stormi Skye. You ought to talk to Lydon about Jim; he may also be Jim's drug connection."

"Okay." Cox nodded and worked at concealing his elation; here, at last, was new information.

"Third, I suspect that Jim may have had some involvement beyond the professional—that is, beyond the *legal* professional—with Stormi Skye. I've been trying to find her all day to talk to her about it, but she's not at home, and she's not at Lydon's store."

"Pleazures."

"You know of it?"

"Sure."

"And there's another thing. I'm currently representing Stormi in a possession case. She was picked up two nights ago in Campbellville, drunk at the side of the road, her keys locked in her car. When the IPD stopped her, they found a Baggie of cocaine on the floor of the car."

"The night of Barris's murder."

"Yes."

"Anything else?"

"Yes. Because I'm Stormi's attorney on the possession charge, you can't talk to her about that charge unless I'm present."

"Of course."

The two then sipped their coffees in silence, the heart of their business done. Nora looked up to find Cox staring at her face, seeming to examine her.

"Tell me about James Barris," Cox said. "What kind of man was he?"

"I think he was intensely lonely," Nora said quickly, surprised by the emotion in her voice. "He never spoke much about his family, but he told me once that his father died when he was quite young, maybe six, in an automobile accident. His mother never remarried.

110

He had an older brother. He's mentally ill—schizophrenic, I think—and lives on the East Coast. I think Jim . . . needed love desperately, yet he could not let down his guard long enough to receive it; he had something to prove to everybody."

"Hence the drugs."

"Yes, I think so."

"And the prostitutes."

"Yes. And the womanizing. He had this thing . . . about promiscuity being a kind of sexual honesty. But I think it's because he never could trust anybody."

Cox stirred the grounds at the bottom of the espresso cup. "Maybe he was right."

"Yes, that's the obvious answer, isn't it?"

"I don't know."

"I think he couldn't trust anyone because he was so untrustworthy himself. I mean, how can you trust anyone to love you if you're always looking for the next opportunity to score, the next piece of ass. To trust, you have to—" Oh shit, Nora, she scolded herself, lost for words, what on earth are you talking about?

He smiled at her pitifully. "Be worthy of trust."

"Yes. Have you ever been married, Mr. Cox?"

"Yes. I was, once. Why do you ask?"

"Because I think people who've been married for a long time or who marry young forget what it's like to be lonely . . . and not to have someone to trust completely."

"I don't know many marriages where that's the case."

"I've known one or two. So what happened? Are you divorced?"

"No. My wife died in a fire. Nine years ago."

"Oh. I'm sorry." Nora flushed with embarrassment, her heart aching at the idiocy of her assumption, wishing miserably she could disappear. She spread her fingers on the table's wooden surface and looked down at her hands, avoiding Cox's gaze.

Cox watched her face, then looked down, too, at the floor, where his eye was caught by the up-and-down motion of her foot as she slipped the back of her shoe, a brown loafer, on and off her heel. As he watched her heel disappear into the shoe and be revealed again, it occurred to him that he hadn't made love with a woman since a disastrous affair shortly after Julia's death. Nine years. Odd how that number kept increasing. He couldn't imagine having a relationship with a woman now. Desire came so rarely that it was less an inspiration to action than a bitter reminder of loss. But as he glimpsed the ripples of her sole, the bare foot creating a sensation of texture and odor and warmth in his mind, he felt a lunge of terror in his heart. He realized how deeply he wanted the intimacy of love, and that he would always want it. But he knew that he would never love another woman. Ever. Even this woman.

Cox looked up and found her watching him. He smiled and nearly blushed.

"Have you solved the mystery, Detective Cox?" she asked.

"See those paintings up there, the three above the aquarium?" Cox motioned toward a series of three views of the tiny pond south of his cabin, the reflections of the woods and sky distorted in the rippled surface of the pond. They were painstaking efforts, and he was uncharacteristically proud of these works.

She turned to look, then turned back quickly. "Yes, not bad, actually. What about them?"

"Just caught my eye," he said.

She left him in the café, having promised that if she managed to locate her client, she would urge Stormi to come down to the Harrison police headquarters and give a statement about her relationship with Barris. Cox had seemed satisfied with that, for now, though he insisted perfunctorily that Nora make herself available for further questioning, something Nora knew was inevitable in any event.

What a strange man, Nora thought as she drove southwest through the darkening afternoon toward Stormi's trailer. How dour, how blunt, how humorless. Still, she sensed that he was at least honest, contrary to what she had heard about the Harrison cops, and maybe he cared enough to put some effort into solving this case.

Nora crept through the trailer park and pulled up behind the Impala belonging to Stormi's mother. Leaning against the side of the trailer was a motorcycle with a license plate that read STORMI above the rear wheel.

As Nora stepped down from her pickup and turned toward the trailer, the metal door swung open and Stormi emerged, wearing a tight checked blouse knotted below the sternum and cutoff jeans shorts that traced the line between the tops of her legs and her pelvis. She smiled a vaguely mocking smile, seemingly oblivious to the chill air, and descended the three metal steps to the ground.

"Hi," she said, moving toward Nora.

"Hi, Stormi." Nora held out her hand to Stormi, who shook it uncertainly. "I need to talk to you about a few things."

"Well, I hope you're hungry, 'cause my ma and I are about ta eat. And we got extra, 'cause my sister ain't showed up."

Nora followed her toward the trailer. "I don't want to impose."

"You ain't got a choice."

"Well, in that case, thanks."

"Hell of a place, huh?" Stormi moved her head to indicate the whole trailer park. "I can't tell ya how much I wanna git the fuck outta here."

"I think I know."

Stormi led Nora to Garth, still in the sandbox; the boy had stopped his playing to watch the two women.

"Nora, I'd like you to meet Garth," she said in the singsong cadence of a kindergarten teacher.

"Hi, Garth. We met a little earlier today." Nora extended her hand; Garth shook it for about half a minute.

"My mom's a country music fan," Stormi said.

"I see," Nora replied. "Whose child is Garth?"

"You could say he belongs t' all of us."

"Who's his mother?"

"My sister."

Nora followed Stormi into the trailer. In the galley kitchen, at the front end of the trailer, Weesie stood bent over an oven door, her backside shaking as she worked. Nora glanced at Stormi, who rolled her eyes.

"Stormi, izzat you?"

"Yeah, Ma."

"Them pork chops is almost ready ta go in." She grunted as she closed the oven door and stood. "Taters is done."

"We got company, Ma," Stormi said.

Weesie turned abruptly and wiped her hands on a dishrag. "Oh, well, how ya doin', Miss—"

"Lumsey. Nora, I mean."

"So glad ya could come on back," she said, grinning.

Nora shook the woman's hand. "Thanks for having me."

Weesie turned her attention to the sink, which was piled with dishes. "Stormi says yer a darn good lawyer. Ya gotta go to school fer a long time ta do that, don't ya?"

"Law school is three years. After you graduate from college."

"I wish one o' my kids'd gone ta college. At least one of my girls finished high school, though, and I ain't lettin' Garth do like his uncles done and drop out."

"Yes, I think—"

"Stormi coulda gone ta college. She ain't stupid."

"Ma," Stormi moaned.

"Maybe I coulda gone ta college, too, if I'd finished high school. I spent just too much time havin' babies." She bounced on the balls of her feet whenever she stopped speaking, as if impatient for a cue to start talking again.

"How many—"

"Seven. Five living. I had 'em tie a knot in it at the hospital after Randy was born. That wuz enough for me."

"I see." Nora smiled.

"There's Johnny and Kenny. Them's by my first husband, Delbert. Then there's the twins, Sunni and Stormi, and my boy Randy with my second husband, Levon. My third husband, Elvin, passed away just fourteen month ago."

"I'm sorry."

"Well, all the kids are up and gone now, 'cept Sunni 'n Stormi, and I do believe they're not long for this place. Damned if I know what I'm gonna do alone here, with a boy yet to raise, at my age."

"Ma—"

"None o' mah kids are any damn good, ya know. Kenny been in jail twice, Randy's on parole, Johnny's a goddamn drug addict—"

"Ma, please, she don't want ta hear—"

"Sunni's wild, too, drinkin' way too much fer her age and runnin' with those bikers and those weird dykes downtown."

"They ain't dykes!"

"She always stuck up for Sunni. Even as a baby, she wouldn't—"

"Ma—"

"She—"

"MA! Shut up!" Stormi breathed deeply, shaking her head. She glanced at Nora as she shucked some corn and threw it in a pot. "She is so fuckin' stupid."

"Do ya see th' way she talks ta me?"

Nora smiled, her head spinning. She picked up a framed photograph from on top of the TV. It was of Weesie and a sullen-looking, balding black man in a green polyester suit. "Is this—"

"That's Elvin Phipps. Our wedding day. Hard to believe it was just six years ago. Poor bastard drank himself to death."

"I'm sorry—"

"Speakin' o' which, can I get ya somethin'?"

"Um, a beer, please."

"Stormi?"

"Yeah, the same."

A motorcycle roared up outside, its unmufflered engine pelting the air with great angry sobs. The sound died abruptly and was followed by the loud clanging of boots on the metal steps. The door was thrust open and a young woman in jeans, flannel shirt, and leather jacket burst in, flinging back her shoulder-length neon pink hair.

Sunni Skye.

When she saw Nora, Sunni stopped, startled, and glanced around fearfully, as if Nora had been sent to repossess the place.

"Hi," Nora ventured. Stormi continued to mix frozen vegetables in a pot; Weesie glanced over at Sunni, shook her head, and continued to set the folding table.

"What th' hell's goin' on here?" Sunni cried, ignoring Nora. "Stormi, I gotta talk ta ya."

She dried her hands. "Nora, this is my sister, Sunni."

Nora, about to extend her hand, was met by a look of barely suppressed fury. She watched as Sunni pushed past her mother, grabbed Stormi by the upper arm, and pushed her out the other side of the kitchen into a small pantry area.

"What th' fuck are ya doin'?"

Nora stood at the grimy window, watching Garth outside as he swatted the air with a plastic sword, and she listened as Stormi murmured indecipherably and Sunni spat angrily back at her.

"The shit's hittin' the fan and you're— Izzat her? *Izzat the cunt?*" There was the sound of a slap, of a grunt, then whispers, quieter now, between the two. Suddenly, Sunni emerged, face afire, trembling. She pushed silently past Weesie and Nora and disappeared out the door. Nora returned to the window. She watched Sunni kick-start her motorcycle, hers bearing a SUNNI license plate, and take off, roaring through the trailer park, kicking up dirt. The sound terrified Garth, who huddled against the side of the trailer.

"Hell of a gal, my sis," Stormi said, emerging. She turned down the electric burner under the vegetables, then stirred them slowly.

Nora had planned to find a few moments before or after dinner to sit Stormi down and speak frankly with her about Barris, but four beers later, Nora found herself staring into Weesie's face with a mixture of revulsion and wonder, fascinated by the quiver of Weesie's jowls, the slow pucker of the sagging skin beneath her eyes, the crinkle of her crow's-feet. She was saying something to Nora about dancing, and Stormi, who had nursed one beer throughout the meal, was shaking her head and saying over and over, "No, Ma, please. No, Ma, please," as Garth, seated at the end of the table, shook his head in rhythm with Stormi and murmured, "No, no, no, no." But then the fat lady was out of her chair and turning up the volume on the clock radio on the kitchen counter. It was a George Strait record they were playing, a Texas swing number called "Now and Then," and in an instant, Weesie had Nora on her feet and she was twirling her around the six-foot-square patch of floor space between the kitchen table and the living room couch.

"Can ya do the two-step?" she called, and when Nora shook her head, Weesie released her and stood still for a moment, waiting for the right beat. Then abruptly, she exploded into movement, her huge body shimmying, her feet describing arcs on the dirty vinyl floor. After a moment, Weesie reached out and pulled Nora into her orbit, and even Stormi, who had been sitting with her head in her hands and a sour, bored expression on her face, had to laugh. Weesie motioned for her to join in, but Stormi shook her head. "There's no room," she yelled.

"Sure thur is," yelled Weesie, and she reached her arm out and pulled Stormi into the dance. The three formed a circle, Nora grinning as she tried to follow the steps that the other two women knew well. She watched Stormi closely, and Stormi returned her gaze. But then the music faded into a commercial, the dance ceased like the running down of a windup toy, and Stormi's expression clouded.

"Shit, I've got to get to work," she said.

Outside the trailer, the night was loud with televisions and cars and motorcycles, with laughter and music and fighting, with things banging and children crying.

Stormi and Nora stepped slowly together in the gravel driveway, then stood between Nora's pickup and the Impala.

"Your mom's wild," Nora said.

"No shit," said Stormi.

They stood for a moment, Nora with her hands in her pockets, Stormi rubbing her arms against the evening chill.

117

"Stormi, I need to talk to you about James Barris. Do you remember him? He was the lawyer who took over for me when—"

"Sure I remember him." Stormi took a cigarette out of her purse and lighted it with a small plastic lighter. "He's the one who got killed."

"That's right. How do you know about that?"

"The paper. And I remembered him."

Nora looked at Stormi in the glare of the streetlight illuminating the trailer park's main drag. The shadows on Stormi's face made her skin look old, older than her mother's; pity and protectiveness welled up in Nora.

"How well did you know Jim Barris?"

"We'd talk."

"Was it just about your case? Or were there other things you'd talk about?"

"Other things."

"Like what?"

"All kinds of shit."

Nora put her hand on Stormi's shoulder. "Stormi, I'm your lawyer. You've got to be honest with me if I'm going to help you."

Stormi wrenched her body away from Nora's hand. "I don't know what the fuck I need your help for. So I got picked up with a little coke."

"It's a serious offense, Stormi. And you've already got two felonies on your record. If you get convicted for cocaine possession, you've got a third. That makes you a habitual offender. You could spend the next twenty years in prison."

Stormi threw her cigarette to the ground. "Fuck," she muttered, blowing out smoke.

"You may be a suspect in Barris's death. You're going to be questioned, at the very least. There's a detective on the Harrison police, Luther Cox, who's looking for you."

Stormi stood still now, and she stared at the ground.

"I told him that you'd go to the police station and give a voluntary statement."

Stormi was silent.

"Will you do that?"

"Yeah, sure."

"What will you tell them?"

"What should I tell them?"

"Did you have a sexual relationship with Barris?"

A pause. "Yeah, but it's not like you think."

"What do you mean?"

"I knew Barris since I was fifteen. Since I knew Lydon. He was a customer, a john."

"You had sex with Barris when you were fifteen?"

"Yeah."

Nora felt herself choke with anger and disbelief. "Long before he became your lawyer."

"Yeah."

Nora opened her eyes wide, looked at Stormi's face, and fought the images that were crowding her mind, images of herself and Barris, of Barris and this tiny young woman.

Then Stormi said, "He told me not to say nothin' to ya."

"Oh, he did. Why?"

" 'Cause he was doin' you, too."

Stormi tried not to smirk as she said this, but Nora saw the smirk and the effort and her heart sank as she thought of how thoroughly Barris had used her.

"Don't feel bad," Stormi went on, now sisterly. "He was a pig. I hated him."

"Why did you hate him?" Nora whispered, her voice failing, her throat choked with humiliation.

"He was a pig. He liked to hurt me."

Nora felt her head grow heavy with the weight of what she had heard, and she could hear no more. "You must go to the Harrison police and speak with Luther Cox. Will you do that?"

"Yeah, sure."

"Don't fuck with me, Stormi," Nora said, feeling her self-control slip away. "Will you do it?"

"Yeah, I swear."

"When?"

"Tomorrow."

"When?"

"Well . . . I guess around one."

"I'll be there. I'll be with you."

Stormi shrugged. "Thanks."

Nora began to open the door to her pickup but stopped, trembling; she could not leave without asking.

"Stormi?"

"Yeah."

"What did Jim Barris do to hurt you?"

"You don't wanna know."

"I want to know."

"No you don't."

"I . . . want . . . to . . . know!" Nora shouted the words, stunned by her anger, and she had to clutch the pickup door to keep from grabbing Stormi.

Stormi stepped back and leaned on the hood of the Impala. "He liked to burn me. 'Punishment,' he called it. For smoking. He would take my cigarettes away and light one and touch me with it." Stormi lit a cigarette and stared at the burning tip of it, as if to demonstrate. "Happy now?"

"Why'd you let him do it?"

"Once he cut me . . . with a razor. . . . He wanted to see the blood come up, he said, but that was too weird, and it stung like hell. I wouldn't let him do that again."

"Why'd you let him do it in the first place?"

"Money. He ever try that shit with you?"

Go on, sister, add insult to injury. Nora shook her head.

"That kind of shit wouldn't happen to you, would it? I got used to being hit and burned and shit when I was a kid, so it wasn't so bad."

"It was bad."

120

"I can take care of myself. I don't mind a little pain, a little messin' around. Sometimes pain can make you feel good. It's when it stops feelin' good but you do it anyway that you're fucked. Then you start hatin' yerself fer wantin' it. Then you start to die. And if you can't run away, can't break from it, you do die."

From Cox's stereo, the sinuous whine of Jerry Garcia's guitar leapt forth in the midst of an extended jam on "Dark Star" as Cox doodled on a twenty-four-by-thirty-six-inch pad. The sound's controlled chaos, its cerebral intimacy and sense of improvised architecture had created in him an unaccustomed mood of freedom and playfulness, and he let his hand move almost without thought, the representations taking form with an eerie unconscious predestination.

Cox started with a short horizontal line and watched it turn into what looked like a stack of folded towels. It blossomed into three dimensions, then became a neat square stack, like the stack of folded clothing found next to Barris's body. Yes. Cox drew a pair of shoes, wing tips, next to the clothes, and then tried to reproduce Barris's body in the position in which he had come upon it.

Next to his drawing, Cox made from memory a list of the physical evidence taken from the scene of Barris's murder.

- fibers—polyester blanket
- fingerprint from body
- pubic hair combing
- scattered clothing fibers
- soil and vegetation samples
- Barris blood sample
- Barris car—impounded
- pattern of rope impression in neck
- fibers and hair from Barris car—vacuumed samples
- tire tracks by side of road
- Barris clothes, shoes, wallet
- Barris fingernail scrapings

It was an amazingly good collection of evidence—lots of items that were capable of establishing links between a suspect and the crime scene—but it wouldn't do him a damn bit of good until enough evidence pointed to a particular suspect to establish a definite connection. Barris had certainly spilled a lot of blood; some of it must have gotten on the murderer's clothing. A single bloody sock in the trunk of somebody's car would be all Cox needed.

The fingerprint was significant. Farrell had run the print through the FBI's automated fingerprint identification system, a computerized fingerprint comparison program that searched a database of more than 20 million print records of offenders for possible matches. The system's success depended, however, on the clarity of the fingerprint's minutia points—ridge endings, bifurcations, directions, and contours—which are mapped and digitized. Sixty minutia points are considered a good number for matching; the print lifted from Barris's body yielded only nine, and consequently the search turned up thousands of possible matches in Indiana alone. But if they had a suspect and a set of prints to work with, nine minutia points would be plenty to establish probable cause.

But who? What person amid the worlds in which Barris moved would be the one to kill him? Who among the faculty? There was no dearth of motives to go around—Blau, his wife's infidelity; Rosen, the violation of trust; Mtoyo, the jealousy and the rage over Barris's racism. And academic competitiveness, a motive they all shared. Who among Barris's friends? Don Hedstrom? What motive? And his lovers? Who were they? For all the talk of Barris's sex life, the only known lovers they'd been able to come up with were the wives of a couple of faculty members, a prostitute, and Nora Lumsey.

Before turning in for the night, Cox went to his bookcase and carefully lifted an old shoe box down from the highest shelf. He took the shoe box to his table, where he opened it and took out a thick bundle of bamboo sticks and his copy of the *I Ching*.

The time had come to ask the help of ancient wisdom.

Cox had made an infrequent ritual of consulting the *I Ching*, the Confucian system of prophesy, since his undergraduate days, when a yearlong infatuation with Eastern philosophy led him nearly to abandon his major in art in favor of Asian studies. It was his complete ineptitude at languages that stopped him—or saved him; confronted with the daunting task of learning thousands of Chinese and Japanese characters, he decided he would be satisfied knowing enough Chinese to study the basics of Tao and to use the *I Ching*. But more than that, Cox realized that he was neither a teacher nor a scholar. His natural Tao was that of a hunter, a tracker, a lone pursuer.

Now all that remained of Cox's foray into Oriental mysticism was a shelfful of books by Alan Watts, a collection of marble and jade Buddhas and incense burners that graced the odd nooks of his cabin, and an enduring faith in the prophetic power of the *I Ching*. Over the years, Cox had memorized the *I Ching*'s sixty-four hexagrams, internalizing the *I Ching*'s catalog of cosmic forces, its universe of ideas and images, warnings and enticements, possibilities and dead ends.

Early in his career, Cox discovered that the *I Ching* and its commentaries had a subtle power to settle his mind and evoke new perspectives on difficult cases. He'd taken plenty of shit from Bieberschmidt about it at first, after Bieberschmidt caught him counting the sticks one lunch hour, the last time Cox ever did such a thing at the office.

But when the advice of hexagram 36—*Ming I, K'un over Li,* Earth over Fire, "Concealment of Illumination"—led to the arrest of a rapist-murderer, the smirks ceased instantly.

As Cox had explained to the gape-mouthed chief, *Ming I* depicts the concept of illumination, which represents goodness, being nurtured in concealment, which represents evil. The commentaries explained that while goodness can grow within evil, evil can likewise grow within good, and it occurred to Cox that a facade of goodness might have been employed to shield the rapist. Cox's attention was thereby drawn to an evangelical preacher who had performed in Harrison on the date of the murder.

Two days later, the preacher was arrested in Indianapolis and was linked to similar crimes in six states.

Cox put out the cigarette, breathed deeply to remove the smoke from his lungs, closed his eyes, and sat without movement, attempting to empty his mind of subjectivity and predispositions. He tried to formulate a question that would seek a direction, a path, a clue—a way to awaken the answer within him. The voice in Cox's mind asked, Oracle, is the murderer known to me?

Cox put one of the sticks on the desk in front of him, then divided the remaining forty-nine sticks into two bundles without counting them. He held one bundle in each hand, then took one stick from the right-hand bundle and held it in his left hand between his ring and little fingers. Cox then removed the sticks from the left-hand bundle, two at a time, forming groups of eight, until no more groups of eight could be made. As it turned out, the sticks divided exactly by eight. The number for the lower trigram was therefore zero—for the number of sticks left over—plus one for the stick held between the ring and little fingers. The numeral one, he knew, corresponded to *Ch'ien*, or Heaven.

Cox drew the three solid lines on his pad.

———
———
———

He repeated the process again to produce the upper trigram; after dividing the sticks into groups of eight, he was left with three sticks, plus the one held between the ring and little fingers of his left hand. The number four corresponded to *Chen,* or Thunder. Cox drew the two broken lines and one solid line above the lower trigram, forming the complete hexagram.

—— ——
—— ——
———
———
———
———

He recognized the hexagram, surprised at its clarity: *Ta Chuan*, Thunder over Heaven—"Great Power."

Cox opened the book of commentary and turned to the page explaining *Ta Chuan.* It read: "Thunder, intense and powerful, dwells above heaven; that is its proper place, and it does no harm. But thunder on earth is explosive, deadly."

> Great power has the capacity to be used for good or for evil, for productivity or for destruction. The four strong lines at the bottom of the hexagram are rising, driving out weakness, and there is an implicit warning that the abuse of power, or the lack of wisdom in the use of power, will lead to misfortune, conflict, and harm.

Cox stared at the page and let his mind explore the interplay between the hexagram and the world of James Barris.

"Great power." The phrase, taken literally, pointed to Barris's power as a scholar. Or lover. Or to his ideas—to the notion of power as survival, regardless of the cost to others. Was Barris's notion of a Darwinian society a corruption of great power?

"Great power." Could it also, Cox pondered, refer to Barris's illusions of importance? Or to the powerful people he knew—the university administration, those of Harrison's politicians with whom he was acquainted, or Don Hedstrom?

"Thunder on earth." The image that occurred immediately to Cox was of an explosive—a bomb or a firearm. Are such devices a perversion of natural law because they empower the weak? Or are they simply the accoutrements of the fittest in our society? Or is "thunder on earth" a phrase for amorality—the separation of power from any constraining moral code?

It is difficult, Cox thought, to reconcile the Taoist vision of natural life with Barris's libertarian-Darwinist vision of natural law. The former sees life as simple, joyful, flowing, in harmony with the essential nature of the world and creation; the latter sees life as an endless struggle, a battle for survival against others, and only through vanquishing the weaker will the stronger survive.

Perhaps I live too much in my Tao, Cox fretted. I trust too much, tolerate too much, forgive too much in myself and others. I'm getting too damn soft watching the river flow.

125

Maybe it's time to live in the Darwinian world for a while.

Cox resolved to take a stroll through Barris's little black book to see if he couldn't raise a few ex-girlfriends. And he'd call Blau's wife, despite his reluctance to stir up marital discord with unpleasant memories. Unpleasant for Blau, anyway; the wife might have had a wonderful time. And he'd talk to Barris's prostitute himself, a certain Stormi Skye.

13

FRIDAY, DECEMBER 9

As the night progressed, the temperature plunged into the single digits. At 1:45 A.M., the cold penetrated Cox's plaid flannel blanket sufficiently to awaken him, and he forced himself out of bed and over to the cedar chest, where he rummaged for his down comforter through piles of ragged sweaters. He found the comforter at the bottom of the chest and pulled it out in billows of linen and feathers, dragged it back to the bed, and burrowed into it, shivering. Cox reminded himself that if he didn't repoint the log exterior of the cabin, he was going to freeze his ass all winter.

At 4:10 A.M., the telephone rang. He picked up the phone and put it to his ear without opening his eyes.

"Cox."

The voice that responded belonged to Sandy, the night dispatcher.

"Sorry, Luther. Got a homicide at the Sleep Tite Motel. Fourth Street and Eustace Avenue. Caucasian woman, twenties, believed to be a prostitute. Perry and Adams are at the scene. Bieberschmidt and Farrell have been dispatched."

Cox's heart started to pound. It was the girl, he knew, the one he should have interviewed yesterday.

"I'm on my way," he said. "Listen, Sandy, get Quade down there, okay?"

———

Twenty-two minutes later, Cox pulled up at the motel. Eyes burning, he squinted into the glare of four sets of police flashers as they swept the streets and surrounding buildings in pulsing blasts of color. An ambulance was there, too, but it was clear from the way the emergency medical technicians were huddled together over cups of coffee that their services hadn't been needed. He hoped that they hadn't disturbed the corpse—and the evidence in and around it—with futile efforts at lifesaving.

The Sleep Tite Motel was a two-story redbrick barracks, a dormitory for Harrison's transient down-and-out. The place was well known to the HPD as a flophouse for the wide variety of trash that floated through town—the dealers, the con men, and the "promoters" who preyed on student athletes—and it was the only place in town where you could buy a room for an hour.

Cox nodded to the five cops guarding the entrance to room 126, a ground-level room in the middle of a block of about fifteen rooms. Behind the cops on either side were small congregations of the curious, lured by the flashers, rubbernecking to catch a glimpse of the activity inside.

As he entered the room, Cox was met by bursts of light. He blinked and quickly closed the door behind him. Farrell was there, shooting film, and Quade was scribbling in his field notebook.

Farrell glanced at Cox soberly. He looked at her, tight-lipped; the grim, unspoken message between them was one of failure, of tragedy, and of responsibility. Then Cox looked at the body on the bed, and he saw that the girl had been mutilated.

He breathed deeply. His nostrils cringed at the foul tang of the corpse and the faintly salty odor of blood—an odor that always reminded him of summer days on a Virginia beach when the ocean was calm and the sand was so hot that it scorched the soles of his feet.

He stood and took in the scene.

On the floor in front of the nightstand, a red-and-yellow plastic cord lay curled, the ends frayed and dirty. On the floor near the foot of the bed, a single-edge razor, smeared with blood, lay flat on the carpet.

There were clothes thrown over a chair in the corner nearest the door, but there was no pocketbook, no towel, no Bible, no ashtrays, no suitcase, no toiletries. Nothing. Just the lifeless remains of a young woman, dimly illuminated by two dusty wall-mounted lamps.

The top sheet and covers were pulled off the front of the bed. The girl lay on her back, arms at her sides, her legs spread slightly—at about a forty-degree angle—with one leg oddly twisted, probably the beginning of rigor. There was a stain of blood and excreta between the legs and it had spread down to the area between her knees. Her genitals appeared to have been slashed. Her torso, pale and thin, was free of bruises and clean, except for some blood spatters. Her eyes were open, showing, even from where Cox was standing—a distance of seven feet—the dark blotches of petechial hemorrhaging. The girl's pink hair lay neatly around her face, in odd contrast to the violent disfigurement of her body. Ringing the upper portion of her neck was a thin red line, a friction burn, no doubt from the means of strangulation.

It took Cox a moment to realize that the girl's pubic hair was pink as well, a garish pink tuft crowning the hideous mutilation of her genitals.

Farrell and Quade watched Cox consider the scene; no one felt the need to say what they all knew—that this was either the work of Barris's killer or a good facsimile. The only difference was the mouth—the girl's mouth had not been slashed.

Looking at the girl, Cox was reminded of a domestic case he'd worked on, where, in an abused child's room, clippings of magazine advertisements were found with the faces and bodies graphically mutilated—the eyes and mouth messily crossed out, the groin and chest ripped or blackened.

Cox made a mental note to call the FBI's Behavioral Science Unit, where the particular pattern of this killer's MO might be matched against a profile indicating something about the killer's lifestyle—family life, job, income, psychology. Cox felt his body tense as the thought surfaced in his mind that these murders were the work of a serial killer.

He approached Quade. "Talk to me. What have you got?"

Quade glanced at his notebook. "The name's Sunni Skye. Body was discovered by a Larry Crowder. Cashier in the porn shop. Works for Gene Lydon. Seems like it's also Crowder's job to keep an eye on the girls. If they've been with a john too long, he checks it out." Quade flipped through his notebook as Cox rolled a cigarette. "Looks like this girl was with a john too long. Crowder says it was a slow night. She only had two johns that he knows of—one at about ten, the other at eleven-thirty. Doesn't know the names, but we'll be getting descriptions. He said she told him she wouldn't be around after midnight because she was meeting somebody, but she didn't say who. I told Crowder to take a seat in the squad car. Didn't want the little sleazeball to make a quick exit."

"Good." Cox lighted the cigarette and exhaled slowly. "Is there somebody to notify? Family?"

"Crowder says she lives with her mother and her sister on the west side. The sister also works for Lydon. Crowder says he called Lydon after he called nine one one."

"Tina?"

Farrell, bent over the girl's face, looked over at Cox and shook her head. "Looks like we got another genital slashing, though I'll leave the details of that to Ivan. Otherwise, the good news is that we've got the twine and the razor blade. It'll be a piece of cake to see if they're the same instruments used in the Barris homicide. Looks damn close to me. Of course, that raises the question of why the perp left the stuff here."

"Better to leave it than get caught with it," Quade suggested.

"Maybe," Tina said. "Or maybe the perp is telling us he's finished, that he accomplished what he set out to do."

Cox nodded. "Or he's ready to be caught."

Farrell went on. "We've got the clothes, but the whole damn thing's incredibly clean, even more so than Barris's murder. Not much of a struggle, either, though the strangulation line looks deeper.

We've also got some blood and skin under the girl's fingernails—look for a perp with some scratches."

"How long has she been lying here?"

"Three to six hours." Farrell stood, stripped off her latex gloves, and went over to Cox. "Damn room is too hot."

"Witnesses? Did the desk clerk see her come in with anybody?"

Quade shook his head. "No. The couple who run the motel are outside. They'll talk to you, but they claim they don't know anything. They also work for Lydon—he owns the joint."

"Have you tried to get hold of Lydon?"

"Not yet. Crowder says he's out of town, but he gave me Lydon's home and office numbers and addresses. I'll try them later. Anyway, he says the girls who work the place have their own keys to four of the motel rooms—they don't bother checking in. Sometimes they pick up guys in the bookstore, sometimes they meet guys in bars around town and bring them here to the motel, and sometimes they just meet guys at the motel. There's a phone in the back room at the bookstore where they can get messages. The girls are pretty independent for this kind of operation. They pay Lydon a hefty fee for protection and use of the facilities. Works on the honor system."

"Is this what happens when you cheat?"

The sudden crescendo of an unmuffled motor roaring to a halt outside the motel was followed by shouts and the sounds of a scuffle. Cox checked his watch—4:42—then opened the door and stepped outside, where a motorcycle now lay on the sidewalk, rear wheel spinning, and Adams and Perry were restraining a leather-jacketed young woman, apparently another of Lydon's whores, trying to get into the room. Behind the young woman, a wild-eyed, obese woman in her late forties, her face raw with hysteria, emerged from a rusted Impala.

"Lemme go!" the young woman cried. "That's my fuckin' sister in there!"

The two relaxed slightly as Cox approached; the young woman was fresh-faced and surly, and Cox noticed immediately the resemblance between her and the girl whose body lay inside the room—

the pale skin, the reddish tinge to the cheeks, the wide, soft features. The older woman, who he assumed was the girl's mother, appeared to be near collapse with grief and shock, and he knew that in his presence, with its implicit authority and promise of taking care of the mess, she would permit herself the freedom to fall apart completely, to get angry, to scream, and to blame him for her daughter's death.

Cox showed them his badge, then asked quietly, "Mrs. Skye?"

"Phipps," the woman whimpered and started to weep. Cox turned to the young woman. "What's your name?"

"Stormi Skye." She strained to extract her arm from the light hold Perry had maintained on her upper arm. The cop let her go. "That's my sister, for Christ's sake."

Cox touched the older woman lightly on her hands, which were folded in front of her. When he spoke, he instantly assumed the blunt, official tone of bad news, a slow, even inflection, without affectation.

"Mrs. Phipps, your daughter died tonight from wounds inflicted by an assailant. Did the person who called you tell you that she had been murdered?"

The woman's face seemed to swell for a second with suppressed emotion; then she shook her head. Stormi wrenched her head around wildly. "Aw fuck," she cried. "Fuck!" And then she kicked at the curb. "Lemme see her, okay? I just wanna see her."

Cox asked the mother, "Are you ready to see her?" Weesie nodded, her face knotted with grief.

Cox took Weesie by the arm and walked her past the cops at the door and into the motel room. The body lay exposed, as before, with Farrell hunched over the girl's torso with a magnifying glass. When Farrell saw Cox and the two women enter, she backed off and went to her evidence bag to take care of some paperwork.

Weesie pulled away from Cox and began to let out a low whimpering moan as she rushed toward her daughter's body. She held the girl, kissing her face frenziedly and stroking her hair as she called her name. Cox felt his stomach churn in sympathetic agony; he knew

132

how cold and stiff that body would feel three to six hours after the life had been snuffed out of it.

Stormi stood at the foot of the bed and gazed at her sister silently for a moment, her expression slack and defeated; then she said, "They'll pay for this, sister. Be damn fuckin' sure."

The mother turned to her, eyes blazing. "You little shit!" she screamed. "They'll pay for this? Ain't that what got her here?" She stood, went swiftly to Stormi, and grabbed her face between her hands. "You did this, you shit! It's your fuckin' fault!"

"Ma . . . I didn't . . . I didn't . . ." With that, Stormi began to cry, and the mother held her and cried with her. Then they sat on the edge of the bed, Stormi sobbing as the mother regained composure.

Cox, Farrell, and Quade stood at the small reading table in the room. The raw emotion between Stormi and her mother made Cox's skin grow cold. To distract himself, he watched Farrell label her evidence packets and Quade write up field notes, though Quade could not seem to take his eyes from the two sobbing women. After waiting a respectable three minutes, Cox walked quietly over to the bed and asked the inevitable question.

"Do you know who might have done this?"

The woman shook her head. Stormi said, "I dunno. Shit, I dunno." Sniffling, she wiped her eyes and nose on her jacket, leaving shiny streaks on the sleeves. "Some john."

"Which one?"

"I dunno. You gotta ask Lydon."

"What do you do for Lydon?"

"Anything."

"Do you know any of Sunni's johns?"

She shook her head. "Some." She bit her lip.

"I'm going to need names."

"I don't know no names."

Cox examined Stormi's face and saw that her temper was spent, leaving numb grief, and something else—the froglike blink, the fingers absently scratching her cheek, the vacant stare. The girl would soon need a fix, he knew.

"You're out on bail, aren't you, Stormi?"

"Yeah." Stormi looked pleadingly up at him, her face streaked with tears. "You ain't gonna take me in, are ya?"

"Afraid so."

"Then I want my lawyer."

Sunni. Nora trembled with cold and disbelief as she stood naked at the telephone—which she had, in a moment of masochism, placed across the room to force herself out of bed if it rang. Stormi. What would this new horror do to her already-volatile mind?

It had been Cox on the phone, not Stormi herself, informing Nora of the murder and that Stormi was being held for questioning. Nora was under no obligation to rush out to Harrison to serve as Stormi's counsel in the investigation of Sunni's murder—as Stormi's public defender, her representation was restricted to the charges for which she had been appointed as counsel—but she could not leave Stormi to face Cox's questioning alone. Cox was all right; he was a human being, unlike so many detectives, for whom the monthly bottom line of number of cases resolved, tied as it was to raises and promotions, was a Pavlovian motivator, sapping the humanity from them. Cox seemed different, though not different enough to trust.

Nora dressed hurriedly, throwing on a dark blue suit for maximum assertiveness, heated up yesterday's coffee in the microwave, and then headed out to Harrison.

Stormi was handcuffed, then transported to the station in the back of the squad car, Cox and Farrell sitting silently in front. She was herded through the station's side entrance into a foyer where a woman behind a shield of thick glass buzzed the inner door. When it unlocked, Cox reached forward and pulled the door open, all the time keeping one hand firmly on Stormi's shoulder. Then the three of them walked swiftly through a labyrinth of corridors to a metal door with a small window at eye level. Cox unlocked it by slipping a card through a slot at the side of the door; suddenly, the door was open and Stormi was inside the bright white room.

Inside was a desk and two swivel chairs, one on each side of the desk. There was a cassette tape recorder and a pitcher and cups on top of the desk. The walls were bare except for a poster-sized mirror opposite the desk, obviously a two-way mirror, and a ceiling-mounted video camera.

The room was warm, and Stormi felt flushed and vaguely sleepy for the first time since hearing of her sister's murder. She was alone now, Cox and Farrell having excused themselves with the promise to return shortly. What's the fuckin' deal? Stormi wondered. Do the bastards really think they can wear me down? Then she remembered why she was there, and the thought that Sunni was dead seized her. An image of Sunni's corpse surfaced in her mind—motionless, pale, unclothed—but she felt no grief, only a cold horror.

Stormi watched the tiny window in the door. She saw several faces flash by, eyes peering in at her briefly, then disappearing. She felt like an object under a microscope, resentful of the power these observers had over her, and then she realized in a bolt of intuition that she had been watched the whole time from behind the two-way mirror. She turned quickly and glared at the mirror. Where's the fuckin' lawyer? she wondered. Irritation crept slowly across her skin, and she felt herself grow painfully withered, shrunken, squeezed dry.

Cox stepped into the observation room to look in on Stormi Skye through the two-way mirror.

Stormi sat almost perfectly still, exactly where Cox had left her a half hour before, except now she was hunched over in the chair, hands over her mouth, eyes half-open. She looked to Cox like a caged rabbit, edgy with fear.

Deciding that the girl needed a comforting word, Cox went inside to her. Stormi looked up quickly when the door opened, and she followed Cox expectantly with her eyes.

"Miss Lumsey should be here any moment. I'm sorry."

Stormi rubbed her face, and Cox thought she was about to cry.

135

"Someone will be coming by shortly to get you something to eat," Cox said softly.

"I'm not fuckin' hungry," replied Stormi.

Nora hated waiting, particularly when she'd driven at illegal speeds to get somewhere, and to be kept waiting in the reception area of the Harrison Police Department for twenty minutes was an affront for which someone would pay. It would be Cox.

When she was finally buzzed in and directed to Cox's office, Nora strode swiftly past a wall of file cabinets and presented herself at Cox's open door and said words she had not planned on saying, not when she'd hoped to insist amicably on Stormi's release.

What she said was, "What the fuck are you doing?" And she said it testily, emphasizing each word, and then she waited for Cox's response with her fists on her hips.

Cox looked at her impassively. "I need to get answers. Now. I can't wait around for her to decide to cooperate."

"You can't hold her without probable cause."

"She has information that's critical to the investigation of her sister's murder. Unless she gives that up, she's chargeable as an accessory."

"Her sister's dead! Murdered, for Christ's sake! Have some compassion! There will be time for questioning later."

"She's here now. There will be time for grief later. All I want are the names of Sunni's johns."

Suppressing her fury, Nora demanded, "And then she's released?"

"Yeah, depending on what she has to say."

Nora considered this. "I need to see my client."

Nora found Stormi sitting hunched and trembling, her face resting on her knees, on the floor of the interrogation room, under the mirror but in the full, inescapable view of the ceiling-mounted camera.

"Jesus," Nora muttered. She crouched by Stormi, briefly stroked her hair, and stood, taking Stormi by the arm and pulling her unceremoniously up with her. "I need a room without a camera," she said to the mirror. "And without a fuckin' mirror."

Cox met her at the door, nodded in silent apology, and opened a door across the hall. It was a tiny closet-sized office, a penitent's confessional, with walls and ceiling of acoustic tile, three stiff-backed wooden chairs, and a writing desk.

Nora sat on the desk. Stormi compressed herself—legs, feet, and all—onto the seat of one of the chairs. Cox shut the door behind him as he left.

"What happened?" Nora began. "Do you know what happened to Sunni?"

Stormi slowly, just perceptibly, shook her head.

"Do you have any idea who might have done this to her?"

Again, Stormi shook her head.

"Do you know who she was with last night?"

Softly, Stormi said, "No."

"They're going to want the names of men who patronized you and Sunni. Do you know some names?"

Stormi shook her head.

"I understand that you feel you need to protect these men, but it's time to give it up, Stormi. It's time to give up that life. The whole thing. Stop using. Stop selling sex."

Stormi did not move.

"Don't you know that what happened to Sunni could happen to you? Your life is in danger."

Lifting her head, her face swollen, she said, "Don't ya think I fuckin' know that?"

"Then why won't you cooperate?"

Stormi covered her face with her hands and began to sob. "I jus' wanna go home."

"Where's your mother?"

"Home. I made her go. I didn't want her here." She was sniffling now, wiping her face on her knees.

"What happened last night when Sunni came to the trailer? What were you arguing about?"

"Nothin'," she said coldly now, abruptly.

"Don't tell me 'nothin'! For Christ's sake, Stormi, I can't help you unless you tell me what's going on."

Stormi put her chin between her knees and stared at Nora.

Nora ventured, "Does it have something to do with Gene Lydon?"

Stormi looked away.

"They need names, Stormi."

Nora looked at Stormi, who remained silent, and wanted to shake her hard, but she promised herself that she would not touch her again.

"Stormi, you want to go home. You want the police to catch whoever did this to Sunni, don't you? Why protect them?"

Stormi looked at her.

"Why protect them, Stormi? You know who did this, don't you?"

"No."

"They need names, Stormi. Then you get to go home."

Stormi sighed. "They want names? Okay. I'll give them names."

Nora opened the door and found herself face-to-face with Cox, who was standing directly outside, listening, Nora was sure.

"Come in," she said, and Cox stepped inside somberly and closed the door behind him.

"Stormi will provide you with names of Sunni's johns, to the extent she knows names, on the condition that she be released. Do we have your agreement?"

"Yeah, sure," Cox said. "And I have a few other questions. But I won't take up too much of your time."

Cox opened a slim drawer at the back of the desk and took out a pad of lined paper and an ashtray. He sat down, took a ballpoint pen from his shirt pocket, and clicked it into writing position.

Stormi glowered at him. Nora leaned gingerly against the wall, fearful of breaking through the acoustic tile, and prepared herself to object if Cox's questioning violated their agreement.

"Do you smoke?" Cox asked Stormi.

"Yeah."

"Do you mind if I do?"

Stormi hesitated. "Got one for me?"

"No. Not yet." Cox took the pouch of Top from his jacket pocket and began rolling a cigarette as he spoke. "Where were you born, Stormi?"

"Harrison."

"How old are you now?"

"Twenty."

Cox lit the cigarette. "Ever been married?"

"No."

"Jim Barris was a customer of yours, wasn't he?"

"Yeah."

"A regular customer?"

Stormi shrugged.

"When did he start using you?"

"A long time ago. Four, five years, maybe."

"How often?"

"I don't know."

"Once a month?"

"Yeah, sometimes. Once, I didn't see him for a year."

"How often in the past year? More than a dozen?"

"Prob'ly not."

"How many in a dozen?"

"Twelve."

"All right. How'd you connect with Barris?"

"He knew Lydon."

"When was the last time you had sex with Barris?"

"Three nights ago."

"The night Barris was murdered."

"Yeah." Stormi looked away.

Cox sat back. "What time were you with him that night?"

"It was probably around ten-thirty or eleven."

"And you were with him for how long?"

"A half hour, forty-five minutes, maybe."

"Where?"

"At his house."

"What did you do after that?"

"Went home."

"Tell me what you've been doing for the last twenty-four hours."

"I ate dinner. With her"—she tilted her head toward Nora, who kept her eyes on Cox—"at my ma's."

"Then what?"

"Then I went to Pleazures. Did a couple college guys. And went home."

"What are the names of these college guys?"

"I don't know."

"Did you see Sunni?"

"No."

"Do you know if she was there?"

"No."

"Would Crowder know?"

"Yeah, prob'ly."

"How much did Barris pay you?"

"He usually give me a hundred."

"Who do you think killed Sunni?"

Stormi shrugged.

"Come on, help me out here, Stormi. Who killed your sister?"

"I don't know. I don't fuckin' know." She looked at Cox. "Prob'ly the same guy who killed Barris."

Cox rolled a cigarette, passed it to Stormi, and lighted it for her. The tiny room was by then hazy with smoke from Cox's cigarette, and Nora felt the back of her throat growing sore, but Stormi was loosening, and Nora would not break the spell.

Stormi sucked the small cigarette gingerly, inhaled the smoke, and coughed slightly.

"I need names of Sunni's johns, Stormi, whatever you know."

"There's a lot of her johns I don't know about. I only know the ones she'd tell me about. And ones I had, too."

"Names, Stormi."

"Do ya want one-timers or regulars?"

"Everybody."

"How far back do ya want me ta go?"

"Let's start with the past year."

Stormi took a long drag on the cigarette, exhaled it thoughtfully, and began reciting a litany of names, mostly first names only, with brief descriptions: the frat boys, Jim, Jack, Joe, Albert; a business student, a physics-religion double major, a number of football, basketball, and soccer players; the truckers who were in and out of the metal powders factory down the street from Pleazures; Tom, the roofing salesman; Fred, the travel agent; Stanley, the lawyer; Ed, the bail bondsman; Pete, the orthodontist with a bondage fetish; BHU faculty members, in particular an English professor named Newton, whose name Cox recognized as a renowned specialist in Joyce and Pound, and a law professor, a friend of Barris's, a guy named Harvey.

Cox grimly noted that he would need to pay a return visit to Harvey Blau. "How about Coach Hedstrom?" he asked. "You've admitted to the players. How about the coach?"

"No," Stormi said sharply. "I've never done the coach. I don't know about Sunni."

Cox glanced at Nora, whose eyes were focused impatiently on his own.

"Sometimes we get cops, too, ya know," Stormi said abruptly, cocking her head defiantly. "Mostly from out of town, but we get some from here. Like that guy who was at the motel this morning."

Cox felt the blood drain from his face. "Who?"

"That other cop, the fat one. I think his name is Teddy."

"Has he paid you for sex?"

"Yeah. Twice. And he mighta had Sunni."

His mind hard with anger and a sharp sense of institutional humiliation, Cox released Stormi, instructing her to stay close at hand; he thanked her sincerely, perhaps too much so, and he thanked Nora for her time and cooperation.

"With your help, we'll catch the bastard who did this," he said. "Call me immediately if you think of anything else."

Cox handed cards to Stormi and Nora, knowing it was a perfunctory, almost ludicrous gesture under the circumstances. Of course, they would be seeing one another soon. They were entwined in this horror, the three of them, and it was far from finished.

It was 8:20 A.M.

"Where the fuck is Quade?"

Farrell shook her head as Cox sipped stale coffee and stared at the many circular stains on the surface of his desk.

"I left him at the scene with Ivan," said Farrell. "Those guys'll probably be gabbing all morning as they pick over the corpse."

"Well, then, talk to me, Tina," said Cox, exasperated. "What have you got?"

"Same MO as with Barris. Strangulation with nylon clothesline-type cord, then the mutilation. Clothesline found at scene matches the one used in Barris's murder. Here we have just a couple perfunctory slashes across the pubic bone and the labia. Not nearly as bad as Barris got. Looks like death occurred at about one or two A.M. We'll have to see what Ivan says about that. As regards evidence, aside from the usual body work-up, the razor blade, and the clothesline, we've got the fingernail scrapings I told you about"—Cox made a mental note to check for scratches—"and hair from in and around the bed, though God knows how many people have been shedding hair in that room."

"Among other things."

"Right. I've done a thorough vacuuming, dusted the place for fingerprints. We've got the girl's clothes, but they're not telling us much—except that she shopped at Target, had white-trash taste, and didn't bathe often."

"Nothing in the wastebaskets?"

She shook her head. "Not even a Trojan wrapper."

Just then, Quade appeared, carrying a take-out container of coffee, on the other side of the glass door to Cox's office. Cox glanced at Farrell, then waved Quade in.

"Where the fuck have you been?"

"No need to snap at me, for Christ's sake. A man's entitled to have breakfast."

Cox sipped his coffee and stared at the table, annoyed. Quade sipped his coffee in turn. Farrell waited.

"What does Ivan say?"

"He says the girl was strangled with cord and slashed with the single-edge razor blade. The strangulation took place from behind. We're not talkin' thumbs on the throat here. The perp got the twine around the girl's neck from behind, pulled it tight fast enough so the girl couldn't grab it, and then he choked her. Never saw the victim chokin' to death. Then, when the girl's good and dead, he has his fun with the blade. Some sick bastard, huh? Whoever did it wasn't no surgeon, either." Cox lifted his chin toward Quade. "The cuts are very superficial incisions. Strictly for show."

"Was she raped?"

"Ivan doesn't think so. There was semen swirlin' around in there, but what a surprise that is."

Cox nodded. "What about the witnesses?"

Quade looked at his notes and sighed deeply. "Okay. I spoke with the Millers, the couple who run the motel. They've known Sunni for the three years she's been turning tricks for Lydon. They just see her come and go, don't have anything to do with her unless she comes by to use the vending machine or to get some ice. Last night, Mr. Miller was asleep by midnight, but the missus was up watching TV in the office until one. She heard a lot of car traffic out on Eustace Avenue, but she didn't see anybody. Says she minds her own business."

"Always a good policy," commented Farrell.

"Spoke to a Randy Sturgeon, who was working late in his auto-body shop about half a block up Eustace. Says a well-dressed man parked a Mercedes in front of his place at about midnight and walked

143

south. Has no idea where he went or what happened to him. He didn't see the guy come back to the car, but it was gone the next time he looked in that direction, which he says was probably around three A.M."

"Okay, that's something."

"Spoke to Crowder. A real prick, made zero effort to cooperate. Wouldn't show me the business records. He's been working for Lydon for three years. Calls himself the bookstore manager. Gave me some descriptions of regular customers. Crowder denies knowing Barris. I tried calling Lydon from his phone, got no answer at any of his numbers, no response at home, cell phone, nothing."

A silence. Cox looked at Farrell, then stared at the top of his desk and drummed a pencil on the edge. He threw the pencil down, took out his tobacco, and rolled a cigarette.

"Tina, I need a moment alone with Teddy."

14

Quade stiffened as Farrell left the office.

"I hear you've used some of Lydon's girls, Teddy," Cox said quietly.

Quade shrugged, as though unsurprised. "Yeah . . . a couple of times. Nothing I'm proud of, but . . . it happened."

"Do you know Lydon?"

"Never met the man. I didn't talk to any guys there, just the broad."

"Same one both times?"

"Yeah."

"Did you see Crowder there?"

"I might have. I happen to have been pretty loaded. On both occasions."

"Does Millie know about this?"

"Hell no."

"Does Hank?"

"No."

"Is there anything you think I ought to know?"

"About me, no."

"But?"

"If you're going after Lydon, you ought to know that he's connected up the ass. Knows a lot of people. Pulls strings in politics. He's also one of the richest men in this town."

Cox did not expect to find Pleazures open at 9:30 A.M.—he could not imagine someone needing to run out for pornography at that hour of the morning. But when he tugged at the door, expecting it to be locked, it swung open fast and almost hit him in the face.

Cox stepped into the large powder blue room and took two steps down into the aisles of magazine racks, where Larry Crowder was bent over a bundle of magazines, busily cutting the plastic straps that bound it together.

Cox approached Crowder and tried not to be distracted by the photographs of sex acts all around him. Crowder seemed unaware of Cox's presence until Cox's legs were next to the stack of magazines he was sorting through.

Crowder looked up. Cox flashed his badge.

"Remember me?"

Crowder nodded and stood up.

"Don't you ever get an hour off?"

"Yeah, sometimes." Crowder shrugged. "The hours suck, but the benefits are great." He grinned and held up a magazine displaying an oral sex act.

Cox looked at Crowder and did not smile. "Where do I find Gene Lydon?"

"I don't know. I think he's out of town." Crowder bent back down and continued to stack the magazines.

"Tell me where Lydon is—now, Crowder."

"I can't help you," Crowder mumbled. "I got work to do."

Cox grabbed the back of Crowder's collar, pulled him upward quickly, then thrust him down against the floor, put his knee in Crowder's back, and handcuffed his wrists behind his back.

"Listen up, asshole," Cox murmured through gritted teeth. "You tell me now exactly where I can find Gene Lydon, or else I'm arresting you, taking you downtown, and booking you for distribution of obscene matter."

"You can't do that, motherfucker," Crowder spat out. "We got protection."

"Try me," said Cox.

Crowder was silent.

"Don't make me hurt you," said Cox.

Crowder remained silent.

Cox closed his eyes, shook his head slowly, then picked Crowder up by his wrists until his face was a foot from the floor. Cox let him drop. Crowder's face made a smacking, crunching sound, like a bone-shattering belly flop into a shallow pool, as his cheek hit the linoleum.

Then Crowder told him where to find Lydon.

It was an office under the name Artistic Enterprises in one of the stately limestone office buildings surrounding Harrison's town square. Lydon, it seemed, maintained two offices, the other being a room with an answering machine in back of an employment agency across the street from Pleazures. That was the office address and phone number his employees were instructed to provide to anyone who asked, particularly the police.

Cox walked through the marble foyer, checked the directory to be sure Artistic Enterprises would be found on the third floor, then punched the elevator button and waited. The building was cold and illuminated with a dull yellow light, a simulation of gaslight that Cox guessed was intended to have the effect of enhancing the antique elegance of the place. He found it depressing.

At the third floor, the elevators opened onto a long hallway, similarly lighted, with doors on each side. Cox found Suite 370 and entered a small reception area redolent of decades of burning tobacco. A secretary sat behind a long desk next to an open inner door, from which the music of Vivaldi's *The Four Seasons* emanated loudly. Cox showed his badge to the secretary, a pinched woman in her seventies who looked like she had been sitting there since 1945. The woman waved a lipstick-smeared cigarette as she buzzed Lydon and identified his visitor. Then she used the cigarette to point toward the door, and Cox went in.

The man stood behind a wide glass table, playing the violin as Vivaldi blared from two tall speakers behind him. He smiled as Cox entered, held up one finger as if to ask Cox to wait, then deftly continued playing the long sequence of eighth notes that comprises the main theme.

Cox had met Lydon twice on official business and had seen him on other occasions socially. Lydon was a patron of the arts in Harrison, and he never missed an opportunity to show off his largesse at concerts and gallery openings—even when the artist happened to be a police detective. Lydon affected a nouveau bohemian image that didn't quite succeed on his rotund, six-foot-tall figure. Balding, with a fringe of hair that curled out from his head and billowed to his shoulders, he wore small oval wire-rimmed granny glasses and had an overgrown walrus mustache that nearly covered his mouth. He always dressed in black—black turtleneck, black pleated pants, and black boots.

Lydon nodded to the detective as he put the violin down on his desk.

"Forgive me," he said, his voice smooth and crisp, a disc jockey's voice. "I'm performing the Vivaldi tonight with the Harrison Symphony. Of course, what you just heard was the Chicago Symphony. We won't sound quite that good. Except maybe in our dreams." Lydon clicked a knob in the stereo cabinet behind him, then turned and extended his hand and smiled, exposing a gleaming set of teeth. Cox was momentarily disarmed by Lydon's warmth, and he shook Lydon's hand politely.

"Good morning, Detective," Lydon said. "I've been expecting to speak with you today."

Cox nodded. "I need to—"

"It's a terrible thing about Sunni," Lydon said, interrupting Cox and looking down at the table. "She was one of the good ones." He looked at Cox. "Do you have any idea who's responsible?"

Cox looked at Lydon, annoyed at having been interrupted, then said firmly, "I'd like you to answer some questions about the murders of Sunni Skye and James Barris."

Lydon's face assumed a quizzical expression. "Do you think there's a connection?"

"Yes, I do. But let's begin with you telling me your movements of last evening."

"I was here until about seven. Then I went home. Made myself dinner. At about ten, I went to my club, the Aztec, where I drank and danced and had a terrific time until about one. Which was when I went home. Plenty of people at the Aztec will corroborate my being there."

"When did you hear about the girl's murder?"

"One of my employees called me this morning."

"Which employee?"

"His name is Larry Crowder. He works in the adult bookstore."

"When I spoke to Mr. Crowder this morning, he was very reluctant to give me the address of this office."

Lydon shrugged.

"That kind of behavior might be considered interfering with the investigation of a homicide. Considering the other charges that could be brought against Crowder and yourself, I'd say we have a right to expect more than complete cooperation with this investigation."

"Larry can be a little overzealous in protecting my interests. That's what he's paid for, and I apologize."

"I don't want your apologies, Lydon. Two murders have been committed in the past three days, and you happen to be implicated in both of them."

Lydon shrugged again. "I don't know what to tell you. I wish I could help, honestly. But I had nothing to do with these murders."

"Were you aware that James Barris was a client of Sunni Skye's?"

"Sure. But she had other clients. And he had other girls."

"How long had he been a client of your girls, Lydon?"

Lydon leaned back in his chair and looked at Cox. Suddenly, he sprang forward, picked up his violin, and plucked a string. "I'm going to make this easy for you, Cox. I'm going to save you a lot of trouble and me a lot of time. I'm gonna tell you something."

Cox nodded. "I'm listening."

"I've known James Barris for about eight years, but my relations with Barris took a serious turn for the worse shortly before his death. So frankly, I wasn't terribly upset to hear about it. I can tell you that because I'm perfectly innocent of any wrongdoing, as you know. And because you, Mr. Cox, are yourself involved—in a collateral way—but involved nonetheless, and so I suppose you really have a right to know."

Cox's face grew hot.

"You may or may not be aware that my escort service has for many years been patronized by Coach Hedstrom to provide entertainment for alums visiting from out of town, for players as a special reward, for other coaches, for his friends, and for himself, now and again. And of course we operate with the implicit approval of the city administration, the mayor's office, the police department, et cetera. Okay? It goes without saying. We provide a necessary service, and we generate a little extra income for public employees who really aren't paid anything close to what they're worth.

"Now, Mr. Cox, as you know, there was an unpleasant situation a year or so ago involving a basketball player who got a little too aggressive with a coed—they had sex and she called it rape. Remember? And Coach Hedstrom needed the player, right? And he didn't want to see a promising young man's career—his life—go down the toilet because of one chick's second thoughts the morning after. Know what I mean? So the coach asked the mayor to do him a favor. And the mayor asked Chief Bieberschmidt to do her a favor. And Chief Bieberschmidt asked you to do him a favor. And you did the favor. Thank you."

Lydon bowed slightly and made a gesture of deference to Cox, who sat stolidly immobile.

"Of course, all of this is not well known. Because people's loyalty to a basketball team—and its coach—only goes so far, even here. A few of us know the story. But fewer know the whole story." He paused, took a pack of Marlboros from his shirt pocket, and offered one to Cox.

Cox looked at him and did not respond. Lydon tapped a cigarette out of the pack and lighted it.

"Coach Hedstrom has a problem. He talks too much. And he drinks too much. That's a bad combination. One of the people he liked to talk to and drink with was Jim Barris. And so he told the whole story to Jim, for Jim's amusement, of course, but also because Hedstrom, for all his talent and success, can't get over what a big shot he is. So he likes to talk about it. And Jim Barris, who was a nobody, thought that because he knew the coach, because he was the coach's friend, he was a somebody, too. And he thought, Well, this is an interesting bit of information. How can I use this information to benefit myself? Just the kind of selfishness you'd expect from a guy like that.

"Another thing about Barris. He liked to think that he could live in two worlds, you know? Be the law professor, the intellectual, but also play on the street, hit the clubs, run with the bad boys and the bad girls. No can do. Not really. You can't live in the straight world and play in the crooked world. But you can live in the crooked world and play in the straight world. That's what I do. And I have a wonderful time, too.

"So Barris went to Hedstrom with a scheme. He saw what a good business I have here with the bookstore and the escort service and my other ventures. Barris wanted a piece of the business. He wanted to recapitalize, build a new bookstore, a new motel, find a location outside of town, make everything modern and clean, decorate like some Nevada chicken ranch, the whole bit. He had all these stupid ideas.

"Now you have to understand that my business doesn't have a lot of class, but that's the way it has to be in a town like this. We have our university here, but my business is eighty-five percent redneck. That includes the local businessmen, the local lawyers, judges . . . even cops, right?"

He raised an eyebrow to Cox and waited for a response. He got none.

"So what do I have here? I have a few rooms in a motel, I have a classified ad every week in the *Harrison Voice*, and I have a room in the back of the bookstore with a phone for the girls to hang out in. And that's all I need. But Barris thought otherwise.

"So Barris went to Hedstrom because he wanted them both, being buddies, to be partners in this new business. Hedstrom loved it, and so they came to me. Now this is not something I wanted to do. Why should I? I was doing just peachy on my own. But they wanted this thing badly enough, and they thought enough of themselves to suppose that they could exert pressure on me to go along.

"I persuaded them otherwise. Hedstrom dropped out of the deal; he had too much at stake elsewhere to worry about a business of questionable legality. But Barris came back later that night. He came to me with the kind of wild glint in his eye of someone who's hooked on playing with fire, who thinks he might enjoy living dangerously. He came to me and told me that if I didn't agree to go into business with him, he'd go to the police—namely, our friend Chief Bieberschmidt—and force him to shut me down by threatening to go to the press with the whole story about how Hedstrom got his boy off the hook."

"When did you have this conversation with Barris?"

"About ten days ago."

"Did you have him killed, Lydon?"

"I had absolutely no reason to do that. His threats were meaningless—to me. Of course, the truly amazing thing is, the scheme might have worked. There's been a lot of pressure on the chief lately to have me shut down. It used to be the damn evangelicals who harassed me; now it's the fuckin' feminists on an antiporno crusade.

"But if the chief had shut me down, I could have taken the story to the papers myself. Not that I have Barris's credibility. But I have the same leverage with the chief and Brodey and the bunch of them that Barris had. And of course Barris would have screwed Hedstrom in the process. Why would he do that? Maybe he was pissed off at Hedstrom; maybe he wanted to bring Hedstrom down, get him in trouble with the NCAA.

"I don't know. It's not my problem anymore. Barris was an asshole. One of those guys who think they have it all figured out. I'm

152

not sorry he's dead. And I'm not losing any sleep thinking about who killed him."

"Then who killed him, Lydon?"

"As God is my witness, I sure as hell don't know."

"What about Sunni Skye?"

He shook his head. "Some sicko, I'm sure."

"Who were her regular clients?"

"I thought Crowder gave you that information."

"Don't you know?"

"No. I don't get that involved. I just provide the facility. The girls are independent contractors."

"Do you patronize the girls, Lydon?"

"Are you crazy? Think I want to catch something?"

Cox stood slowly. "I'll be in touch. Don't leave Harrison without informing me. You will be needed for further questioning."

Lydon stood and put his hand out. Cox looked at the hand, then at Lydon, and turned to leave.

"Kind of interesting, isn't it?" Lydon said as Cox reached the door.

Cox turned. "What?"

"The position you find yourself in." Lydon picked up the violin and slid the neck between his thumb and forefinger. "I mean, it seems like it's all got to come out sooner or later, doesn't it? And who do you think is going to get his dick caught in the zipper? Who's going to take the fall for the department, the chief, the mayor, the coach— for everybody? I mean, just imagine I did kill Barris. Would you arrest me and have the whole mess come out? How my businesses survive thanks to the consent of our town fathers and mothers? And the whole rape cover-up? I mean, what can one poor cop do?"

"Who killed the girl, Lydon?"

"I don't know. Really. It's a dangerous job these girls do."

As Cox left the room, he heard the bright harmonies of the Vivaldi behind him; he moved swiftly, seething, and resolved to get some answers from Hedstrom.

153

15

Stormi leaned her cheek against the passenger-side window of Nora's pickup and closed her eyes as Nora drove her to recover the motorcycle Stormi had left at the Sleep Tite Motel early that morning. Stormi rubbed her face; she wanted desperately to be home, sleeping, and then to get high and go out, forget about Sunni, forget about everything.

"We need to talk." Stopped at a red light in downtown Harrison, Nora turned to Stormi and said again, "We need to talk."

Stormi shrugged and shook her head.

"I was surprised to hear that Harvey Blau had been your client," Nora ventured. "Did he always come with Barris, or sometimes alone?"

Stormi clawed at her face and stared forward.

"Did Barris or Blau use Sunni, too?"

Stormi rasped, "We'll never fuckin' know now, will we?"

"I need to know the truth, Stormi," Nora said. "About you and Sunni and what Sunni was upset about yesterday."

"I told you, it was nothin'."

When the light turned green, Nora made a left turn into a McDonald's parking lot and pulled the truck into the drive-through lane. "Let's get something to eat," she said. "What can I get you?"

"Nothin'."

Nora ordered two Egg McMuffin Value Meals, and when the food and coffees had been passed to her, she drove the truck to a parking spot and placed one of the sandwiches in Stormi's lap.

"No thanks," Stormi said.

"Suit yourself." Nora took a sip of coffee and unwrapped her sandwich. "I distinctly remember Sunni saying something about 'shit hittin' the fan.' What was she talking about?"

"I don't remember."

"Bullshit."

"I don't!"

"Sunni also referred to someone as a 'cunt.' Who was she referring to?"

"You." Stormi unwrapped the Egg McMuffin and began to eat it, at first tentatively, then ravenously. "Happy now?"

"Did Barris do something to Sunni? To hurt her?"

Stormi chewed the sandwich rapidly, swallowing with some difficulty. "Lemme the fuck alone," she murmured through the food in her mouth.

"Tell me."

"You don't know shit about it," Stormi said after a time. "You don't know what it's like, lettin' guys fuck you for money. A lot of 'em stink. They got bad breath; they're sweaty. It ain't like bein' with somebody you want to be with. And sometimes they hit you or they want to choke you while they're fuckin' you. You know what I'm sayin'? There's all kinds of weird fuckers out there."

"You think that's what happened to Sunni? You think she had problems with one of these guys?"

"Maybe."

"And you know which one it was."

Stormi stared at her and chewed the sandwich, chewed it and bit at it and stared, like a raccoon caught in headlights.

"You know who it was."

"Yeah."

"Who?"

"I'm not gonna tell you. Not in a million fuckin' years."

155

"Why?"

"I ain't gonna say another fuckin' thing. I shouldn't a told you I knew. But I'm sick of your fuckin' questions. I don't have to tell you shit. You ain't the law."

"No. But I'm all that stands between you and prison. Keep that in mind. I'm here to help you. I represent you in court. I'm your lawyer."

"What if I don't want you to be my fuckin' lawyer?"

"Then you can tell the court you want somebody else. And you ought to know that I'm only your lawyer on the possession charge. I'm here taking my own time today to do you a favor and get you released."

"Don't do me any fuckin' favors! I'll get somebody else."

"Stormi—"

"You think I had something to do with this! You think I killed my own fuckin' sister!"

"I don't."

"You think I killed Barris!"

"I don't!"

Stormi dumped the contents of her lap—sandwich, home fries, and wrappings—onto the floor of Nora's truck and opened the passenger-side door.

"I'm gettin' the fuck out," she said. "I can walk."

Stormi slammed the door and stepped down to the asphalt. "You're fired. Get the fuck out of my life."

Nora knew Stormi's anger had little to do with her and everything to do with her sister's death, but still she wondered whether or not to take the firing seriously; it was Stormi's prerogative, she knew, to fire her, but there were hoops that Stormi needed to go through before the court would appoint a new public defender for her, a fact of which Nora was sure Stormi was unaware.

Nora resolved that she could not consider herself fired until Stormi took action with the court to replace her; Stormi would need her, she knew, while the investigations of her sister's and Barris's murders continued. Unlike Lydon, Nora would not let Stormi hang out to dry.

What is it about academics? Nora thought as she ascended the law school steps, passing a trio of professor types. Why do they dress so badly?

Nora smiled as she made eye contact with the two men, both pear-shaped and ungainly, and a woman, hunchbacked from incipient osteoporosis. One of the men was wild-haired and bushy-bearded, the other had tied the few strands of hair left on his skull into a Ben Franklin ponytail, and both of them wore wrinkled corduroys. The woman, emaciatedly thin, was dressed in a sheath of what looked like burlap. Why is it that so many academics eschew grooming? Is it a sign of one's devotion to a life of the mind?

That wasn't Barris. No, not Jim, who had, Nora was sure, been fastidious even as a child, been savvy, a teenage seducer. He was like those born car salesmen, a winning smile from the get-go.

Nora lamented that she had been so easily won.

Harvey Blau's secretary found him in the faculty lounge, a dark-wooded room in ersatz imitation of an exclusive men's club of the last century, where the professor sat in front of *The New York Times,* which was spread open on the surface of a coffee table. The secretary called to him, and he glanced up, scowling, clearly irritated at the interruption. Nora strode gingerly onto the room's plush scarlet carpet.

"Good morning," she said as Blau stood to shake her hand. "I'm Nora Lumsey. I'm an attorney representing Stormi Skye. Does that name ring a bell for you?"

Blau smiled cautiously and gestured toward a wide leather chair opposite his.

"Take a seat," he said, sitting. "You say you're the attorney for whom?"

"Stormi Skye."

"In what capacity?"

"I'm defending her on a drug charge, but the police have been questioning her in connection with Jim Barris's murder."

"Oh." He looked down, glanced up at Nora blankly, and then his torso bolted upright and he said with recognition, "Oh!"

Nora smiled.

"You knew Jim," Blau said.

"Yes."

"You and he . . ."

"Dated, yes," she said, her throat constricting. "He mentioned me?"

"Yes."

"You were good friends, then?"

"Yes, for twenty-five years." He looked uncomfortable. "What can I do for you, Nora?"

"Stormi tells me you . . . were a patron."

Blau looked around the room. "I'd prefer not to answer questions about that. Please."

"I'm sorry, but I need to know. I assume it was Barris who introduced you to Stormi, and not you who introduced Barris to her."

He avoided Nora's eyes. "You assume correctly."

"Stormi is connected to Barris's death, somehow, and I need to understand how Barris came upon Stormi, what connected Barris to Stormi. I know he was more than her attorney."

Blau stared at the carpet and held one finger up, as if running a computer search in his brain.

"I don't know for sure," he said finally, "but I think it was Don Hedstrom who introduced Jim to Stormi."

"The coach."

"Yes. He and Jim were great friends."

"Oh?" she said, interested to hear Blau's version.

"Yes, and they were closest a few years ago, around the time of the coach's most recent marriage. I was lucky enough to be among the thousand or so people invited to the coach's wedding, and Jim was escorted to this affair by Stormi Skye."

"I see."

"That was Jim's famous *Pygmalion* experiment, a wager between Jim and the coach. We all knew at that time that Jim had this local girl he was seeing, common as dirt, really, unadulterated white trash, and probably underage, but no one really knew. So Jim dressed her up and took her to this wedding, where there would be every stuffed shirt in the university. I mean, she may have been sixteen years old, for all I know, but he had her there like he was Henry Higgins and she was Eliza Doolittle. He bought her a gorgeous dress, paid to have her hair done up. It was really something. And she was very well trained. She shook hands with everyone, smiled demurely, and did not open her mouth the whole day and night. I mean, she couldn't. Jesus . . . when people tell you that mass communication is destroying the richness of our regional dialects . . ." He raised his eyebrows and grinned. "It sho ain't so."

"Why would he and the coach do that?"

"Oh, it probably had something to do with one of Jim's cocka-mamie theories." Blau laughed. "He had this fixed idea about the inherentness of class distinctions. Jim's politics veered dangerously close to fascism at times. I think he really believed that the eco-nomically privileged class really does breed more intelligent, better-looking, and physically healthier beings. In other words, that the fittest really do survive best. The ones who defy the rule—that is, the ambitious sons of white-trash hillbillies who get themselves an education—are mutations—freaks—who are able to switch classes. Just crazy, I think." He smiled and then looked up suddenly at Nora. "Of course, the coach thinks it's the kids who have the toughest upbringing who become the strongest adults. Like so many of his players. I never found out who won that bet, but it never seemed to affect Jim's friendship with the coach."

As he drove through campus toward Aberdeen Hall, Cox's mind was a vortex of anger, mortification, and fear. He should have known, of course, that the truth of the Chappelle cover-up would come back

159

to haunt him. In Harrison, any gossip remotely involving basketball could not stay under wraps for long.

His mind replayed the events surrounding the blunder. He didn't need to remind himself why he'd done it; like so many things at the HPD, it was done because somebody needed a favor. But there was something different about that time. Maybe it was the pleading desperation in Bieberschmidt's voice, or maybe it was the appeal, made straight to his Hoosier heart, of the notion of saving the team and a young man's future. But at what price? A young woman's dignity? The lives of other, unknown victims? Justice? Cox allowed himself a moment to lick the wound by reminding himself that it was the only moral blemish on an otherwise-spotless career. But it was a big one. And it was spreading.

Cox breathed slowly and acknowledged to himself that he would never have done it if Julia had been alive, uncompromising Julia, who had been his moral compass. Now he was reaping the just desserts of his stupidity, compromised by the awful truth that at least two of the prime suspects in the murders of Barris and the girl had information that could end his career. His credibility was shot and his judgment was clouded by the fear—conscious and unconscious—that probing too far into Hedstrom's and Lydon's worlds would trigger a revelation of the facts of the rape cover-up.

"Shit!" he cried, and he floored the accelerator and pounded the steering wheel with his fists.

Cox found Hedstrom at Aberdeen Hall, where the team had taken the court in preparation for that evening's game against Ohio State. Despite everything, Cox couldn't help feeling his spirits lift as he walked up the ramp rising between the bleachers and stepped out onto the court. That evening's game was only the third game of the regular season, and expectations were not high after the Sagamores' disastrous performances against Butler and Notre Dame, but there was a palpable optimism in the air, a brightness in the ringing echo of the footfalls and the crisp splash of the basketball hitting hardwood.

The team was playing a red shirt/blue shirt practice match. Hedstrom was there, pacing the sidelines in front of half a dozen assistants, cursing and fretting with the same manic energy he displayed when the game was real. Except that on this day, he was happy—clapping, gesticulating, jumping, imitating the players' moves and showing them the right ones. Happy, that is, until he spotted Cox.

Hedstrom noticed Cox walking up the sidelines toward him, and he took the time to put on a brief demonstration of contempt. He looked hard at Cox, squinted as if he couldn't comprehend what he was seeing, and shook his head in disbelief that Cox would have the nerve to bother him again.

This time, Cox did not wait for a break in the action to approach Hedstrom. He walked directly in front of Hedstrom, stepped up to within six inches of Hedstrom's face, and held his badge at eye level so everyone around the coach would know what he was about. One by one, the players stopped moving. The ball, passed to a player who had abandoned his position, went bounding away noisily until another player scooped it up. Hedstrom was so stunned, he stood immobile. And then the room was silent.

"I have a few questions for you," Cox said firmly.

Hedstrom turned swiftly and walked toward the exit to the corridor, evidently expecting Cox to follow. Cox did so. Halfway there, Hedstrom turned to the players and shouted, "What the fuck are you doing? Did any of you ever see a fuckin' cop before? The man wants to ask me some questions! Did I say to stop playing? Keep playing, motherfuckers!"

"Let's make this quick, Cox," Hedstrom said. "I've got a damn important game tonight."

"A young woman was murdered this morning," Cox said. "Her name was Sunni Skye. She was a prostitute who worked for Gene Lydon. Does any of this ring a bell with you, Hedstrom?"

Hedstrom paled, then shrugged. "I know Gene Lydon."

"I had a long conversation with Gene Lydon this morning. He had a number of interesting things to say about you and Jim Barris."

161

Hedstrom leaned against the cinder-block wall. "So?"

"So now you tell me everything you didn't tell me yesterday. About business arrangements and anything else between you and Barris."

"Look, Cox, do yourself a favor and lighten up, okay? You're making way too much of this. If Lydon told you the truth, then he must have told you that I had next to nothing to do with any kind of business that Barris had with Lydon. Okay? Barris was too fucking ambitious, as you know. He had this crazy idea about him and me buying into Lydon's business. I went along with it so far as bringing up the idea with Lydon, but that was all. Anything Barris did after that was on his own. You may think I'm pretty stupid, but I'm not that stupid."

"Where were you last night between ten P.M. and two A.M.?"

"I was in my office at the Hole until midnight, alone. And then I went home."

"Did you ever pay Sunni Skye for sex?"

Hedstrom laughed. "Hell no. Let's hope it never comes to that!"

"Did you ever hire any of Lydon's girls for other men? Or for parties?"

Hedstrom shrugged. "What can I say? Sometime you've got to grease the wheels. Call it social lubrication. Strictly business."

Cox faced off against Hedstrom, and said, "People do time for that kind of social lubrication."

Hedstrom smiled wanly, then said softly, "Look, Cox. This conversation is unnecessary. And it could be dangerous to our careers. I didn't have anything to do with the murders. You know that. But you and I are involved . . . in a situation that just wouldn't look good to people who don't understand the way we do that a talented young man shouldn't have to pay his whole life for one misjudgment that in the end really didn't hurt anybody. Okay? So we went out on a limb. We took a risk."

Hedstrom moved a step closer to Cox.

"You have a lot of power right now, Cox. Don't blow it. You

and I, we share a secret. If it comes out, no matter how it comes out, we both get hurt. I look bad, but I can probably survive it. All I did was ask for a favor. I didn't do anything against the law."

Hedstrom's voice rose with anger.

"It's when the people who are charged with the administration of justice start doing favors for people like me that the public gets up in arms. Okay? So don't fuck with me, Cox. Don't threaten to prosecute me for silly shit like hiring a few girls. And don't drag me into these murders."

Cox stepped back. Hedstrom took another step toward him.

"You know how this is going to end, Cox? It's going to end with you resigning. With you off the force." Hedstrom jabbed Cox in the chest. "You're the only one who's going to get hurt."

Cox drove back to the station feeling compacted, small, and hard, as if the part of him that was capable of anger, of taking offense, had rolled up into a protective ball like a frightened insect. Abject submission. He smoked with the windows closed, turning the car into a kind of nicotine tent, letting the drug do its work of deadening the pain. And he distracted himself by reasoning through the case. Just let me do my job, he thought. That's all I ask.

Cox wondered if Hedstrom knew that Barris had gone back to Lydon and used the Chappelle situation to threaten Lydon. Barris certainly wouldn't have told Hedstrom; you wouldn't inform someone if you were about to air his dirty laundry unless you wanted something from him. Or unless you got a perverse pleasure out of watching him squirm. It was certain, Cox thought, that Hedstrom was vastly underestimating the impact upon his life of the revelation of the rape cover-up. Hedstrom was right that he hadn't committed a crime by calling in a few favors; but the NCAA might well take action against him, and there was a damn good chance that he'd lose his job. If Hedstrom knew that Barris was about to reveal his secret— their secret—he had more than motive enough to murder Barris. But if Barris didn't tell Hedstrom of his plans, who did? Would Lydon have called Hedstrom after Barris's visit? And how was Sunni's murder connected? Did she know? Had Barris told her, bragging across a pillow one night?

"It's over, Hank."

Bieberschmidt looked up from the plastic bag of Oreo cookies that his wife had packed with lunch that day, then brushed the scattering of crumbs from his desk. "Hmph? What? What's over?"

"The Chappelle cover-up."

Bieberschmidt stopped chewing, and for a moment he looked like he didn't know whether to swallow or spit it all out.

He swallowed. "What are you saying?"

"Hedstrom told Barris everything. So Barris told Lydon, hoping to use the knowledge to get Lydon to give him a piece of his business." Cox chuckled softly and began rolling a cigarette. "It's funny as hell, really. If Lydon didn't cooperate, Barris was going to put the squeeze on you."

Cox smoothed the cigarette and lighted it. Bieberschmidt watched impassively as Cox inhaled. "His plan was to come to you and threaten to expose the cover-up unless you shut Lydon down. Isn't that a riot? Is that a double squeeze play or what?"

Bieberschmidt looked away, rubbed the back of his neck, and muttered, "Oh, Christ . . ."

"So Barris gets whacked. But by who? By Hedstrom or by Lydon, take your pick."

"What about the girl?"

Cox shrugged. "I haven't figured that out yet." He took a long drag on the cigarette. "But it's all got to come out now, Hank. The whole fuckin' story. Everything."

Bieberschmidt sat back in his chair and absently fingered an Oreo, slipping it between and over his fingers like a coin. After a few moments, he said simply, "Why?"

"Because if we're afraid of this thing coming out, we're paralyzed. We're dead. We can't investigate anybody, because what we find out screws us. Okay? Barris was probably killed because of either or both

164

of two reasons. One: what he knew about the fuckin' cover-up. Two: how he planned to use that knowledge. Lydon is a suspect because of number two—he'd squash Barris like an annoying fly. Everybody else is a suspect because of number one." Cox paused. "And that includes you. And me."

"Does that make us suspects or potential victims?" Bieberschmidt shoved the Oreo into his mouth and mumbled, "Or both? And what about the girl?"

Cox frowned. "I don't know."

"And what about the MO? Why the goddamn mutilation?"

Cox shook his head. "I don't know. I just don't know. . . . Okay, listen. We know that Barris paid Sunni for sex, and that Sunni was working for Lydon. If Lydon wanted to kill Barris to keep Barris from attempting to shut him down, he might have used the girl to bait Barris. So he tells Sunni that he's going to hurt Barris. Maybe he doesn't tell her what he really has in mind. So he has the girl meet Barris while a goon is waiting in the closet."

"Maybe. Just maybe."

Cox scratched his forehead. "So while Sunni's getting it on with Barris, all the goon needs to do is to slip behind Barris, get the twine around Barris's neck, and hang on for the ride. Ivan said he was shit-faced and coked up at the time of death. Probably didn't put up much of a fight."

"So why cut out his tongue?"

Cox shrugged. "I don't know. Maybe he wasn't nice to the girl. Maybe it was his payback for some nasty sex."

"And what about the girl? Why the same MO?"

"If Lydon and the girl participated in Barris's murder, then Lydon had a clear motive for getting rid of her. He might have copied the MO to cast suspicion elsewhere." Cox shook his head. "That's why the instruments were left at the scene. So we'd think it was the same perpetrator. Or maybe he wanted it to look like a psycho or a serial killer."

"In which case, they're either telling us that it's over or that they plan to do it again, if only to reinforce the impression."

"Does Lydon have a record?"

Bieberschmidt shook his head. "He's clean."

The two men sat silently. Bieberschmidt watched Cox as he smoked thoughtfully, staring at the floor, and let a few moments pass before saying, "Do you realize you're the last smoker left on the force?"

Cox looked at him. "No, I didn't realize that. Hard to believe."

Bieberschmidt shook his head.

Cox crushed out the cigarette and stood. "It's time to put some people on Lydon. He's got to be watched. Twenty-four-hour surveillance. Do an FBI check. The works."

"Good thought," said Bieberschmidt. He glanced at Cox and smiled tentatively, as if waiting for the other shoe to drop.

Cox sighed. "And get ready for all hell to break loose. If we pick up Lydon, he'll have a long story to tell the good folks of Indiana."

Bieberschmidt nodded solemnly.

"Heard anything from Ivan on the girl?" Cox asked.

"Huh-uh," Bieberschmidt murmured.

Cox leaned over Bieberschmidt's desk, picked up the phone, and punched in the four numbers of Ivan Sarvetnikov's extension. On the seventh ring, Ivan answered.

"Coroner."

"Cox here, Ivan. How's it going?"

"Mr. Cox, how nice to hear from you."

"Yeah, thanks, Ivan."

"Sunni Skye."

"Right."

"There's a high likelihood that it's the same killer as Mr. Barris's. It's the same twine-pattern impression in the neck. The cuts to the genital labia are superficial sharp incisions, probably made with the same blade used to cut Barris."

"Time of death?"

"About one A.M., judging by the degree of rigor."

"Evidence of intercourse?"

"Yeah. We've swabbed it and bagged it. That's all you want on that now, right?"

Cox sighed. "Yeah."

"You'll have it in writing by the end of the day."

"Thanks."

Cox put his hand on Bieberschmidt's shoulder as he stood to leave the chief's office. He thought of what it would be like to tell Farrell what he'd done, the awful humiliation of it, the loss of her respect. He thought of how Quade would enjoy seeing him fall a notch or two, and of how appalled Perry would be, with his Boy Scout idealism. And then he thought of Nora Lumsey, of how little she seemed to think of him already, and of how he would now come to justify the low esteem in which she and so many others in the Indianapolis criminal bar held the Harrison force.

The time had come for a purification—his own.

16

Cox found Farrell waiting in his office, sitting attractively on the edge of his desk, flipping through Barris's law journal article.

"Fascinating." Farrell made a sardonic face, lifting a corner of her mouth into a quizzical smirk. "Listen to this," and she read a passage in her countrified version of an upper-class British accent:

> The nature of sex may be analogized to the game of basketball, a game that echoes the primal feral animal competition of males to mate with a female in heat. Like pack wolves, the males drive for the goal, with its net, which hangs like pubic hair around the rim—the hole—that which must be penetrated for the male to prevail in planting his seed. The other males frantically attempt to block the driving male, try to steal the ball from him to make their own drives for the goal, and the prize goes to the fastest, the biggest, the most fearless, the one with sufficient guile to fake a pass, the one with the ruthlessness to knock an opponent down, the one with the courage to take a hit and be fouled.
>
> Yet in sex, there is no referee to call foul and permit the male a free shot at the goal, unless it is the female, the mercurial goal herself, who, through the mediating exercise of

emotion, permits a lesser male, perhaps a fouled male, an opportunity to score. Emotion operates to dilute the Darwinian nature of sex, just as the referee serves to level the playing field, perhaps unrealistically.

And how interesting it is to consider that the marvelously sexual game of basketball should have begun in Martinsville, Indiana, with a peach basket, the peach being the most sensuously female of the fruits.

Farrell shook her head. "Jesus! Who do you think reads this crap?"

"No one."

Farrell held the reprint up by a corner. "Is this evidence?"

"No. Except of who Barris was. And of his attitudes."

"He must've gotten knocked around a bit by women," Farrell said. "Poor baby."

Cox dropped into his chair. "So what's going on?"

"We've got a couple of guys watching Lydon. Other than that, I've been writing up the evidence report, Ivan's report is on its way, and my father is gasping his last breaths."

"I'm sorry."

"Well, I've got to get my ass over the hospital for a while." She glanced at him apologetically.

"Then get the hell out of here; take the rest of the day."

She shook her head and stood. "No, but thanks. That's too much time. One can sit in silence for only so long. I'll be back this afternoon."

Cox took a breath. "Tina, there's something I need to talk to you about."

Farrell registered instantly that there was something different in Cox's tone, an unfamiliar hesitancy. "Now? I can wait if—"

"No, later, when you have some time."

"Are you sure? Is everything okay?"

"Yeah, it's fine," Cox said. "Fine."

Nora's feet rang on the metal steps, and she saw the trailer door open a crack. A thin slice of Weesie Phipps's face appeared there, and Weesie's voice barked out at her.

"Git away! Ya bitch! Git away from here!"

The door slammed shut.

"Weesie! I need to talk to Stormi! Please!"

Weesie's voice came muffled through the door. "Git the fuck away!"

"Please, let me talk to her!"

A silence. Then, through sobs, she said, "Git th' fuck away. I don't care what you say. My Sunni girl is gone. And her baby ain't got no momma. Stormi's all I got, and you ain't takin' her."

"I'm not here to take her, Weesie. I'm her lawyer. I want to help her."

Nora listened through the door to the sound of Weesie whimpering, and she imagined Weesie collapsed on the floor on the other side, leaning against the door. Then she heard a shuffling behind the door. The doorknob turned, the door swung swiftly open, and behind it stood Stormi, her hair stuck up wildly, as if she'd been pulled out of a fitful sleep.

"What the fuck do *you* want?" Stormi said, her voice thick with anger. She stepped outside, crowding Nora backward down the stairs. The air was freezing cold, yet Stormi, barefoot and wearing only a sleeveless undershirt and panties, pulled the trailer door shut behind her as she pressed toward Nora. "What're ya botherin' her for? You haven't done enough, have ya?"

Nora held both hands up in front of her as she moved backward. "Hey . . . wait a minute. What's your problem, Stormi? I need to talk to you."

Nora jerked from side to side to evade Stormi's hands thrusting out at her, pushing her backward like a schoolyard bully. "Stop it, for Christ's sake!" Nora said. "I didn't—"

"Mother . . . fucker," Stormi said, teeth gritted, now jabbing her fingertips into Nora's chest. "I thought I fired you, mother-fucker. . . ."

They were in the driveway, moving toward Nora's car, when it occurred to Nora that Stormi was neither as tall nor as strong as she was, just meaner. Nora stopped short.

Stormi's face butted up against hers. Nora took one last hard shove on the chest and shoved back.

The flesh of Stormi's upper chest, exposed above the undershirt, felt oddly hot against Nora's palm as she pushed hard at her, force meeting force.

"Why can't you believe me?" Nora said, breathing hard, now intercepting each of Stormi's thrusts with her hands. "I want to help you."

Stormi put her arms down and looked at Nora, then looked away. Nora took one step back and gradually brought her hands to her sides.

Stormi breathed deeply, and Nora could see Stormi's face working to suppress emotion. Behind Stormi, the door opened and Weesie stepped outside, now wearing a long, dirty pink coat. Nora glanced up at her with embarrassment, like a child caught fighting.

Then Stormi landed a hard right to Nora's cheekbone.

Nora never saw it coming; she heard something crack and felt the pain radiate from the point of impact up through her eye and across her skull. She stumbled back, touched her face gingerly with her hand, then instinctively swung at Stormi, connecting lightly with Stormi's ear and part of her neck. Stormi came back with a shot to Nora's stomach that Nora managed to block, and then the two flailed at each other carelessly, bad fighters both, grunting and staggering and rocking.

After a moment, Weesie was in there too, crying, "Stop it, Stormi. Stop it! Stop it!" and pulling on her shoulders and arms.

"Get away, Ma," Stormi yelled. "Get the fuck off!"

Nora stopped swinging; she continued to fend off Stormi's blows, waiting for Stormi to tire, but suddenly Stormi exploded with fury.

She swung hard with her right, missing as Nora pulled back. As Stormi wound up for another blow, her left arm went back and struck her mother just above the mouth. Weesie let out a wail and dropped to the ground, clutching her face as blood emerged between her fingers.

"Goddamn you, Ma!" Stormi bent down to her and peered around her mother's hands to see the damage she'd done.

Nora ran the few steps to her pickup, fumbled for her keys, and quickly turned the ignition. Before putting the truck into gear, she twisted around to see Stormi glaring after her as she helped Weesie to her feet.

After much fussing over a leaky ice pack, her mother had finally lain down, and now, at last, she was asleep. Stormi went into Sunni's bedroom and rummaged in her sister's makeup drawer, where she knew she would find the tiny Ziploc bag that contained Sunni's weekly bonus from Gene Lydon.

Stormi went into the bathroom, where she shook a small amount of pale pink powder from the bag into the bottom of the shallow metal measuring cup that she'd taken from her mother's kitchen, then let a few drops splash into it from the bathroom sink.

She took it to her bed at the back of the trailer and placed the cup on the bandanna that was spread out on top of her night table. The rest of Stormi's works lay scattered on the bandanna.

Stormi lighted a candle in a shallow dish, then loosely tied off her upper arm with a thin rubber strip. She proceeded to cook the heroin-cocaine mixture, the speedball, by moving the cup slowly back and forth above the candle, letting the flame caress it.

She breathed deeply through her nose and let the instant expand as her thoughts focused on her target and the task ahead of her. It was all predestined, always had been, and there was nothing she could do to change it. She should have seen it coming, should have known that the murder and money would lead to this.

Trust. The bastard had paid her and Sunni, but he'd failed to trust them, and so he'd killed Sunni. And now, for that crime, the bastard would have to die.

Stormi stared into the flame, letting the movement of the shiny metal cup paint burning smears across her retina. The world had been out of balance since Sunni had died. There was a kind of static in the air, an electricity that made her skin itch and her head feel dizzy and kept her from concentrating. All day long, she'd wanted to cry, but she could not, not even when she conjured the face of her sister, the soul with whom she had shared her mother's womb, not even when she closed her eyes and put Sunni's face in front of her, imagining Sunni's hand reaching out to clasp the back of her neck and pull their foreheads together with joking affection. But there would be a resolution, a life for a life, because it was predestined and she was only a tool of God's justice.

The liquid bubbled up in the measuring cup and Stormi withdrew it quickly from the flame. She held it still for a second, then tilted the cup and dropped a cotton ball into the liquid. She dipped the tip of the needle into the cotton. Holding the cup with one hand and the shaft of the needle with the other, she simultaneously pulled the plunger up with her teeth and pulled down on the shaft. The chamber filled with the speedball, gently churning. Stormi dropped the cup and held the needle up. She tapped it a few times, pulled the rubber strap tight around her bicep, pumped her arm, then easily hit a healed spot on her usual vein. Stormi pressed the plunger slightly, then let it rise as flowerlets of blood burst upward into the drug. Stormi let the chamber fill, then pressed the plunger again, booting four times before shooting up the entire fix.

Stormi managed to put the needle down when her body imploded, heart pounding as if she'd been running like mad, stomach burning like it'd been kicked hard. She lay back on her mattress as the sweat popped out all over her, then she closed her eyes and waited.

Five minutes later, she opened her eyes, snapped her fingers, grinning, and stood. She felt great. She reached under her bed and pulled out the fishing tackle box that had once belonged to her brothers. She flipped it open. Under the top tray was her .22 pistol. She took it out and pulled out the clip to be sure it was loaded. It was. She grabbed her leather jacket, stuck the gun in the inside pocket, and crept silently past her sleeping mother and out the door.

17

Nora drove to the law school, where she hoped Marjorie could help her pull herself together, but Marjorie was gone for the day.

So Nora went to the ladies' room, where she confronted herself in the mirror. She was not a fighter by nature or ability, and she knew she'd been injured as much from the awkwardness of her self-defense as from anything Stormi had done to her. Her shoulders, sides, and back cried out in jolts of muscular torment with every shift of her body. Worse, the side of her face where Stormi had nailed her pulsed agonizingly, and the mirror revealed that she was developing a remarkably ugly black eye, a classic shiner. At least it would be no worse than that; her eye would not be swollen shut.

She needed to get to her doctor, she knew, but she could not take the time. So she scrounged three extra-strength Tylenol from the bottom of her shoulder bag and downed them with water from the tap.

It was imperative that she speak with Cox, to tell him that Stormi was crazy from heroin withdrawal and that she was in danger of doing violence to herself or others. She wanted him to know, too, that Coach Hedstrom's connection to Stormi was deeper than Cox might have realized.

She would urge him to pick Stormi up, lock her up, and force her to endure sustained withdrawal, then get her into rehab and on her way to the clean, new life Nora envisioned for her.

It was a tragic joke, Nora knew. But she could not help her absurd hopes.

Nora blotted her black eye with a wet paper towel, scolded herself for indulging in sentimental fantasies, and wondered why she couldn't get good and angry with Stormi for being such an irresponsible little shit.

"Because there but for the fucking grace of God go I," she said out loud. "That's why."

As Nora was leaving the ladies' room, a pair of young women entered, laughing, relieved at the conclusion of classes that day, discussing their weekend plans.

Under her open jacket, one of the women wore an I KILLED JAMES BARRIS T-shirt.

Nora's heart jolted at the sight of it, the cruelty of the words, and she was shocked no less by the words themselves than by the thought of how thoroughly Jim Barris had demonized himself in the bizarre predatory culture of the law school.

He made them hate him, she thought, and then it occurred to her that he would have loved this, would have laughed himself silly at the sight of the T-shirt, would have been proud of the trouble these women had taken to create it.

The two women stared back at Nora, frightened, and she could not help but grin at them, despite the sharp pain shooting up from her cheek into her eye.

Stormi needed a drink, but not for courage. She needed that drink to lose a measure of her bravado, her high, her reckless confidence, to slow herself down enough to act rationally. A Southern Comfort and beer chaser would do the trick, she thought, and so she drove Sunni's motorcycle into the parking lot of the Red Bud Inn on her way into town.

Stormi drank slowly and watched the five o'clock news. The weight of the .22 in her inside jacket pocket felt snug and warm against her chest, as if it were a small, still creature burrowed in her clothing.

"We may be favored, but we sure as hell don't expect to roll over this Ohio team." Don Hedstrom was speaking from courtside, his image on a screen at the back of the newsroom set, the two news anchors listening attentively. "They've got a superb center in Kent Robinson, and if we can't keep the ball away from Kent, we ain't gonna do diddly out there."

"What can you tell us about Dan Bilby's knee? Is there a chance he'll start tonight?"

"His knee is looking better than we had any right to expect, but I won't start him. He'll get some playing time, but I won't start him."

"One last question, Coach Hedstrom. Is there any truth to the rumor that there may be a civil action in the Mike Chappelle case? Against you, Chappelle, and the city of Harrison? Are you aware of—"

"Don't ask me about that shit! What's the matter with you? I can't comment on—"

Hedstrom's image faded quickly to black. "Thank you, Coach Hedstrom," said the smiling anchor. "Back after this."

But then Hedstrom's face was back on-screen, this time hawking pizza. "Hey, you want to score some fresh, hot pizza delivered right to your door for free? Then make a fast break to your phone and give the full court press to these numbers—five five five–seven six five two. . . ."

Stormi threw back the last half of her shot, chugged the rest of the beer, pushed her money across the bar, and stood to leave. Yes, that was good, she thought, a little buzz to top things off. But it was getting late, and she had no time to waste.

Cox rolled a cigarette and licked it shut with three flicks of his tongue, lighted it while it was still wet, then sucked down a fat wad of smoke just as the telephone rang. It was Bieberschmidt, who'd gotten a call from his wife, who'd been watching the news.

"Who's the leak?" Bieberschmidt demanded, his voice edgy with fear.

"Could be a hell of a lot of people," replied Cox, "even Hedstrom himself, just to give us a scare, an elbow in the ribs."

"But you know we're going to be getting calls from every reporter in the state, wanting to know about Chappelle. What the hell do we say to them?"

"We say there's absolutely no truth to the rumor. Because that happens to be the truth. And maybe that's what Hedstrom wants to hear us say."

"I hate to give him the satisfaction."

"Yeah." Cox rubbed his forehead and sighed. We've just learned the number-one rule about cover-ups, he thought: They never end, never go away. "Listen, Chief, I think we may have a break in the Barris and Skye murders."

"Oh!" The chief's voice brightened instantly. "Terrific! What have you got?"

"Umm . . ." Cox hesitated. "I'm waiting to hear from Tina over at the state police lab. She's checking some prints. You going to be around for a while?"

"Yeah, but who—"

"Let me get back to you, Chief."

"Damn it, Cox." Bieberschmidt hung up.

Cox held the phone against his cheek, thought about the phone call he had to make, and muttered curses to himself. He depressed the receiver button and held it down for a moment while he glanced over at his notebook for the number. Then he let the receiver button go, pressed the numbers, and waited. A feminine voice answered, a young voice.

Cox said, "I'm trying to reach Don Hedstrom."

"He's not available at the moment," the voice said, well rehearsed. "May I take a message?"

"Ah, yeah, please tell him that Detective Cox called and to give me a call at the Harrison Police Department. It's five five five–four thousand."

"Thank you."

"Ah, wait a sec. When do you expect him in?"

"Not until late tonight, sir. Don't you know there's a game on?"

"Right. See that he gets the message, please."

Cox put down the phone and reached for his tobacco. A cigarette, he thought, to help him work through probable cause.

Don Hedstrom. "Great power." It scared Cox to think it was Hedstrom who had done it, done the murders, both of them, but the evidence was becoming too strong to ignore. There was motive enough—more than enough—in the threat of exposure by Barris of the rape cover-up, and then by Sunni of Barris's murder. But to convince a judge to issue a warrant, he needed more than motive; he needed probable cause, and for that, as the law told him, he needed "facts and circumstances within the officer's knowledge that would lead a reasonably prudent person to believe a crime was being committed or had been committed." In practical terms, that meant evidence establishing a direct link between the suspect and the crime. A fingerprint would do marvelously, he thought, and he glanced at the phone, as if willing it to ring, with Tina on the other end, offering the news he wanted to hear. There was at least a chance; Hedstrom's fingerprints were already on file from a thirteen-year-old DUI arrest, but if the fingerprint didn't come through, he wouldn't complain if he got a fiber or hair match. But that meant getting samples, and getting samples meant getting a search warrant for the Hedstrom place. He had enough evidence to justify a search, but Don Hedstrom would raise holy hell. And what if he were wrong?

The phone rang. Cox stared at it a moment, then took a deep drag on the cigarette. He crushed it out before he reached for the phone.

"Cox."

"Happy days, handsome. We got a match."

"Hallelujah."

"It's not perfect, but we've got thirteen points. That should be plenty."

"Good. Listen, I need you back here, Tina, like fast, okay?"

"Yeah, but I got something else for you. The state fuzz've got this incredible new computer, you know—it digitizes the print so you can superimpose bits of print on top of an image of your file print—"

"Yeah, Tina."

"I took some blurred prints from Barris's car—dashboard, door handle, steering wheel, whatever wasn't leather—and compared them to the files and the prints from Sunni Skye's body."

"Yeah?"

"We've got Sunni in the car, Luther. Driving, or at least sitting in the driver's seat. I can't say when, but she was there not too long ago, or another driver or passenger would have smudged them worse than they are."

A silence. Cox extracted a rolling paper from the Tops pack and smoothed it between his fingers.

Tina took a deep breath and went on. "The Skye prints probably won't make it in court. But I think we can start assuming that Sunni was in that car on the night of Barris's murder."

"Don Hedstrom!"

"Uh-huh."

Bieberschmidt glared at Cox, then looked away, his face undergoing a transfiguration from shock (dropped jaw), to panic (bulging eyes, livid complexion), to fear (tight jaw, pale complexion), to acceptance (furrowed brow, eyes brimming with tears). Then he covered his face with both hands. "Oh shit, ohhh shit," he moaned.

"There's nothing to be done, Chief."

Bieberschmidt sniffled. "It's an evil business, Luther."

"Mm-hm."

"Think the whole Chappelle mess will come out?"

"Yeah, no doubt about it."

Bieberschmidt pulled a handkerchief from inside his jacket and wiped his face. "Don Hedstrom!"

Cox nodded. "Uh-huh."

Quade and Farrell appeared at Cox's door, as had been requested moments before. Cox motioned them in with a quick beckoning gesture.

Farrell handed Cox a thick file, which he opened to a series of laser-printed blowups of fingerprints, profusely scribbled upon and labeled. Cox glanced at the prints, then took a file from the stack of papers to his right and opened it to a sheaf of crime-scene reports, forensic results, and statements from witnesses.

"Okay," Cox said. "So now we know Don Hedstrom was at the scene of Barris's death. Of course, that could be during or after the crime. We've got Sunni Skye in Barris's car. Of course, that could be any time recently."

"That depends," said Farrell, "on how often Barris let other people drive his car."

Cox waited.

"Sunni's prints were on the steering wheel, gearshift, and on the door handle. She probably put her hands there when getting out of the car. The next person to sit there would have wiped the prints off the seat and at least smudged the prints on the handle."

"Was she the last person to drive Barris's car?"

"Difficult to say. We've got Barris's prints in and around hers. Definitely the last but for Barris perhaps."

"So what's our theory, then?" Quade chimed in, stepping forward with arms folded, an aggressive posture that Cox found irritatingly out of sync with the humility he expected from Quade. "Are we saying that Sunni Skye and Don were coconspirators? That Sunni was the bait and Hedstrom killed Sunni to eliminate the lone witness to the crime?"

"Maybe," said Cox.

"So how does he do it?" asked Quade. "And what is Sunni doing in Barris's car that night?"

"Well, what if Sunni was the bait?" Cox reached for his tobacco and rolling papers.

Farrell sat on the edge of Cox's desk. "Why would Hedstrom

want to kill Barris? In what way could Barris pose a threat to Hedstrom? They were buddies. Did Barris know something Hedstrom didn't want revealed?"

Bieberschmidt glanced uneasily at Cox. "We've all got people we'd like to kill."

"I don't," said Quade diffidently.

"But there are plenty of people who'd like to kill you," Farrell joked, then pushed herself off the edge of Cox's desk. "So Hedstrom convinces Sunni to help him murder Barris, eliminating the threat. Sunni lures Barris somewhere for sex. Hedstrom brings the cord and the blade. Sunni arranges for Barris to be in the right position, and Hedstrom sneaks up from behind with the twine. Don't forget he's an athlete, a damn powerful man. Hedstrom garrotes Barris, with Sunni helping keep Barris from pulling free. When Barris is dead, they dump him in the woods and they cut him up for good measure. I mean, whoever cut off the tongue and went apeshit with the razor blade must've been pretty pissed off, right? Maybe they wanted to cut off the prick, too, but lost their nerve."

"And Sunni's murder?" asked Quade.

Farrell looked away thoughtfully for a moment. "I don't know. Maybe Hedstrom figured he'd rather not worry that Sunni was going to get scared and talk to the police. So he meets Sunni at the Sleep Tite Motel. Brings the cord and the knife and slashes the genitals to make it look like the work of a serial killer."

"That's good, Tina," said Quade. "But you still don't have a motive. What threat could Barris have posed to Hedstrom?"

Farrell shrugged. "I don't know," she said softly, and shifted her gaze to Cox.

Cox's eyes met hers, and then he looked at Bieberschmidt, who drew in a breath. "We have information," Cox said, "regarding a motive, but it's going to have to stay under wraps for now. There are sensitive issues . . . involving the force."

Farrell blinked. "The force."

Quade paled.

"It's nothing to do with you, Teddy," Cox said, frowning.

Recovering, Farrell said, "We have the evidence to pick up Hedstrom for the Barris murder, motive or not. We could use more evidence of Sunni's involvement in Barris's murder."

Cox licked his finger and turned a page in the case report. "We've got the prints from the car, for one thing. The cord and the blade. We've got a pubic hair combing from Barris. There's no reason why we can't check it against a sample from Sunni. Have we done that?"

Tina shook her head.

"Do it. We've got some tire tracks by the road, fibers and hair inside Barris's car, fiber from the blanket on the ground. All of that's useless until we have something to compare it to. On Sunni, we've got blood and skin samples from the fingernails, a shitload of hair and lint and dust from the motel room, Crowder's descriptions of the two johns." He shrugged. "And then we've got our auto mechanic, Randy Sturgeon, who says he saw a Mercedes parked out by his shop and what he described as a 'rich guy' walking away from it. What else would come out of a Mercedes?"

"Wait a second." Tina moved around the desk and leaned over Cox's shoulder. Cox inhaled the warm scent of her body and fought distraction as Tina thumbed backward through his notes. "The tire print I got from the Barris crime scene is from . . . a Michelin two-one-five-P-eight-oh-one-seven. And I've got a list of cars that it commonly fits." She turned the page over. "Mercedes two sixty SL. No shit."

"The question is why didn't Randy Sturgeon recognize Hedstrom?" Cox looked at Quade. "Let's ask him. Teddy?"

Quade nodded.

"I'm going to write up an affidavit to support a warrant to arrest Hedstrom and to search his home and car. If the garage guy has a reasonable explanation for not recognizing Hedstrom, great, we'll throw that in, too. And let's check with the BMV to see what vehicles Hedstrom's got registered."

"Gotcha," said Quade.

"And Teddy," said Cox, "do me a favor and find out what time tonight's game begins."

"Seven-thirty-five," said Quade.

Bieberschmidt remained seated across from Cox after the others had filed away to perform their respective tasks. Cox had never seen Bieberschmidt look so depressed; the chief's body appeared to be melting down into the orange fabric of the cheap swivel chairs the HPD had furnished for Cox's office.

"It looks like we'll have to make the arrest at the game tonight," Cox said softly. "It's five-fifty now. We're not going to get the warrant in time to do it before the game. And I'm not gonna wait till it's over just for Hedstrom's sake."

Bieberschmidt sat staring.

"Halftime's a decent compromise. After the buzzer sounds, we'll nab him before he heads downstairs."

Bieberschmidt said nothing. Cox turned to his computer, flicked it on, and watched as the booting-up sequence flashed its usual string of incomprehensible commands.

"There'll be a plea bargain," Bieberschmidt murmured. "Hedstrom will tell the prosecutor everything he knows about Chappelle in exchange for immunity and a reduction in charges."

"We've got two homicides, Hank. They won't plea that down."

Bieberschmidt shook his head. "No, this is Don Hedstrom we're talking about. The rules for mere mortals don't apply."

Cox spread the evidence file next to his keyboard and began typing, his fingers tapping the keys with rapid precision. "What makes you so sure Hedstrom wants the world to know that he tried to hide a rapist?"

"Ah, but that's where you're wrong," said Bieberschmidt, getting to his feet. "The one who offers the bribe never looks half as bad as the one who takes it. And Hedstrom was just protecting his boy from that vengeful slut." Bieberschmidt leaned over Cox's desk. "No, Hedstrom didn't do shit compared to what I did. And what I made you do."

Cox stopped typing and looked up at him. "You didn't make me do it, Hank; you asked me. That was shitty of you, but I made my choice. It just happened to be the wrong one."

"I'm sorry, Luther."

Cox nodded and turned back to the computer.

Bieberschmidt made for the door. "Guess we'll have plenty of time to talk about it after tomorrow." He smiled ruefully. "Maybe we can finally do some fishin' together."

Cox kept typing. "It's the middle of the fuckin' winter, Hank, and I'm not into ice fishing." He licked his finger and turned a page in his notes. "Listen, I'm gonna get this affidavit delivered to Judge Kohrman's house within a half hour tops and hopefully get the warrant back by seven-fifteen. Let's be ready to roll with three squad cars by seven-thirty. If we haul ass, we can catch most of the first half."

The woman at the front desk winced when she saw Nora's black eye, and there came across her face an expression of pathos that Nora found excruciating. No, she was not the victim of an assault, not a battered wife, she would have liked to have told the woman, but she simply asked for Detective Cox and took a seat on a wooden bench.

Cox winced, too, when he came to the lobby to get her. "How'd that happen?" he asked as he led her back to his office.

"I got crosswise with Stormi," Nora said. "I went to see her at her mother's trailer to talk about Sunni's murder, among other things. She came at me, and we mixed it up a bit."

"Have you been to the hospital?"

"Not yet, no."

Cox closed the door to his office, then stood close to Nora and examined her eye.

"Are you seeing all right?" he asked.

"Yeah."

"What sort of pain are you having?"

"A wicked headache."

As he looked at her, Nora examined his face in turn. How peculiarly sculptured he is, she thought. How odd that such a face should be on a living, breathing man, the lines chiseled so deep, the skin textured like worn leather, the mustache sprouting thickly, like salt-and-pepper porcupine quills. After a moment, his eyes—clear blue, weary, sad—met hers, and he smiled.

"No sharp pains?"

"No."

"The swelling's not too bad. So long as you haven't cracked your eye socket, you should be all right. I'd see a doctor if I were you."

"Tomorrow," she said.

Cox moved a chair away from his wall for her, then sat on the other side of his desk and turned to his computer.

"Forgive me a moment while I finish an affidavit."

"No problem," she said, relieved to have another moment to collect her thoughts.

Cox typed the final words of the affidavit, the affirmation under the penalties of perjury, words he had written hundreds of times, but now he felt a stabbing sense of guilt and humiliation, knowing that his perjury in the Chappelle case would soon come to light.

"You a basketball fan?" Cox asked as he pulled the affidavit out of the printer.

"I was once," Nora said, "when I had the time and the peace of mind to enjoy the game. Now I can't sit still long enough for it."

Cox reached into the top drawer of his desk, pulled out a ticket, and handed it to Nora. "As long as you're in town, why not see the game? I won't be using my ticket, and I can tell you that it promises to be a historic evening."

"What team are we playing?"

"Ohio State."

"What's historic about that?"

"You'll see."

"You're being awfully mysterious." Nora tried to smile, but the movement of her cheek muscle sent a spasm of pain across her face.

"So are you," Cox said.

Nora looked at him quizzically.

"You came to see me," Cox said.

"Yes, of course." Nora sighed. "It's Stormi. I think she's going through heroin withdrawal, but I'm not sure. I know she's been shooting heroin, cocaine, and speed at various times and in various combinations."

"Not much we can do about that, except arrest her when we catch her for a drug offense."

"But it's more than that. She's becoming delusional, schizophrenic—hell, I don't know what it is, but Sunni's death has put her over the edge."

Cox nodded, understanding.

"She's gonna hurt herself. Or somebody."

"Do you think she was involved in Barris's death?"

"I don't know." Nora touched her eye, trying vainly to quell a stabbing pain. "I don't think so, but maybe. I don't know."

"Do you know where we can find her?"

Nora shook her head. "She's left home by now. At Pleazures, maybe."

"I'll have somebody stop by there later tonight."

"Thanks."

"You're welcome." Cox smiled and opened his office door.

Relieved, Nora's thoughts turned toward the game and the unexpected pleasure of possessing a coveted ticket to see the BHU Sagamores in action. Before leaving, Nora turned to Cox to thank him and was struck by the anguished expression on his face. She said, "Are you all right?"

"No," Cox replied, abashed, suddenly, by his honesty. "I've got worries."

"Yeah." Nora nodded. "Me, too."

18

The sun had completed its turgid winter sunset, and the lights had eased on gingerly over the Aberdeen Hall parking lot when Stormi rode in, the sputter of her motorcycle ripping a long tear in the cold air as she crossed the asphalt. It was an hour before game time, but the lot's four thousand parking spaces were a third full, mostly with idling cars crammed with students engaged in winter tailgate parties, drinking and smoking to keep warm.

Stormi drew her motorcycle up to a lamppost and dismounted, shivering in the battered leather jacket she wore, with nothing but a threadbare flannel shirt beneath. She trotted toward the box office, hands in pockets, evading the patches of ice shining in the reflection from the parking-lot lights. A frigid breeze blew steadily across the wide expanse of blacktop.

Inside the lobby, only one window in the wall of six box office windows was lighted. A sign hung crookedly above the face of the smiling young woman who sat there: TONIGHT'S GAME SOLD OUT/ ADVANCE SALE ONLY. Stormi looked at the sign, eyed the girl, and stood in the lobby a moment, rubbing her hands. Folding metal gates had been pulled across the turnstiles, and behind them, in the wide entrance way that funneled the fans onto ramps that snaked up to the stadium's three levels, stood four guards, talking animatedly about the Illinois–Michigan State game the night before. Stormi bounced on her heels and listened, staring out the door at the parking lot. Cars drifted in steadily now, and there were men waving orange lights, directing the cars to spaces.

The girl's voice broke in behind her. "You can't wait in here." Stormi turned. The guards had stopped their chattering and were looking at her.

"Okay," she said, and she pushed the door open into the cold air.

She walked close to the building, following its curve north from the box office, moving in and out of the darkness, which was interrupted by splashes of yellow light from the huge halogen lamps atop the parking lot lampposts. Aberdeen Hall, an entirely round structure, resembled the cutoff trunk of a striped tree, its exterior bark composed of alternating panels of concrete and tinted glass. The interior ramps wound corkscrewlike inside the building. From the parking lot at night, the ramps resembled one long cattle chute, and the crowds moving within the stadium looked like a slow-moving herd.

Stormi moved swiftly, past loading docks, behind cars and trucks parked up against the building. She knew there was a way inside. There was always a way inside. How many houses had she broken into in the days before she worked for Lydon? Jewelry bought a fix, sometimes many fixes; that was lesson number one, and she'd learned it early. Lesson number two: Try the door. People were careless. Doors that should be locked often were not. Give the door a tug.

Nearly halfway around the building, out of sight of the crowds streaming toward the stadium entrance, Stormi began testing the metal doors set into the building. She hopped up the two or three steps that led to each of the doors, swiftly pulled the cold metal handles, and moved on. She slowed down as she neared the back of the stadium, the players' entrance, where a wedge of the building had been entirely blocked off, with its own fenced-in parking area and entrances for the exclusive use of coaches, players, and officials. There were lights there, and looking through the fence, Stormi could see guards at the doors. A radio was on, just loud enough for Stormi to hear, tuned to a basketball game somewhere.

Stormi stopped thirty yards short of the fence. She could go no farther. There were two doors in the metal fence, but both were chained shut, and even if she could pass through them, the guards on the other side would turn her back. Stormi stood a moment, sizing up her options, her hands shoved into her pants pockets. A blast of wind got her moving again, and when she turned to go back, she saw a tiny square of light at the base of the building, just on her side of the fence.

Cautiously approaching the light, Stormi saw a concrete stairwell leading down to the basement level, where a metal door with a head-sized square window was lighted from within. She descended the cement steps slowly, praying hard not to be seen by the cops, who were less than twenty feet away on the other side of the fence, and without breaking her stride, she gave the door a forceful tug.

She was inside.

In a long, dimly lighted corridor, Stormi rested against the cool surface of the concrete wall. The air throbbed faintly with the buzz of electricity and the sounds of a boiler room. When she heard distant shouts, she pushed off and walked quickly down the corridor.

At the end of the corridor, the walls changed from concrete to glazed cinder block, and instead of bare bulbs, there were fluorescent fixtures. The shouts had grown louder, and the echo in the voices told Stormi that she was near the players' locker room. She touched the wall and stood absolutely still, listening; she grinned at the thought of eavesdropping on these heroes, these gods, a good number of whom she'd had the pleasure of servicing. And then she heard that other voice, that unmistakable brittle, staccato bark: "What the *fuck* are you *doing*, Ahmad! Get your *dick* out of your hand and get dressed!" Stormi crouched down, overcome with giddiness, struggling to stifle the laughter bubbling up in her throat. Unable to contain it, she laughed once, loudly, crazily, then stumbled forward and ran headlong down the hallway, searching for a way upstairs.

Around the next corner, she saw a way—a pair of freight elevators in a dead-end corridor—but to get to them she had to cross a wide hallway. Here, the floor was linoleum and the light fixtures were set into a dropped ceiling. Stormi knew she was close to the entrance to the locker rooms and the practice gym. She approached the hallway with long, even strides, trying hard to look like she knew where she was going, in case she was spotted.

An instant later, she was. Just as she was about to reach the other side, she heard a voice say, "Hey," quiet the first time, but then loudly a second time, and then there were footsteps moving quickly. Stormi didn't turn her head. From the sound of the footsteps, she could tell the man was somewhere down the hall, maybe far enough away for her to make it. She pushed the elevator button. The elevator on the left opened instantly. She stepped inside, had a momentary crisis when deciding which floor to push, then pushed 5 for no reason at all. The doors slid shut just as the man—not a guard, thank God, but some chubby guy in a suit—came around the corner to the elevator bank. At the fifth floor, the elevator opened onto a shabby lounge containing some spongy-looking couches, round vinyl-topped tables, and metal chairs. Corridors ran off on three sides of the room, each lined, from what Stormi could see in the dim service lighting, with a series of doors.

Stormi stepped off the elevator and walked through the lounge toward the corridor on her right. She was frightened and suddenly very weary, but as she neared the corridor, she heard the subtle murmur of a crowd, and she knew she was somewhere above the hall.

The first door would not open, nor the second, and with mounting frustration she tried them all, until she got to the end of the corridor, which took a sharp left turn and dead-ended into a door with a large window in its upper half. Peering through the glass, Stormi could see rows of shelving filled with lighting equipment and, beyond the shelving, a metal stairway. She tried the door, without luck, but she could see that it was a simple lock, not a dead bolt, and in an instant she had her keychain penknife out and was working the blade in the tiny slot. Within five seconds, the door popped open and Stormi was through.

The sound of the crowd was suddenly much louder. She bounded across the room and down the metal stairway, which descended from the floor of the storage room and ended on a catwalk high above Aberdeen Hall.

The catwalk swayed slightly as Stormi stepped onto it, and she crouched low to stabilize it and to avoid being seen. She was nearly over the court, far too high above the seats to jump down, but ahead of her there was another catwalk, perpendicular to her, which ran across the hall and back to the top of the seating. Stormi stood, holding the rails on each side of the catwalk, and made her way slowly across. Below her, people were beginning to move up into the seats, the ushers were selling programs, guards were patrolling the entrances, and, in the press boxes immediately below and to her right, men were smoking and staring at tiny TVs.

At the end of the catwalk, there was a twelve-foot drop to the highest row of seats. Stormi crouched and considered the jump. There was no one nearby at that moment; it was her best chance of making it unseen, and the moment would not last. She looked around quickly, heart pounding, then swung herself down over the end of the catwalk, hung for a second by her hands, and then dropped. Her heels hit the top of the upright seat bottom, pushing it down and causing her to bang her knees on the seat in front and to jolt her backside against the armrest.

It was over in a second. Her body reverberated with the impact, and the pain began to seep into her brain. But there she was, sitting in the last row of Aberdeen Hall. She looked around. A man sitting about ten rows down glanced back at her, made an annoyed face, and turned away.

Stormi was safe.

And the game was soon to begin.

Waiting for the warrant to be delivered to him, Cox sat alone in his office and smoked. Five freshly rolled cigarettes lay in a neat row on his desk, prepared in advance for the long night ahead. Now he smoked slowly and rested. It was 7:06 P.M.

He knew it was his duty to arrest Hedstrom at the first possible moment—that is, the first moment he had access to him. Even waiting until halftime was a stretch. But he wondered about his motives. He would be arresting Hedstrom in front of the press, and in front of Hedstrom's adoring public. He knew, of course, that no matter how he made the arrest, Hedstrom would go to the press with the Chappelle story. By arresting Hedstrom in such a spectacularly public way, he'd be telling Hedstrom and the world, I've got nothing to hide. I can't be bought. I'm just a good cop doing his job. Yeah. But what was it really about? It was about his vanity, his ego, his pride. It was his way of saying to Hedstrom, I'm not going to let you bully me, motherfucker. I don't care what you've got on me. It embarrassed Cox that he could feel that way, that he could ever use his authority as a cop to satisfy a personal beef. But where the personal beef and the professional duty coincide? Shit, he knew he wasn't immune. Who was?

Barris's law review article lay open and overturned on a corner of Cox's desk. He reached for it idly.

In the postmodern world, sex ultimately needs no defense, for events stripped of meaning are mere happenings in time, moments unfettered by consequence. We have arrived at cat consciousness. The evidence is everywhere—in the ever-increasing incidence of violent crime, the ever-decreasing age of sexual maturity, and in the awful poverty of our culture, our arts, our politics. It's the moment that matters. Memories are short, or nonexistent. There is no such thing as history or historicity.

It is as if our obsession with information has returned us through the ancient night of time back to an age when there was no information—when there was mere day-to-day survival, no choices to be made, and it would have occurred to no one but a madman to consider his place in the world. Selfish or selfless, we are but worms with clothes and TV and the Internet. Male or female, we are nothing but our grotesque appetites.

And we are returned as well to a predatory consciousness.

193

We must pursue our game to survive, without morality or the mediation of any law but the natural law: survival of the fittest. The strongest, smartest, quickest, the most fertile—in short, the best-adapted creatures survive. And this is not merely a defensive philosophy; if survival means destroying one's enemies first, then the offensive must be taken. The natural world is no place for bleeding hearts and no place for lawmakers.

Lawmakers and those who interpret and implement the law will doubtless continue to operate on the assumption that their formulaic responses to events have real-world consequences beyond the lives of the individuals engaged in the instant controversy—that is, their interventions serve to "make the world a better place," or serve to "do justice," or serve to "put the injured party back in the place he would have been in had the injury not occurred." The antiporn feminist is the paradigm of this wrongheadedness of the law; she would legislate safer relations between the sexes by banning pornography and any other material that didn't meet her sexual standard. But no, it simply can't be done. Paradoxically, these strenuous efforts serve only to render unreal the realities of the natural world in all its glorious danger, disease, and disaster. The law is antievolutionary, anti-Darwinist, antiliberty, antitruth. As the current locution would have it, "Shit happens." I would add, "Sex happens." Let sex happen in the frankly naked, unencumbered, postmodern now.

Death happens, too. That was one Barris hadn't counted on, Cox mused, vaguely annoyed. Having reached the end of the article, he felt suddenly included among the objects of Barris's derision, being one of those who implement the law. Was the man really suggesting that we'd be better off in a natural world where the strongest, least scrupulous survive? Without laws and those who enforce them? Or was that a prescription for the extinction of humanity?

Cox looked up to find Farrell materialized at his door, smiling at the sight of him reading Barris's article, her concern and regard for Cox apparent in the gleam of her eyes. "Reading for pleasure?"

"No," Cox replied dourly. "Quite the opposite."

"Is this a good time for that talk we were going to have?"

Cox's heart sank; he'd forgotten it, deliberately, he knew. "Well, actually, no," he said, cursing his cowardice. "Another day. I've got a lot on my mind."

"You say when," she said, and she left him with a chaste wink.

Twenty minutes later, Cox leaned his elbow on top of the squad car and rested his head in his palm as he watched the other officers slowly exit the station. Nobody said a word. The four cops who were to accompany him and Farrell—Perry, Adams, and McMichael and Stewart, two experienced cops, whom Cox could count on if things got nasty—had sat somberly through the briefing, stunned upon being told the identity of the subject of the arrest warrant that Cox held in the inside pocket of his coat. Now the cops fell into their cars and contemplated arresting the coach in front of fifteen thousand basketball fans. The TV cameras would be there, too, although it was expected that the local stations carrying the game would have gone to their halftime commercials before the arrest was made. But it would surely be captured on video for replay on the news for days to come.

The six of them would have to do. Cox couldn't bear the thought of bringing more cops along to arrest one presumably unarmed man. Of course, the worst he expected of Hedstrom was a nose-to-nose shouting match or a thrown punch.

He waited fifteen more minutes to be sure the crowd was settled and the game had begun before they arrived. At 7:45, they took off, a phalanx of three cars gliding up Chestnut Street toward Aberdeen Hall, about eight minutes from the HPD. The streets of Harrison were deserted, as they always were on game nights, and when the cops arrived at the parking lot, the ocean of cars surrounding the hall was tranquil, the parking lot lights shimmering gently on the car tops.

195

They stopped directly in front of the main entrance. As Cox emerged from his car, the muffled roar of the crowd inside washed over him.

"Shhhit," Cox whispered, feeling the adrenaline begin to surge. He and Farrell led the four others into the building. Cox nodded to the girl in the box office, exchanged greetings of "Hey" with the two security guards—retired cops—and then ascended the left ramp into the hall.

At the top of the ramp, the cops stopped and surveyed the crowd. They stood just behind the box seats, which put twenty rows between them and the court. Their vantage point was to the left of midcourt, not quite even with the basket, on the home side of the court. Down and to their right, Coach Hedstrom paced on the sidelines, his green sweater, absurdly long on his huge back, forming a kind of bright green marker, a point of reference around which everything else in the hall seemed to orbit.

Ohio State was leading, 18–16, with twelve minutes and change to go in the half. The other cops had already settled themselves in, leaning against the ramp walls and following the action. Cox folded his arms across his chest and did the same.

By the time the game had started, even the last row had filled with ticket holders. Stormi moved out into the aisle when her seat was claimed, mumbling politely to avoid creating a scene, and then stood leaning against the outer wall of the press box to her left.

Below her lay the arena and its row after row of seats, and there, the center of everyone's attention, was her prey.

It's so different to see him here in his glory, she thought, our hero, our beloved, the man upon whom all our hopes rise and fall. They don't know him, don't know how evil he is.

I know. And soon they'll know, too.

Nora observed the game with an absence of interest only associated with the dead in Indiana. She was barely aware of the score, needing to remind herself now and then of who had the ball at any given moment.

She knew she should not have come. Her body ached with pain and exhaustion. She needed sleep desperately. And the game's ceaseless drive from basket to basket, the empathetic straining effort of everyone around her to score Sagamore baskets, set in relief her sense of the unreality of all that had happened in the past twenty-four hours. With periodic glances at her watch, she reminded herself that a day earlier at that time she had had dinner with Weesie and Stormi, that she had not known the depth of Stormi's relationship with Barris, that she had not known that Stormi knew of her affair with Barris. Her face grew hot with a deep, excoriating shame.

As halftime approached, Nora decided that she'd had enough of waiting for Cox and whatever historic event was going to happen. She got up out of her seat, gathered her coat and cap and bag, and made her way apologetically across the row of seats and out toward the aisle.

Stormi noticed a tall woman stand up a dozen rows in front of her. She knew that the woman was familiar, but she could not place her until a guy in back of the woman shouted for her to get out of the way, and the woman turned briefly and frowned before making her way out to the aisle.

Stormi's heart started beating very fast, and she sensed her hand moving, almost involuntarily, to touch the gun in her pocket, to feel its weight in her palm.

Her mind raced. Why is *she* here?

When Nora reached the aisle, Stormi pushed herself from the wall and slipped quickly into the shadow of the press box.

A foul was called on Indiana, and Ohio's giant Todd Alpert was sent to the line, quieting the crowd.

Nora had taken two steps down the aisle toward the exit when she felt in her coat pocket for her keys and realized that her gloves were missing. She cursed to herself at the thought that she'd have to go back across the row of seats, past the gauntlet of knees and feet, to where she was sitting and search the floor for her gloves. But as she

197

turned and started up the steps, she glanced up, and her eyes met Stormi's.

The sight of Stormi knocked the breath out of Nora, and she had to pause for a moment to recover. Her black eye suddenly pulsed with pain, and Nora touched her fingers to it, cooling it with her cold fingertips, as she stared into Stormi's face in the shadows.

Nora took two steps up the aisle toward Stormi. Stormi took two steps down, and with eyes locked, the women moved toward each other, Nora still gingerly touching her face, Stormi with her hand on the gun in her jacket pocket.

As Nora approached Stormi, she looked hard at the girl, at Stormi's ashen, terrified face, and her own startled fear turned to pity.

"Stormi," Nora said, "are you all right?"

Stormi stared at her, disbelieving, immobile, unable to speak.

Nora observed the confusion on Stormi's face. "Listen, I'm glad I ran into you," she said. "I'm sorry about what happened today. Maybe I shouldn't have gone to your house. I just wanted to explain to your ma that I—"

"I need to talk to you," Stormi blurted. "I mean, private."

Nora nodded. "All right."

"Let's get outta here." Stormi stepped around Nora and headed down the aisle toward the exit.

Nora followed, hoping for an answer.

Stormi led Nora down the exit ramp and into the outer corridor, where Stormi glanced quickly around her, searching for a place to do what she had to do.

Lawyer Lumsey. There was no escaping this woman, this smothering creature, and Stormi cursed herself for not having known better than to call her, no matter how bad it got, no matter how much trouble she was in. At the time, she thought it was funny to wake up Lumsey and beg her to come down to the lockup to rescue her, perfect, in its way, to call Barris's bitch, the uptight one, the one Barris mocked as weak, the big girl with the weak heart.

And it was true. Now Lumsey was following her like a dog;

Stormi almost laughed to think of it, Lumsey so full of warmth and concern, so oblivious, so pathetic, as deserving of death as Hedstrom.

Across the corridor was a refreshment concession, where a boy behind the counter glanced up from a magazine to give Stormi the once-over. Down the sloping corridor, she knew, about a third of the way around the stadium, was the main entrance, where the guards were on duty. Up the corridor, there was nothing but a concrete wall, interrupted by a shallow alcove, about seven feet across and five feet deep, beyond which was a set of rest rooms.

Stormi touched the sleeve of Nora's jacket and clumsily guided her up the corridor a few yards, where she glanced into the alcove, hardly believing how easy it had become. Set within the alcove was a maintenance closet, about six feet deep, with sink, mop and bucket, and shelves full of rolls of toilet paper.

There, Stormi thought.

Stormi led Nora into the alcove, then stepped into the maintenance closet, which was dark, cool, dank. Nora followed, mystified by the secrecy, but not suspecting that she might be in danger until she was inside the murky, narrow room, looking into Stormi's shining eyes, and Stormi drew the dull black pistol from inside her jacket.

19

With seven minutes left in the half, the Sagamores took a one-point lead on a couple of three-point shots by Tommy Owens, the six-foot-ten-inch sophomore who was Hedstrom's fondest hope for a championship season two years hence. Hedstrom clapped his hands and grinned with pleasure. Cox watched the other cops watching the game and exchanged glances every few moments with Farrell, who felt guilty enough about enjoying herself to check in with the boss.

Hedstrom's grin faded when a whistle was blown on Owens for interference. Hedstrom flew into an apoplectic rage. The action stopped as Hedstrom went nose-to-nose with the official who'd made the call, and the crowd was abruptly quieted by the hope of catching a few of Hedstrom's choice words.

Cox watched Hedstrom do battle.

The gun hung in the air between them, suspended at the end of Stormi's arm like a dog held at bay.

A jolt of fear rushed through Nora's body. She wanted desperately to lift her feet and flee, but she could not will herself to move. She stood there, panting ridiculously, trying to catch a breath.

"Don't you move," Stormi murmured. "You ain't goin' nowhere."

Nora stared at her.

"Ya piece a shit."

Stormi leaned back against the closet wall and laughed; now she and Nora were three feet apart, against opposite walls, with no place to back away. The rise and fall of the crowd noise and the ragged yells of the cheerleaders echoed across the corridor and into the alcove. Nora felt herself begin to sweat, and suddenly the stench of ammonia and mildew and urine overwhelmed her senses.

"Why?" Nora whispered. "Why are you doing this?"

"Because I got a job ta do," Stormi murmured. "And you make me sick."

"What job?"

"None of yer fuckin' business."

"What do you want me to do?"

"Die."

"Why?"

Stormi laughed. " 'Cause I hate you."

"What job do you need to do?"

"I'm not gonna fuckin' tell ya!" Stormi shouted.

"Is it about Sunni?" Nora whispered, her throat constricting painfully.

"Sunni! Yeah, it's about Sunni."

"What is it?"

"Yer such a fuckin' idiot." Stormi waved the gun back and forth at Nora's chest. "You're never fuckin' satisfied, are you? Right? Am I right?" She gripped the gun with two hands and pointed it directly at Nora's chest. "*Am I right?*" Her voice rose with anger. "*Am I right?*"

Nora whispered, "I don't know what you're talking about."

Stormi laughed. "You can be damn sure I'm right." She wiped her forehead on her sleeve. "She trusted that bastard, you understand that? Man, that was my twin got blown away. And for what?" She scratched the back of her head, shaking spasmodically. "Uh-uh, man. He didn't have to do that. She never would have said a word. Never."

Nora stared at her, uncomprehending. "Never would have said a word about what?"

Stormi straightened her arms and held the gun up toward Nora's face. "You stupid bitch! Don't you know? I'm the one she got to do it with her. I'm the one who helped her kill that bastard."

The game seesawed for a few minutes, the teams trading buckets and the lead, but with a minute and a half to go, the Sagamores had posted three in a row for a five-point advantage. The crowd was riotous with joy, but Cox's heart was heavy with anxiety as he watched Hedstrom pace, growl, curse, and fret.

When the clock ran below one minute, Cox gestured to Farrell to tap the other cops and to begin to prepare to move. It was clear that there'd be at least a couple time-outs before the end of the half, eating up another five minutes. The first one came with fourteen seconds, and Cox took the opportunity to point out the route they'd take down to courtside. The second one came with 5.1 seconds left.

Cox rubbed his forehead and waited while the time-out ran down, glancing back and forth from his watch to Hedstrom to make sure he didn't bolt when the buzzer sounded.

Ten seconds before play was set to resume, Cox stepped out in front of the cluster of cops and moved swiftly out the entrance ramp and across the lane in back of the front rows of seats. Play resumed and Cox turned the corner to go down the aisle toward courtside. The Sagamores had the ball out of bounds under their own net. The ball was quickly tossed to Joe Bailey, who shunted it over to Owens. Owens faked a pass to Jones, then boosted a three-pointer that carommed off the rim as the buzzer sounded.

Hedstrom's hand shot out in front of his face and formed a fist, which he hammered against the air in disappointment. He shook his head, lips tight with determination, and he was about to follow his boys into the locker room when out of the corner of his eye he saw Cox step onto the hardwood.

Hedstrom did a double take, and on the second take, he saw Farrell and Perry a step behind Cox and the other three cops at the top of the aisle. He reversed the motion of his body, which was already on its way toward the locker room, with a wrenching twist that seemed to turn the players and assistant coaches around with it. As movement toward the locker room halted, the attention of the spectators was pulled in bit by bit, and a wave of silence passed over the crowd.

Hedstrom charged over to Cox, his face livid with rage. "What the fuck are you doing? What the fuck is this?"

Cox glanced up toward the cops at the top of the aisle, who started to move slowly down toward him.

"I have a warrant for your arrest for the murders of James Barris and Sunni Skye. You have the right to remain silent. You have the right to the presence of an attorney—"

"Hey! Hey! You son of a bitch! What the fuck—"

Cox took the warrant out of his pocket and handed it to Hedstrom, who looked hard at the warrant, his gaze skittering over the numbered paragraphs of the affidavit that set out the evidence supporting the arrest. "This is bullshit. It's crazy." He swallowed. He glared at Cox. "You know what this means, right? You know what's gonna happen, right?"

Cox said quietly, "Do you understand your rights?"

Hedstrom grabbed Cox by the upper arm and bent his frame down over Cox, leaning hard into the detective's face. "You stupid fuck," he hissed as Cox angrily shook Hedstrom's hand away. "You're going down for this, asshole. And not just you—"

"Shut up, for Christ's sake," snapped Cox.

Hedstrom stepped away from Cox and dropped his huge hands to his sides, looking as if he was about to cry.

"Tina, cuff him," Cox said suddenly. "Let's move."

Farrell drew the handcuffs from her jacket pocket instantly and had already slapped them over one wrist before Hedstrom was able to jerk his hands up to his chest. "Son of a bitch," Hedstrom said. "You don't need to handcuff me. It's embarrassing."

"Finish the job, Tina."

An awareness of the crowd closed in again upon Cox, triggering

203

an adrenaline rush. He glanced up the aisle, trying not to gaze around like a tourist, and nodded to the three cops above him on the steps to indicate that he was coming through. Cox then took Hedstrom by the arm and led him up the aisle, accompanied by Adams. Perry, McMichael, and Stewart brought up the rear.

At the edge of the court, the assistant coaches, refs, and players had assembled and now stood horror-struck. As the cops led Hedstrom up the aisle, the people nearest the procession stood to get a better view, and within seconds, every spectator in the hall was standing. From somewhere above in the bleacher seats, a chant began, the word *coach* over and over, accompanied by a resounding hand clap, rhythmic and insistent, and within seconds, it had spread throughout the hall.

The cops tightened their ranks around Hedstrom. Cox wished, too late, that he'd left the squad cars at the players' entrance in back and avoided this march through the crowd. Nothing like hindsight. The cops steeled themselves and continued to move forward.

Students started spilling out of the seats and down the aisles to form a mass of bodies surging chaotically behind the tiny knot of blue uniforms surrounding Cox and his prisoner. The security guards, spread one to a section throughout the hall, were helpless to block the aisles. Cox cursed and pushed Hedstrom tighter between himself and Farrell, praying that none of Hedstrom's adoring fans would have the nerve to block their way.

Sweat stung Nora's eyes as she calculated the odds of escape. Three feet away, across a cement floor slick with mildew and splashes of soap, Stormi rambled on, at times incoherently, still clutching the gun with a grip so rock-steady, it looked like the gun were keeping Stormi from falling over. Nora knew that it would soon be the end of the half, and people would be heading for the rest rooms, coming right past the alcove, and maybe she could dash out into the moving crowd before Stormi knew what was happening. But now it was intensely quiet. Even the crowd noise had faded, strangely, as if there were no one in the place but the two of them, and no sound but the

204

murmuring of Stormi's voice and the intermittent drip of the janitor's sink at the back of the closet.

"I didn't know. . . . She trusted him. . . . There was so much fuckin' money, man, I shoulda known he'd . . ." Stormi's mouth opened in a silent laugh that ended in little shaking coughs.

"Kill who, Stormi? Who? Do you mean Jim? Did you help Sunni kill Jim?"

"So much fuckin' money. Why'd he kill her? If he'da been smart, he wouldn'ta killed her at all. Or did he just not give a shit about money? Or a life?"

Nora said evenly, "Who, Stormi? Who do you think killed Sunni?"

Stormi regarded Nora. "You're a fuckin' idiot. . . . If ya hadn't been here, I coulda wasted the fucker."

"I don't know who you're talking about. And I didn't know anything about Sunni or you killing Jim . . . or anybody."

Nora breathed as shallowly and silently as she could, while her mind struggled to make sense of what Stormi was telling her. She regarded Stormi impassively, trying to project an unthreatening mien. Stormi leaned her head back against the wall and appeared to be in some pain as she grimaced and pressed on her upper stomach with one hand. Her eyelids fluttered and it was clearly with some effort that she snapped herself into alertness.

"Fuck," Stormi muttered.

"Are you all right?"

"No." Stormi pushed away from the wall and shook her upper body, struggling to clear her brain. "I need some crank."

"Crank? You mean like drugs? Like heroin or something?"

Stormi gave her a look of mock incredulity. "Yeah. Ya got any money?"

"Some. Maybe fifteen dollars."

Stormi laughed. "That's not money."

Nora looked at Stormi's face, which was shining with sweat, and at her body, palsied with craving for the drug, and felt a brief surge of pity, followed by a dawning sense of opportunity.

"I can get you more money," she said. "At the bank machine. Please. Let's go there. I'll give you some money and we'll forget this ever happened."

Stormi appeared to consider this for a moment. She kept her eyes locked with Nora's and she held the gun pointed outward from her stomach, her finger curled securely around the trigger.

Nora returned Stormi's stare and assumed what she hoped was a kindly expression.

Stormi said nothing.

Out of the silence, murmurs filtered down from the hall, and within seconds, the murmurs congealed into the sound of a chant, a word shouted out over and over, gathering voices and intensity.

"Turn around."

Nora froze.

"Turn around and put yer hands against the wall."

Nora obeyed.

"Put yer face against the wall. So yer lookin' out."

Nora placed her cheek against the rough, cool cement, facing so that she was looking out toward the alcove. She heard Stormi take two steps across the closet to reach her.

Now's the time, Nora thought. I've got to run for it. But before that thought was complete, she felt the barrel of Stormi's gun at the base of her skull and Stormi's hand pressing her head against the wall.

"I didn't come here for money, ya stupid fuck. I can git all the fuckin' money I want."

Nora spread her hands against the wall, her mind swiftly calculating the position of Stormi's body and the amount of force she could achieve by pushing against the wall.

The chant grew louder, now accompanied by the vibration of feet, of bodies moving in a crowd. What the hell is that? Nora thought. Halftime? If I can hold her off for a few more moments—

"Please," Nora murmured. "Please don't. I didn't—"

"I gotta kill ya," Stormi whispered behind her ear, her voice breaking with emotion. "I got to. They gonna catch me fer sure, but I don't care. If I can't kill him, I'll kill you, 'cause somebody's got to pay. And ya'd probably kill me if ya had the chance." Keeping her hand on Nora's head and the gun pressed against her neck, Stormi slowly stepped back, drawing her body away from Nora. "Ya won't git that chance."

Cox strode evenly forward, clutching Hedstrom's upper arm tightly as they moved down the entrance ramp and out into the corridor. With every step, he was aware of the pressure of the monstrous crowd now squeezing into the bottleneck of the entrance ramp behind him, its chant ricocheting cacophonously, deafeningly. Ahead of them now, too, fans who had exited from the other side of the hall were spilling out of the ramps and forming a phalanx across the lobby, waiting to catch a glimpse of their hero in handcuffs. The press guys, who had managed to take the back elevator from the press booth down to the entrance level, were pushing through the gathering fans. Bright white splashes of the photographers' flashes peppered the air, and shoulder-mounted video cameras were already recording Hedstrom's descent toward the lobby and Cox's steely, terrified expression.

Something was happening, something impossible, and Nora listened and waited as she felt the building shake and the riotous shouting grow nearer and wilder. She could see flashes of light out in the corridor and then figures dashing past.

She waited for the blast, for the end. Stormi's hand, rough and sweaty, pushed against her head. The muzzle of the gun pressed painfully into the small at the back of her skull. Stormi's breath was coming faster, heavier now. Why hadn't she pulled the trigger?

"What th' fuck are they doin' out there?" Stormi murmured.

Nora bolted. She swung her body out and away from the gun and sprinted with every muscle pushing hard, her legs straining against the floor, her arms swimming against the air, every breath putting distance between herself and that gun. She heard herself cry out, an ugly keening groan from the chest, the product of fear, as she prayed not to hear the crack of the gun behind her.

She ran, stumbling, crying, into the corridor, directly into the path of the cops and their prisoner. She could not believe what she was seeing. She pulled up short, trying to stop her headlong rush. Her mouth opened to speak as she saw the cops, their eyes widening, stunned, hands reaching guardedly toward their guns, and Hedstrom contorting protectively away.

Then she heard it, the crack of the gun behind her. Nora fell to her knees, pain radiating from her kneecaps like cracks in a broken windshield, and then she fell forward, her palms smacking the cement floor, breaking her fall as her face came swiftly down to meet the cement. Over the clamorous ringing in her ears, Nora heard three more shots in rapid succession.

Hedstrom slumped, dropping heavily in Cox's grip. Farrell cried out, her scream joining the shrill noise that burst from the scattering throng, and she swiftly knelt to ease Hedstrom down.

The shots from Stormi's gun were answered almost instantly by one well-placed round from Perry; it hit just below the collarbone on Stormi's left side, causing her left arm to jerk spasmodically. The gun flipped from her hand, and Stormi crumpled as Perry and Adams rushed her.

Cox bent quickly to help Farrell catch Hedstrom's collapsing body. As they placed Hedstrom down, Farrell lifted his head, revealing a bloody hole under his right eye, the skin blown open, the bone shattered beneath, blood bubbling gently up from the wound. Hedstrom's facial muscles were still. Farrell lifted her hand from where it had rested on Hedstrom's chest and touched his face. The movement of her fingers left bloody streaks across his skin, and she noticed with a start that her palm was covered with blood. Looking down, Farrell saw that Hedstrom's shirt was soaked with blood, and more blood was silently pooling around his body.

Within seconds, most of the mob had fled up the corridor, out the main entrance, or back into the hall. Then the word was passed around in timid shouts of "It's okay; they got the guy," and people straightened their backs and tried to figure out what had happened.

Word came around first that Hedstrom had been shot, then seconds later that he was dead. Many in the crowd sat down dazedly and burst into tears. Students hugged one another and cried openly.

On the court, the BHU and Ohio State players and coaches knelt together in a ragged formation before the Sagamores' basket. Weeping, some sobbing uncontrollably, they clasped their hands together and prayed. The cheerleaders and the band came out to the court, too, and some spectators ventured down to join them, all falling to their knees in silent, tearful horror.

Luther Cox gripped Nora's hand and smiled as comfortingly as he could into her half-open eyes.

"You're all right," he said. "It doesn't look like you were hit."

Nora's face was contorted with pain, her breathing rapid and shallow. "I'm okay," she murmured. "I just hope I didn't fracture a kneecap."

"That can be fixed," Cox said. "That, at least, can be fixed."

Nora closed her eyes and nodded. Cox patted her hand hard a couple of times and stood as the emergency medical team came rushing toward her.

20

SATURDAY, DECEMBER 10

S hreds of tobacco littered Cox's desk, and there rose from his ashtray a monstrous, stinking heap of ashes and tar-stained cigarette ends, the product of a night that had already extended to 7:15 A.M.

"First of the year, Luther," said Bieberschmidt, yawning. "It's not too far off now. What the hell are you going to do when you can't smoke in here?"

"You're going to have to arrest me, Hank." Cox licked the rolling paper and smoothed the cigarette shut.

"No exceptions, Luther. Every city, county, and state office building goes smoke-free as of January first."

"Maybe I'll quit."

"Yeah, right."

"Why shouldn't I?"

"You'll never quit."

"Have a little faith. I can change. What makes you think I can't change?"

"You're a nicotine addict, that's why."

Cox took a long drag on the cigarette, then blew the smoke slowly through his nostrils. "Smoking is the only pleasure I have left," he said.

"I'm sorry to hear you say that."

"Sad, isn't it?"

"Mmm."

Cox shut his eyes tight and breathed deeply. "Shit, I'm tired."

Bieberschmidt plopped into a chair opposite Cox's desk and regarded him gently.

"You've done a good job, Luther, for what it's worth. We have the girl. We have Hedstrom. A loose end here and there? No big deal."

Cox shook his head. "Thanks, Hank, but I don't like loose ends. Hedstrom will be telling his story as soon as it suits him. And then there's Lydon."

"He won't bother us."

"As long as we don't bother him."

"Right."

"But it's time we bothered him."

Bieberschmidt looked away.

"It's time, Hank. It's time to put Lydon out of business. And if somebody has to take some heat for letting Chappelle go, I'm willing to do it."

"I can't let you do that. I'm not gonna see you lose your job because of something I did."

Cox shrugged. "I don't want this job anymore, Hank." As he said the words, a frisson of fear passed over him; he knew in his heart that he meant it, that he was through at long last, and he felt himself struggling to restrain a flood of emotion.

Cox's hand trembled as he stubbed out the cigarette. "I'm tired. I mean . . . I'm really *tired*. I can't do my job . . . if I'm constantly looking over my shoulder. If I'm worried about getting caught for something *I* did, then how am I going to catch the other guy? How can I investigate a crime if I'm worried that the guy I'm after has something on me?"

Bieberschmidt said nothing.

"I can't," Cox went on. "I just can't do it anymore. So I'm suggesting to you that we pick up Larry Crowder and get the prosecutor to plea bargain in exchange for testimony about Lydon's pros-

211

titution and drug activities. We do the same thing with the girls. And then there's Stormi Skye. The kid hasn't shut up since she got here. I'm sure she'd be happy to talk about Lydon."

Bieberschmidt nodded.

"The only thing Lydon knows," said Cox, "is what Barris told him. Barris heard it from Hedstrom. That puts Lydon one dead man away from the truth. That's far enough to leave lots of room for error. And no proof to corroborate any of it. Until Hedstrom speaks up. So if I want to take the fall for it, I can do that without implicating anyone else. Everything else is just innuendo."

"If that's true, then why bother taking a fall? Who's going to believe Lydon if there's no proof?"

"The point, Hank, is to get the monkey off my back. I don't know who else knows. God knows how many people Hedstrom told about it. Or the mayor told. Or Barris told. Or Lydon told." Cox smiled ruefully. "I hate this shit, Hank. I just want to admit the mistake and get it over with."

"You're an idiot, Cox. And you're so goddamn righteous, you really make me feel like shit."

"How many years till retirement, Hank?"

Bieberschmidt looked at him angrily.

"I wouldn't blow it, either, if I were you."

Through the long, difficult hours of the night, Hedstrom had been alternately hostile and cooperative. His injuries had been far less severe than initially thought; one of the bullets from Stormi Skye's gun had blasted open his cheek, rendering him unconscious, but had passed through the flesh of his face and slammed into the corridor's cinder-block wall. Another bullet had pierced his side, breaking a rib, but he had been more than lucky, and his survival was, to his fans, further proof of God's Hoosier allegiance.

It was out of concern for the behavior of these fans that Cox had allowed the rumor of Hedstrom's death that had swept through Aberdeen Hall to fester; no statement on Hedstrom's condition was issued until he had been safely transported to Harrison Hospital.

Once his wounds had been cleaned and patched, Hedstrom had become almost childlike in his willingness to tell the cops what they needed to know and in wanting in return to be treated with the warmth and kindness an adult shows a hurt child. At times, he was the wary suspect, closemouthed unless he was invoking a constitutional right; at other times, he was hysterical with remorse. It was clear from the start that he did not want to go through the agony of a trial and that he would ultimately be willing to make a deal. Cox had suggested to Bieberschmidt that any questioning of Hedstrom be put off until he had recuperated from the shock of the attempt on his life. Bieberschmidt vetoed the idea; he wanted to ensure that he got a confession of Hedstrom's role in Barris's murder, and the longer they waited to interrogate him, the less likely that became.

Sitting at Hedstrom's bedside through the night had been Cal Gipson, a Harrison lawyer, whose pot belly and folksy demeanor masked a strategic acumen. The call from Hedstrom's girlfriend had interrupted Gipson's preparations for bed, Gipson having for most of his adult life kept farmer's hours—in bed by ten, up by four. Gipson, a former high school basketball star, had known Don Hedstrom for decades, and he had handled Hedstrom's three divorces—with assistance from Barris. A former prosecutor, Gipson also had considerable experience in criminal defense. Within fifteen minutes of the call, Gipson was at the hospital, conferring privately with Hedstrom. An hour and a half later, he was ready to bargain for Hedstrom's life.

Cox kept his team working during the negotiations; while he and Bieberschmidt and the county prosecutor haggled with Gipson, Farrell and Quade executed a search warrant of Hedstrom's home. The search yielded little of immediate use—just a print of the tire tread from Hedstrom's Mercedes, and shoes and other items of clothing that Hedstrom might have worn on the nights in question. Every piece of evidence in their possession supported the theory that Hedstrom and Sunni had murdered Barris, that Hedstrom had murdered Sunni to eliminate the witness, and that Stormi had sought revenge against Hedstrom for her sister's death, but it wasn't nearly enough

213

to overcome a juror's reasonable doubt. Cox's best evidence was in Barris's murder: The fingerprint, footprints, and tire prints all placed Hedstrom at the scene of the crime. In Sunni Skye's murder, Cox had the dubious account of the mechanic who had spotted Hedstrom that evening, and who had agreed upon further questioning that it could have been the coach, whom he idolized and could never imagine seeing up close, but he wasn't sure. There were hair and fiber samples recovered from the motel room yet to be analyzed, and Farrell didn't hold out much hope there. The one potentially crucial piece of evidence was the debris from under Sunni's fingernails; it appeared to contain blood, and there were some fresh scrapes on Hedstrom's wrists and forearms.

But after Stormi Skye's confession, Cox's assumptions evaporated like morning fog, revealing a landscape wholly unexpected.

Following the shootings, Stormi had been taken to Harrison Hospital, just eight blocks from police headquarters. There, the hole Perry's bullet had blown through Stormi's upper chest was patched, and Stormi was given a room on the secure fifth floor—a section of rooms usually reserved for violent mental patients. Stormi was also given two cops for company, and by 11:30 that evening, she had received the first of several visits that night from Cox.

Stormi shook her head when Cox asked the routine questions about whether she had an attorney, whether she could afford an attorney, and whether she wanted one appointed for her.

"I don't want a lawyer," she said firmly, grasping Cox's wrist and looking straight into his eyes. "Lemme just confess and get the fuckin' thing done."

Cox noticed the needle marks on Stormi's inner arm, then wondered if the doctors had given her an opiate derivative to kill the pain from her wound. That would explain the strange forcefulness and clarity she exhibited; along with treating her wound, the doctors had given her a fix. Cox wondered if they had done so deliberately.

Cox was expecting a confession to the attempted murder of Don Hedstrom, a crime to which the state already had Stormi dead to

214

rights, with dozens of eyewitnesses. But Cox wasn't taking any chances. He needed to be sure that Stormi's level of medication and the type of drugs she had been given would not significantly impair her judgment or cause hallucinations, thereby spoiling the confession, which by law had to be rendered "knowingly, willingly, and voluntarily." So Cox asked a couple of doctors to examine Stormi's chart to verify that she was competent to confess. They did so, in the process confirming Cox's hunch that Stormi had been "fixed" to help her through her recovery.

"As I understand it," one doctor noted, "she'll have plenty of time to go cold turkey."

Cox returned to Stormi's room just after midnight with the Miranda waiver forms, a separate right to counsel waiver form, and a handheld cassette recorder. This statement would be provisional, awaiting the more formal videotaped confession, but Cox would not let the moment slip by. He switched on the recorder, identified himself and noted the time, place, and circumstances, and then, for the record, he read the waivers onto the tape and had Stormi verbally consent before signing the documents. Finally, he asked, "Stormi, did you shoot Don Hedstrom three times at Aberdeen Hall tonight?"

"Yeah, I guess I did."

"What do you mean, 'I guess I did'?"

"I just shot; I dunno how many times."

"Were you attempting to kill Don Hedstrom?"

"Yeah."

"Why did you want to kill Don Hedstrom?"

" 'Cause he killed Sunni."

"You think he killed your sister, Sunni?"

"Yeah."

"Stormi, did you attempt to shoot Nora Lumsey at Aberdeen Hall tonight?"

"Yeah."

"Why did you attempt to kill Nora Lumsey?"

"What about the other guy?"

"Who?"

"The guy me and sis killed."

"You and Sunni?"

"Yeah."

"Who did you kill?"

"Barris."

Cox's heart twisted painfully in his chest; the thought that he had wrongly arrested Hedstrom sent a rush of panic across his mind.

"James Barris? Three nights ago? In the pines by the cornfield?"

"Yeah."

"Tell me about it."

"It was a john," Stormi said. "One of Sunni's tricks asked her to do it. He needed somebody he could trust, he said, and he couldn't ask Lydon, 'cause he didn't trust Lydon, and Lydon wouldn't want to fuck up the good thing he got going by gettin' involved in a murder. He trusted Sunni. And he said there'd be a lot of money in it. A lot of money, like winnin' the fuckin' lottery. Fifty thousand. All she had to do was kill this guy. Dump the body out in the country. Don't leave any clues. And forget about it.

"She asked me to help her do it. The john said she could get somebody to help her so long as Sunni trusted her and didn't ever say who was payin' to have it done. So she asked me. I didn't think twice. I didn't know who the john was, not then, but I knew Barris and I didn't have any problems killin' the bastard. And for that kind of money, are you kiddin'?

"It was so fuckin' easy. Barris was a fuckin' regular, for both of us, so she told him we'd have somethin' special for him at home, at the trailer. The guy was a fuckin' coke freak. So she told him I was scorin' some really good blow and he should come to the trailer and we could all fuck there and he could score some blow from me. Sunni had already worked it out with Ma so that Ma would take Garth and stay with Kenny—that's our older brother.

"I got some blow, just to show Barris, like I was gonna sell it to him, and I showed up after midnight. They had already fucked, him and Sunni, and they was sittin' around on Sunni's bed, her in her

216

underwear, him in Sunni's bathrobe, wearin' sunglasses and grinnin' like crazy. He looked like a fool, weird, but like he was so pleased with himself. They was smokin' cigarettes and takin' hits from a bottle of Southern Comfort. Barris passed me the bottle and I took a hit.

"Sunni put on a CD, it was ZZ Top, somethin' loud and noisy in case things got out of hand. Barris was smokin' and bobbin' his head with the music, lookin' like some crazy old freak. We sat around for a little while, drinkin', gettin' comfortable. Like it wasn't polite, you know, just to do the deal.

"I had two grams I was gonna sell him for two hundred. I had it in some tinfoil and after a while I just took it out and said, 'Y'a interested?' He grinned and nodded and touched it with his finger and tasted it, then nodded again like the stuff was okay, then said, 'Fine, that'll do,' and then he offered a line to each of us, his treat, he said. We both said no, we was too nervous.

"So he got his wallet out of his pants, paid me my two hundred, and in the wallet he had a little mirror and razor blade. He cut himself a line and started rolling up a twenty. Sunni looked at me like 'Now's the time,' so I got up. I said I had to take a leak. I had this bit of plastic clothesline in my pocket I picked up in the yard. I walked around in back of him. He was busy gettin' ready to snort the coke. I took the clothesline out, got a tight grip on it with both hands. I waited till he snorted the blow and he was sniffin', sittin' up straight, breathin' it in real hard. Then I slipped the cord real quick over his head and pulled it tight, twisted it around like a knot. He fought like a motherfucker, grabbin' at the line, buckin' his body. Sunni tried to grab his hands, but he kicked her away.

"And then it was over. Just like that. He was buckin' real wild one second, then boom. I thought for a minute he was fakin' it, but he started to piss, and his neck felt like jelly under the cord.

"Sunni and I was both shakin' like crazy. She ran outside and threw up, and once she did it, I had to do it, too. Sunni was actin' really crazy. After she threw up, it was like she was really havin' a good time, really enjoyin' herself. She started laughin', and the ZZ

217

Top was still goin', and she started dancin' to it, out in the yard. I had to sit down. I sat on the steps and had a cigarette, and maybe it was twenty minutes later, the music stopped and we went back inside.

"We figured we'd dump him in the country somewhere. There weren't no point in buryin' him. We figured they'd be lookin' for him sooner or later and so they may as well find him. There was nothin' to connect him to us, anyway.

"So we got his keys out of his jacket, opened up the trunk of his car, and then we carried the body out there in a blanket, him still in the robe, usin' it like a kind of hammock, you know. We put him in the trunk. Sunni and me went back in and cleaned up the place, Sunni foldin' his clothes up real nice. Me, I took care of the blow and the wallet. I took the money out of it, and kept the blow and the mirror. We wasn't tryin' to make it look like a robbery or anything; it just was. We wasn't thinkin' cover-up or any such thing; we just wanted to git the body the hell out of there.

"Then Sunni drove his car and I followed in my mother's car. We was gonna take him to the state forest, but I figured there'd be rangers out there, so we agreed to take him down and dump him in a field somewhere. So she just started drivin' and I followed. I shoulda taken the lead, because she really didn't know where the hell she was goin'. A half hour later, I got fed up and I pulled out in front of her and made her stop. We was up north o' town—shit, we'd been goin' back and forth and in circles. We was by this dirt field, where the corn been chopped down, and I seen this big stand of pine out there, so I figgered that's as good a place as any, there bein' no houses around. So we go around and git ready to open the trunk, and Sunni's already actin' off the wall, but instead of bein' hyper, she's so serious, it scares the shit out of me. She's suddenly barkin' at me, givin' orders. It was weird, 'cause I couldn't catch her wavelength, like I always can, but I went ahead and did what she said anyway just to git it over with.

"So I open the trunk, and as I open it, the moonlight lit up his face, and we both jumped back six feet 'cause the son of a bitch is layin' there with his eyes open. Sunni then hauls off and hits me and we go back and I close the fucker's eyes. It takes both of us to pull his shoulders up out of the trunk. We got to drag him, bit by bit, out of the trunk and onto the ground, and then we sort of half-lift and half-drug him through the dirt and out to the tree, where we just drop him.

"Sunni told me to go back to the car and get the clothes and shoes, and as I go, I see she's doin' somethin' with the body, movin' it around, and I see there's somethin' shinin' in her hand. I don't think much of it until I git back with the clothes and I see the dude's mouth is all messed up, bloody, and she's slicing around the son of a bitch's dick with the razor blade he used to cut the coke.

"I whisper real loud, 'What the fuck are you doin'?' And she orders me to git back to the car. She's lookin' so angry and mean, and she's cryin', too, so I figger I'd just let her do what she got to do. Barris'd done some awful mean shit to me, and maybe he'd done somethin' worse to Sunni, I dunno.

"So she comes back and she asks me if I still got the cord I used to choke the guy. I had it bunched up in my jacket pocket, so I hand it to her. She goes and throws it by the body; then we both git in my ma's car and leave his car there. Sunni has me slow down next intersection we pass so she can see the road signs. Turns out we're just about ten minutes north of the center of town. We're both hungrier 'n hell, so we drive right to the McDonald's at Third Street. We both go into the bathrooms to wash up; then while I order the food, Sunni goes to call the john who ordered the killin' to tell him it was done and where the body was dumped and all that.

"We ate real quiet, comin' down from all the excitement, Sunni lookin' a little more like herself, and then I drive her to work and I go out for a couple beers with my buds.

"I drank too much and I ended up all fucked up—drivin' back, I could hardly see where I was goin'. And then I had to take a leak real bad and I couldn't wait or I was goin' to ruin the car, so I stopped and run out and took a leak by the side of the road, and when I git back, the fuckin' door's locked and—"

Cox let Stormi talk on, thanking God for the confession and for how much easier it made his job, at the same time hating the confession for the way it made him obsolete, swept away the long hours of his effort, highlighted the wrongheadedness of his assumptions. As he listened, he dwelled dreamily in his mind on the various blunders he'd made, wondering if his failure to undo the strands of the case was caused by his fear of the cover-up being disclosed, a failure of imagination, or just plain incompetence. He cringed at the thought that his lapse had resulted in Sunni's death, and in the attempts on Hedstrom's and Nora Lumsey's lives. It was all there at the scene of Barris's death, he thought gloomily, every goddamn thing I needed to know.

Stormi went on: "I didn't know who the john was and I didn't give a shit. Sunni got the money the next day and it was like Howdy, money! Sunni put it in the bank—I didn't have any bank account—she was gonna give it to me bit by bit so's I didn't waste it all at once.

"Then, when I found out Sunni was dead, I lost it, man. I really freaked. I couldn't git the money 'cause it was in her account. I figgered he done it, whoever the john was, and I figgered it had to be Hedstrom. I knew Sunni'd had him, that Sunni'd done players for him. He done it because he was afraid Sunni might talk. And he didn't know that I was the one who helped Sunni. And he didn't know that I knew that he was the one who hired Sunni to kill that guy.

"So I went after him. I didn't give a flyin' fuck what happened to me then, man. I wanted him dead. He killed my twin. That's like killin' me.

"I snuck into Aberdeen Hall and I was gonna go after him, but then the lawyer—Lumsey—was there, and she saw me, and it all got fucked. Then I started to come down real bad, man. I needed a fix, and I was sick in my stomach. Then all that weird shit started happenin', people yellin' and stompin', and then she ran and the coach come down the ramp like he done.

"I just started firin'. I shot the dude and—and I just kept shootin'. He went down real good, and I figgered I was gonna die anyway, so's I just kept shootin'. I couldn'ta stopped myself if I'd wanted to. I just had to shoot every fuckin' bullet I had.

"It's a damn good thing yer guy shot me when he did, or I woulda shot you, too."

The john. A voice on the telephone ordering up a killing just as easily as ordering a pizza. It was some, if small, consolation to Cox to have Stormi in custody, to have at least one of the instruments of Barris's death. But the john. Maybe it had been Hedstrom, and maybe not. Cox guessed that it had been, but it was a damn long road between a guess and a conviction.

After receiving Stormi's confession, Cox drove back to the station, feeling vaguely depressed about the case against Hedstrom in Barris's murder. He knew he'd have to recommend to the prosecutor that Hedstrom's charges be changed to conspiracy to commit murder, but he wasn't ready to do that. And there was no need for him to share the particulars of Stormi's confession with Gipson. Not yet.

And if he wanted a confession to Sunni Skye's murder, he'd need leverage, a bargaining chip.

At the station, Cox found Gipson and Bieberschmidt drinking coffee and chatting amiably in Bieberschmidt's office.

Gipson raised his eyebrows as Cox entered. "Well, Mr. Cox, please join us." He coughed a thick, phlegmy cough. "May I offer you a cigarette? It's ready-rolled, but I guarantee you it's fresh. Just opened the pack not fifteen minutes ago." He grinned and held out a box of unfiltered Pall Malls.

"Don't mind if I do," said Cox, pulling one out of the pack. "Thank you." Cox allowed Gipson to light the cigarette for him, and as he exhaled, Cox leaned over the desk to check the contents of the coffee cups. "Glad to see it's coffee you're drinking."

Gipson laughed and said, "Oh, yeah." Bieberschmidt nodded tolerantly. Despite his long friendship with Gipson, Bieberschmidt had at the start of this long night accepted the role of the hard-ass, do-it-by-the-book, positional negotiator, permitting Cox to act the flexible, sympathetic, accommodating one. Gipson, an experienced plea bargainer, knew exactly how to play off both men.

"How's the coach?" Cox said.

"At the moment, a mess," Gipson responded gravely. "He'll need a few days in the hospital. Then I'd like to take him home. You've got your charges filed. I'd be grateful if you'd leave him alone for a week or so."

Bieberschmidt said, "I'm sorry, Cal, but it's murder we're talking about."

Gipson nodded. "You really ought to let him go home."

"No can do," said Bieberschmidt. "Of course, you may have better luck with the prosecutor. If he charges the coach with voluntary manslaughter, he may recommend to the judge that we send the coach home for a half million in bail. If it's murder, there's no bail."

Gipson smiled. He knew that the charges and therefore the opportunity for bail were largely dependent on Bieberschmidt's assessment of the strength of the evidence. "The coach would be grateful to go home," Gipson said after a long silence. "By the same token, if he's not allowed to go, he'll be talking to the press. About a lot of things."

Cox felt Bieberschmidt's eyes on his face and avoided glancing back. He looked hard at Gipson. "Let him talk," he said.

"On Monday, of course, Hedstrom will enter an automatic not guilty plea," Gipson said softly. "And he'll keep his mouth shut about Chappelle. For the fans, for the university, for his family, for everybody, okay?"

"Uh-huh." Bieberschmidt took out a legal pad and scribbled notes; Cox hung back, glad to defer to Bieberschmidt on the morally questionable business of plea bargaining.

"And there's got to be bail."

"Uh-huh."

"Then later on we plead guilty, but to reckless homicide."

"In Barris's murder?"

"Yes."

"How do you figure that?"

"It wasn't meant to happen."

"And in Sunni Skye's murder?"

"Voluntary manslaughter. He gets a chance at parole."

A rush of relief raised the hairs on the back of Cox's neck.

"That's up to the prosecutor."

"You'll have some say in the matter."

"I want a confession. On video. The whole story. Both murders."

"Perhaps we can give you a confession."

"Good."

"If we get to go home. And the reckless homicide and voluntary manslaughter charges."

"I'll discuss it with the prosecutor. And we want the confession before he goes anywhere."

"I'll discuss it with my client."

Bruised but unbowed, Nora Lumsey padded around her small house wearing sweatpants and wishing she could wear a mask over her damaged face.

At Harrison Hospital, she had been poked, prodded, x-rayed, and CAT-scanned, all to the effect that she became the object of the doctors' marvel, a woman of steel. Her bones were neither cracked nor fractured, nor even the slightest bit injured. There was no structural damage whatsoever; it was only the flesh that had been harmed in her hard fall at Aberdeen Hall, only what showed—just her face and knees and forearms.

She had been offered the opportunity to stay overnight at the hospital, but Nora had insisted upon going home; she could walk, which was enough for her to get into bed that night and to get into her tub for a soak the next day—all she really wanted to do. And so she was released at 2:00 A.M. and driven home by Officer Perry, a handsome boy with a crew cut, about twenty, who helped her inside

223

and discretely waited by her front door until she had turned on some lights and had begun to feel safe.

It was all too horrible for her to feel much of anything.

Nora thought of Stormi's eyes, the deranged hatred in them, the unfocused rage.

Stormi had tried to shoot her, perhaps kill her; the thought of it chilled her, but still she wanted to embrace Stormi, to tell her that it would be all right, that she could triumph over her demons, triumph over all of it—her abuse, her self-abasement, her addiction.

Nora had to acknowledge it now, that her feelings for Stormi were in parts maternal, sisterly, pastoral, that she had added Stormi to the collection of those troubled creatures who had been charged to her care: her manic-depressive mother, her alcoholic father, her tragic Dexter. Now Stormi. How else could she explain her complete lack of anger toward the girl?

And Cox. He had been kind, bewilderingly so, and as he'd bent over her in the corridor at Aberdeen Hall, she had seen in his eyes a startling gentleness and depth of feeling.

She would thank him, soon, when the questioning was done, testimony given, and the world's turning slowed down enough for them to meet and talk about something other than the murder of James Barris.

21

SUNDAY, DECEMBER 11

The videotaped confession, shot at 9:30 A.M., a day and a half after the attempt on his life, showed Don Hedstrom wearing a plain gray hospital gown, the left side of his face bandaged, his left eye and cheekbone covered with gauze and tape, and though his face looked haggard in the smeary video image, his features appeared hard, crisp, and stoically determined. He sat at a gray Formica table, faced the camera, and answered questions posed to him by Tina Farrell, who had been assigned the task by Luther Cox.

There was no hesitation in his voice and little emotion. At points during the night, he had already told his story, or parts of it, to Gipson and Bieberschmidt. If people viewing the tape two weeks later, as millions did when it was released to the television networks, thought him cold-blooded, they were mistaken. His coolness was the result of preparation, and his natural intelligence compelled him to achieve a certain conciseness, accuracy, and simplicity in his statement that some later felt was inconsistent with the pleas to reckless homicide and voluntary manslaughter that the prosecution had accepted. But the outcry over the state's leniency was far overshadowed by the public's deep sense of astonishment and horror at the story Hedstrom had to tell.

225

He was in bed late one night, when the phone rang. He awoke with a start the instant it rang, and it took another ring before he rolled over to the side of the bed, where the phone sat on the night table. He picked it up in the middle of the third ring.

His mouth was in the process of forming the word *hello,* when he heard the voice of Sunni Skye, a prostitute he had met through business connections, telling him that it had been done, the job he'd asked her to do, and that she wanted to get paid.

He couldn't believe she'd taken him seriously. He had said it to her, joking, over drinks at Neidermeyer's—too many drinks—that he'd pay to see Barris dead, and she'd asked how much he would pay, and he'd mused, "Oh, what would it be worth? What's the going rate?" And she'd said fifty grand, and he replied, "That sounds about right," and they had gone on to discuss hypothetically, he thought, how such a crime might be committed.

Now the girl was telling him that she'd done it, and that if he didn't believe her, the proof was in the pine trees in a cornfield off Regner Road, up north of Henderson Street. East side of the street. He said, "Are you crazy?" And she said, "You meet me tomorrow at eleven at the Third Street McDonald's, and be sure it's cash." And she hung up the phone.

Odd how suddenly calm he felt once his heart had stopped thundering. The disembodied voice played again and again in his brain as he lay there in the dark, clutching the covers to his chin. Had he been dreaming? Had she really believed that he would pay her to murder Jim Barris? The very idea was impossible and dreadful, and yet it filled him with awe and a sense of having achieved a kind of power that he hadn't felt since his first triumphs on the basketball court.

He had to go, to see what was there by the cornfield, to see it with his own eyes. Now.

He dressed quickly and went out the back door to the garage; he took the Mercedes, the quietest of his cars, and drove north.

It was easy to find, even in the dark. There was only one stand of pine trees north of Henderson Street on Regner Road, and it stood out, black against the starry sky, spindly peaks pointing upward. He saw the trees before he saw Barris's car at the side of the road. He pulled up behind the Volvo and sat for a moment before getting out, listening to the whine and tick of his engine as it cooled.

It was a chilly night, even for early December, the air crisp and still, and already there was the flapping of buzzard wings to lead him to the body.

He stepped through the pines slowly, fearfully, his legs weak, muscles rebelling against his will to see the corpse. Then abruptly, it was there before him, Barris's skin shining in the starlight, augmented by the pale fire of a quarter-moon. He hadn't expected him to be unclothed. That startled him more than anything, until he saw the dark patches around Barris's mouth and abdomen.

The birds fluttered away as he approached the body. He bent over the corpse, curious now and almost laughing with the awful tension of it, and then he saw that Barris's tongue had been severed, and Hedstrom's stomach contracted in disgust. He fell to his knees beside the body, and then to his hands, and he wanted to vomit but could not let go.

He looked again. He had to. He crouched and looked closely at Barris's dead eyes, open and already pecked bloody by the birds. He looked, dispassionately now, at his mouth and its awful mutilation. He touched Barris's cheek, ran his fingers down to his chin, felt sticky blood there, and instantly pulled his hand away. The abrupt motion set him off balance, and in nearly falling, he instinctively reached out and touched the corpse to steady himself, his bloody finger pressing into the cold flesh below Barris's armpit.

Hedstrom stood and rubbed the blood into his hands, drying his fingers, trying not to get any blood on his clothes. As he stood, he became aware of the birds circling impatiently above. Fear welled up in him again, and his feet began to pull him away, back to his car. Breathing quickly, he looked once again at Barris, then down at his own feet. There, three steps from the body, he saw something curled and bright. It looked in the pale light like ribbon. Without thinking, he bent down and touched it, felt that it was hard, a cord or rope

227

of some kind. And at the moment he touched it, he saw something else glinting in a patch of weeds a foot or so away. Automatically, as if he were cleaning up his own yard, he picked up the cord and pushed it into the pocket of his coat. He took a step toward the glinting and saw that it was a razor blade, a single straight-edge razor blade. He picked it up carefully, conscious now of his purpose, and put it in his pocket with the cord. Then he ran the rest of the way back to his car, started it quickly, and sped home.

The next morning, sitting in a remote corner of the McDonald's on Third Street, he watched Sunni come in, get some food, and sit down to wait. He examined her sadly, her strange stringy pink hair, her pale skin, her boyish body and mannerisms. She seemed to Hedstrom an unlikely choice for a killer; he'd never dreamed she'd actually do it, but at the same time, he wondered if murder were not so far from whoring as one might think. The price was just higher.

After watching her a few moments, Hedstrom walked over to her table and gave the girl a small, fat envelope. Sunni leaned back, pushed her pelvis up, and stuffed the envelope unceremoniously into the front pocket of her jeans. Hedstrom did not tell her that he had never intended for her to kill Barris; it was done, and there was nothing he could do about it but go to the police and open a can of worms he didn't want opened. There was the publicity to be considered, and if the cops didn't believe his story, there'd be a trial and he'd have to prove that he hadn't really hired the girl to kill Barris.

No, it was far better to pay and hope the Harrison police did their usual best. The money was no real issue; fifty grand was a routine bribe in Hedstrom's business.

Hedstrom got up and walked quickly out of the place.

On his way back to his car, he reached into his jacket pocket for his keys and found the plastic twine and razor blade he'd picked up in the cornfield. He carefully removed the twine, leaving the razor to fall to the bottom of his pocket. He stared at the twine, amazed to see it there in his hands, amazed at the bright strands of red and yellow plastic wound together. He stretched it between his hands and pulled it tight. The cord sprang into a straight line and vibrated like a guitar string. Hedstrom laughed at the soft boiiinng sound the cord made. And he knew in that instant that he would use the cord to kill the girl.

Late the next night, he waited in the shadows outside the Sleep Tite, watching the door to the room Sunni used, waited until he saw her enter with a john, then waited for the john to leave. And from then on it was like a dream, he said, as if he were acting, causing things to happen, watching himself act, having no will of his own. He remembered Sunni shrieking when he entered, his hand on the pistol emerging from his pocket, Sunni tripping while moving backward, trying to get away from the gun, babbling, on her knees, begging. He remembered he told the girl to get undressed and lie facedown on the bed, and he heard himself promise the girl that everything would be all right. The girl obeyed, crying, shaking with fright, pulled off her tank top and shorts, and lay down, naked but for her sneakers and socks. He remembered moving beside the girl, touching the smooth skin of her back, the soft skin, as the girl kept crying and sniffling, her hands down at her sides, her face turned toward the lamp on the night table, the light bright on her reddened eyes.

Hedstrom felt his own hand move into his jacket pocket, taking the cord, taking it in both hands, and then, as swiftly as he had imagined doing it, pressing his fists into the pillow and pulling the cord down under the girl's face to her neck and then pulling up hard, twisting the cord around itself and pulling tight, now sitting hard on the girl's back and pulling while the girl's body bucked and strained.

It took a long time for the girl to stop moving. She reached back desperately, twisting her arms to claw vainly at Hedstrom's wrists. Hedstrom's far superior physical strength easily restrained her, but the girl did not cease struggling until a minute or more had passed, her mouth stretched open in a silent scream.

When it was over, Hedstrom turned the girl over and placed her neatly on the bed. He threw the cord on the floor next to the nightstand. He took a pair of latex gloves from his pocket, put them on, then took out the razor blade.

229

Hedstrom spread the girl's legs and cut at her timidly. He waited as the blood slowly rose, beaded along the cut line, then trickled down the cut. He made two such cuts; then, unable to continue, he stabbed flailingly three times at the girl's pubis.

He looked at the girl's mouth and could not.

He threw the razor blade on the floor near the foot of the bed for the police to find. The cord and the razor were the girl's belongings, Hedstrom thought, and here the trail ends.

22

MONDAY, DECEMBER 12

At 9:45 A.M., Farrell appeared on the other side of Cox's door and was ushered in with a nod. Opening the door, Farrell blinked rapidly, shook her head, and slapped at the air with her hand.

"Christ, boss, is the place on fire? You really ought to open a window in here."

Cox grinned. "I don't think that window's ever been opened." He scooted his chair over to the window and bent one of the venetian blinds, sending a cloud of dust into the air. "Exactly right."

"It's fifteen minutes to Don Hedstrom's initial hearing. Didn't want you to miss it."

Cox nodded. "Sit down a moment."

Farrell eased herself into one of the chairs opposite Cox's desk and swiveled the seat back and forth absently; she looked at Cox and waited, innocently expectant.

"Hedstrom will be speaking to the press soon—if not today, any day now. His friend Gene Lydon will also be talking."

Farrell watched him, worry creasing her face.

"They'll be talking about the Chappelle case and the allegations of evidence tampering."

Farrell shrugged, her expression lightening. "So? What does that have to do with anything?"

"The motive in the Barris killing was that Barris threatened to reveal that Hedstrom had pulled strings to get Chappelle off."

"Yeah, so?"

"It was true."

Farrell looked away. "I don't understand."

"I was involved in the destruction of the forensic evidence that would have proved sexual intercourse had taken place between Chappelle and the victim."

Cox could see Farrell swallow hard.

"I don't have any excuse. There are no excuses. I'm sorry I did it. But I did it. And now it's time to pay up. I'm resigning from the force. Effective at the end of the day."

Farrell's jaw dropped. "You can't do that."

"I must."

Farrell stood, her face quivering. "Are you crazy? You can't leave! What are we going to do without you? You expect me to work with Quade?" Farrell began pacing in front of Cox's desk, her hands flying. "Okay, so you screwed up! Take the suspension or whatever they do to you and then move on! Don't resign! You can't!"

Cox almost grinned at the sight of her, and his heart ached with gratitude. "No, Tina. I don't have a choice. I mean, for myself. I need to start over."

Farrell sat. "I don't believe this."

"It will mean new opportunities for you."

"I don't want that."

"You're ready."

"I'm not ready."

Abruptly, Cox coughed loudly and grasped the edge of his desk for support.

"Shit, listen to you. You're going down the same road as my pa, coughing like that."

"By the way, how is your father?" Cox rasped.

"He's fucking dying! From smoking! Get it?"

Amazed at the anger in her voice, Cox scratched his head and looked shyly at her.

Farrell said, "So what are you gonna do with yourself? I predict you'll be crawling back to the job in two weeks."

"I don't know," Cox replied. "You may be right. But I need to find out."

Judge Kohrman's courtroom and the corridor leading to it were jammed with reporters. Cox and Farrell pushed their way through, Cox fending off a barrage of questions and a battery of microphones thrust in front of his face. As the two cops entered the courtroom, the bailiffs held the crowd back, enabling Cox and Farrell to squeeze into the second row up front.

The proceedings were just getting under way. Don Hedstrom was sitting in a wheelchair at the defense table, the set of his lips, from Cox's perspective, one of intense nervousness and despair. He did not move; his hands rested immobile in his lap. But the eye that was visible was ringed with red and the muscles in his face showed the strain of keeping his composure.

Judge Kohrman of the Watkins County Superior Court intoned the automatic plea and asked the lawyers' agreement as to dates for subsequent hearings. The room was utterly silent but for the judge's voice and the sound of deep breathing, and a sense of awful gravity pervaded the room. Cox never took his eyes off Hedstrom, and he barely listened as Gipson and the prosecutor went through the motions of arguing over bail. The business was quickly conducted and Hedstrom led away pending the posting of $500,000 bail.

When it was over, the spectators erupted out of their seats and pressed toward the courtroom doors. The bailiffs held the crowd back to enable Cox and Farrell to exit. The two stepped out into the crowded corridor and moved swiftly to the elevator, ignoring the cameras and the entreaties of more than a dozen reporters.

Waiting for the elevator, Cox noticed that copies of the *Harrison Herald* were suddenly in everyone's hands; the headline read HEDSTROM SHOT, and below, in small type, "Hedstrom held in killing of prostitute." Below that, cryptically, in smaller type, "Prostitute held in Hedstrom shooting; may be connected to law prof murder."

233

The frame around the elevator doors was festooned with boughs of artificial pine studded with shiny red metal balls.

Christmas—it would be Cox's first off the force, a free man, since he'd put on that badge eleven years before.

He took a deep breath.

23

TUESDAY, DECEMBER 13

Nora Lumsey sat at the table she had occupied with Luther Cox on a prior occasion, watching as he made his way across the restaurant toward her. She stood and shook his hand. He smiled shyly, with a certain nervousness that seemed unlike him. She had accepted his invitation to meet here and to talk about what had happened. She had told him that she was no longer Stormi Skye's lawyer, not on any of the several criminal matters now pending against Stormi.

"Being that Stormi had attempted to kill me, I thought it best to withdraw from the representation," she had said.

But he had wanted to speak with her anyway; there were things he needed to tell her, he said, important things connected to the case but which had nothing to do with the prosecution of Stormi Skye.

And so she shook his hand, feeling a certain nervousness in herself, too, wondering what he would have to tell her.

Cox sat down and looked into the eyes of this woman he barely knew and whose life he had endangered by his carelessness. He wanted to take her hands and hold them between his hands—for his own comfort, not hers—but he did not have the nerve. And so he clasped his hands around an espresso cup and told her everything, the story of the Chappelle rape and his role in the cover-up of the crime and how it had led, if indirectly, to the murders of James Barris and Sunni Skye. To his surprise, she didn't withdraw, nor did she explode with anger. Instead, she put her hands on his and looked at him with compassion.

There was disappointment. He saw it in the movement of her eyes away from his and in an unsteadiness at the corners of her mouth. He had betrayed his badge, his honor. It was unforgivable. Yet she held his hands between hers and wished him well.

For Cox, the woman's kindness only made him feel worse for having shamed himself.

24

FRIDAY, DECEMBER 23

During the night, a wave of dry, warm air had moved in from the west, thawing the ground and sending absurdly untimely messages to the natural world.

Outside Cox's cabin, the sun beat down harder than it had in weeks. It lit the bare branches and the bed of dry leaves that extended for miles in all directions from this place, the center of Cox's universe, and warmed the air to an unimaginable fifty-four degrees.

At 8:30 A.M., Cox stood outside at his easel, wearing an old Irish knit sweater, jeans, and a pair of decades-old moccasins, his cup of coffee resting atop a weather-beaten wooden barrel. As he dipped his brush into a puddle of ocher acrylic, he remembered, sheepishly, that he had a funeral to attend that afternoon—Tina's father's—and she would surely need him more now than ever, loath as she would be to admit it. He would wait to tell her the news Bieberschmidt had asked him to convey to her, about Quade—his early retirement next month—and her new rank on the force. Let her grieve fully today, he thought, without a confusion of joy and sorrow.

Cox painted the light, or tried to, while it lasted—a brief morning of yellow spots dappling everything, transforming the somber opacity of winter colors into the translucent hues of autumn, fragrant with decay.

It was the most tranquil moment Cox had experienced in

months, maybe years. His mood was transcendent, and he felt so much at peace with himself, it almost worried him.

In the past week, he had begun to sleep later than he had in ages—clear through to 7:30 A.M. His dream still haunted him, but its immediacy was gone, replaced by a detachment that allowed him to judge himself less harshly. Now his heart did not pound when his dream woke him, he did not scream, and he was able to return to sleep.

And now there were moments, waking moments, when he could think of Julia in life, not in death, and in the time when she had loved him.

In the wake of the attempt on Hedstrom's life, blame scattered like confetti. Everyone in sight got a light dusting of responsibility, but it was easily brushed off. In view of the enormity of the impact of the charges against Hedstrom on the world of collegiate basketball, the details of a minor episode of corruption in the Harrison Police Department interested hardly a soul.

Cox suffered the most. He had arrested Gene Lydon two days after Hedstrom's arraignment on the basis of affidavits from Stormi Skye and Larry Crowder detailing Lydon's activities in prostitution and drug dealing. Pleazures was closed down, and the three girls still working for Lydon were arrested and given opportunities to plea bargain in exchange for testimony.

Lydon made good on his threat. In a conversation with the *Harrison Herald* from a county jail cell, Lydon exposed the rape cover-up and the roles played in it by Cox, Bieberschmidt, Mayor Brodey, and the city council president, Mark Andrews. The paper called around and got unequivocal denials from everyone but Cox, who confirmed his own role in the cover-up, to the extent that he would not jeopardize Bieberschmidt's retirement income. What he told the reporter was that he had become aware that the evidence had been tampered with but that he had not done the tampering and did not know precisely who had.

Few cared, and no one cared enough to take action. The story was printed on the front page of the *Herald* and died there without follow-up. The news surrounding the arrests of Hedstrom and Stormi Skye and the story of the murders of James Barris and Sunni Skye overwhelmed the ramblings of an indicted pimp and drug dealer.

Cox had purged his conscience and was free. Still, an image of Margaret Sanderson, Chappelle's victim, haunted him. He was not responsible for what had been done to her in the media and by Hedstrom, but he'd had a hand in denying her vindication. He could not forgive himself for that. The thought of it shamed him, gnawed at him, made him feel stale, compromised, and old.

Nearly two weeks after his resignation, Cox did not find himself wanting to crawl back to the force. He had a little money set aside. He could start a business. Or teach. Or do nothing for a time but paint and walk his magnificent woods.

Cox breathed deeply of the crisp, cool air. As he exhaled, something caught in his chest and he erupted with a tubercular cough.

"Sainted Christ, Spunk," he wheezed. Spunk, who had camouflaged himself in a pile of leaves, turned his head disdainfully, angered at the interruption in his stalking of an unwary cardinal.

Cox had not had a cigarette for six days, and he felt his body purging itself, a bit skeptically, of decades of poison.

Maybe it's time to call Nora Lumsey, Cox thought. She was wise, and perhaps she could help him overcome his blindness to his own possibilities. Maybe, with a little luck, she could even give him a reason to want to live a few years longer.

Nora sat on a folding chair in a corner of the interview room down the hall from the women's lockup on the fifth floor of the City-County Building, her hands clasping Stormi's hands as Stormi cried copious tears, fat, wet tears that dripped down her cheeks and fell, soaking into the legs of her navy blue cotton prison garb.

Eight days earlier, Stormi had been transferred from the Harrison jail back to Indianapolis, where the drug charges pending against her would be tried before she was returned to Harrison to face charges for the murder of James Barris and the attempted murders of Don Hedstrom and Nora Lumsey. And in those eight days, she had re-

239

ceived daily visits from Nora, who came down from her cubicle on the fourteenth floor to spend a few moments sitting with Stormi, to lend support, to forgive, and to give Stormi the faith that she had the power to end her misery and change her life.

Stormi had promised that she was ready to change, to stay clean, and with each passing day, Nora saw signs of healing in Stormi's eyes—their clarity—and in the return of color to her skin.

Now there were tears of gratitude, wholly unexpected, and Nora was moved to see that the kindness she had shown had broken through a barrier inside Stormi.

Nora had told Stormi that she had asked the county prosecutor to drop the charges against Stormi for her attempted murder. The prosecutor had reluctantly agreed, but in fact, he had little choice in the matter, not if Nora was willing to testify before the jury that she did not believe that Stormi had meant to harm her.

Now Stormi faced her drug charges and charges in the murder of James Barris and the attempted murder of Don Hedstrom. It would be a mitigating circumstance in the Hedstrom case that Hedstrom had murdered her sister, and Stormi would likely be convicted of no worse an offense than battery on that charge, which would bring her a sentence of as little as six to ten years.

In the murder of James Barris, Stormi was looking at a possible life sentence for murder and anywhere from ten to forty years for voluntary manslaughter. There was little chance that Stormi would be eligible for parole for at least twenty years, considering all the charges against her, barring exceptional circumstances.

Exceptional circumstances. Nora believed that if ever there was a case in which a straight-faced argument could be made for the existence of exceptional circumstances, it was this case. There was Stormi's exploitation and abuse by Barris, Lydon, Hedstrom, and the rest. And then there was her addiction, which these men had fed, encouraged, abetted.

Nora would pull strings to get Stormi into the state's best drug-rehabilitation program; she'd push Stormi to work for her GED and then college credit. She would urge Stormi to believe that she could still be somebody, raise herself up, that her life wasn't over.

And Nora had learned that Stormi had received visits from a young man named Joe Tyler, a graduate student, a former client, who had taken an interest in her redemption.

Another sign of hope.

"Thank you," Stormi murmured. "I don't deserve it—when I tell my ma, that's what she'll say—but it'll mean the world to her, and to me."

Nora nodded, tight-lipped, stifling her own tears. "I know, I know," she whispered. "I have hope for you, Stormi."

Instinctively, Nora leaned toward Stormi to embrace her, to seal this moment of faith, but as she did, she saw a dark spot on the sleeve of Stormi's shirt, below the elbow, a spot that looked like dried blood.

Nora withdrew, and holding Stormi's wrist with one hand, she pushed Stormi's sleeve up with the other.

Nora saw a fresh puncture below Stormi's elbow.

Stormi wrenched her arm away and slapped Nora hard.

At her desk, Nora held a cold can of Diet Coke against her cheek and cursed herself and her idiot heart. Why was she such a goddamn chump? She had let Stormi fill a gap in her emotional life, just as Barris and so many others had done. Why this compulsion to save the world, one troubled life at a time?

She thought with envy that Luther Cox had given up the struggle—that he was saving himself, instead of the world, retreating to lick his wounds, fighting internal battles.

Nora had never known an artist before, not a real artist, and she enjoyed the idea of knowing Luther Cox. She feared she did not have a creative bone in her body, and she wondered if meeting him was her destiny, if she had things to learn from him. She did not consider Cox a prospect for love; she thought him rather too ugly for that, physically—his face was gouged and rough, his features too big for his head—and she could not get past that, despite having had more than enough of good-looking men.

But there was something about him that intrigued her.

Nora had not discovered until their second meeting at the Mad Hatter that Cox was the artist whose work she had criticized—but he had laughed about it, relieved, she thought, that she had not bolted from the restaurant in disgust when he revealed to her his perjury in the Chappelle rape case.

At another time in her life, she might have bolted, but she had arrived, she recognized, at an acceptance of compromise—of her own compromised nature, of the need for compromise with her demons, of the need to compromise with her ideals.

She would not give up on Stormi Skye, but she would not expect too much too soon.

And she would pay Luther Cox a visit at his cabin, take a look at more of his work, give it another chance.

He was an artist. She liked that.